ENSNARED...

Chloe sipped her wine and set the glass down on the table beside her, her fingers finding the silver links around her wrist. In the warmth of the evening they were amazingly cool, the perfect ornamentation of each door on the bracelet like Braille beneath her fingers. Who would make such a thing, taking such pride and care in the minute details? She drew in a deep breath and, with that question in mind, opened herself.

The dim light over the water, the reds of the sunset all seemed to swirl and eddy before her, like the deep recesses of a fire opal. Iridescence appeared over the view like light on labradorite, rustle of the bamboo in the breeze came from behind her almost as if something crept there watching. She shivered. What was it about this bracelet that had her nerves jangling and Lila so concerned? Aside from its unique form, it was just another bunch of silver like every other piece that they had in the store.

"But you're special, aren't you? Kylee always seemed to think so, and now I can sort of understand how protective she was of you." She reached for her glass, but the glass wasn't there.

What the…?

The scent of lake water faded and was replaced by a sense of heated earth. The breeze was different, too. Thicker somehow. Yes. Sand particles lightly peppered her skin, and out beyond her patio the sounds of cars from the highway had faded, too. Were those hoof beats she heard? Bringing warning? She stood up, suddenly sure it was a warning. Her cat tumbled off her lap and gave her a dirty look before retreating to the apartment.

Something bad was going to happen unless—unless she did something—and on the dusty road outside, the one she feared had found her. They were coming. They were coming. They were pounding at her door. She stumbled away from her chair and knocked the table. The crash of breaking glass stopped her.

Her wine glass. It was there.

BOOKS BY THE AUTHOR

Romance
Ashes and Light
Shades of Moonlight
Judas Kiss
Second Spring
A Different Nightmusic
Shadow Play
Unlocking Her Heart
Unlocking Her History
Unlocking Her Grace (Spring 2015)

Fantasy
***The Cartographer Universe* series:**
The Warden of Power
The Cartographer's Daughter
Afterburn
Aftershock
Aftermath
Afterimage

Terra Incognita
Terra Infirma
Terra Nueva

Also by the Author
Mutable Things
Emberstone
Ice Dragon
Crystal Courtesan
Impossible

UNLOCKING HER HISTORY

Karen L. Abrahamson

Dedicated to my parents.
Keepers of hearth and home in the Okanagan.

UNLOCKING HER HISTORY

PROLOGUE

The night air off of Okanagan Lake carried the warm, wet heat of the daytime like the luscious heat off a living body. It smelled of deep water, the pine of the dry hills and the faint scent of boat diesel from Peachland marina that was just down the road. The beach lay silent as it was supposed to at this deepest hour of night. Just gentle waves lapping over fine gravel and the occasional splash of the ducks that slumbered with their wings over their heads near the shore. They were as blind to his presence, as were Peachland's puny sleeping residents.

Uphill from the water came the low rumble of the long-haul trucks on their midnight rides down the highway and from farther uphill came the yip of some kind of animal. Dog? No, something wild. He had no time for that sort of thing. He brought his attention down to the stately old white house stained gray by the night, its red trim turned the color of midnight shadows. That was his destination.

Like a shadow himself he crossed the street, keeping to the shade of a huge old cottonwood, then slunk around the corner away from the water and down the back alley until he reached the two-car carport that he had marked when he first assumed this body. It was a good body, ready for action and unassuming. He had located it through his usual agency and then moved into it to regain what had been kept from him.

Darkness filled the carport as he slid past the mini SUV and into the yard at the rear of the house. It was a small yard made smaller by the workshop that filled the left side of the space. He inhaled the forge and solder stink of an artisan. To the right was a high cedar fence and a small vegetable garden, while at the back of the house stood a flagstone patio with cushioned wicker furniture, the cushions tipped up against the night dew. Someone in the house paid attention to details. That was not a good thing.

The rear of the house held the kitchen area, he'd ascertained that during a prior visit. The body smoothly knelt beside the door and used fine fingers to extract tools from a small vinyl case. He relinquished control of the hands and let the body do its work. Lean in and listen for the soft clicks, feel them through the thin metal picks. There, one pin shifted. There, another. A third. A fourth and he stopped, inhaled and drew power out of the darkness, then blasted it into the alarm system that ran through the doors and windows. The bitter scent of burned wiring curled into his nostrils as he shifted the door handle.

The rear door swung open onto darkness and he inhaled the breath of the two women sleeping in the bedrooms above.

He slid inside and pulled the door softly closed behind. The kitchen was rich with the scents of basil and thyme, the dark smoke of red wine, and an undertone of silver. That was what he sought. Like smoke, he followed the scent down the hall, but stopped before the door into the jewelry shop. The scent of silver was stronger here. Silver and gold and the arcane vibrations of stones and crystals, but a silly curtain of plastic beads blocked him from it. Well, he had come this far.

Gently he eased the strings of beads aside. He slid through the curtain, then let the curtain fall back into position, the beads clacking softly.

He sniffed the air again. Silver, but he was not sure. This body was not as attuned to the nuances of scent as the policeman had been, and even that was a far cry from the body he normally rode. But the bracelet had come off the woman. He'd felt it as surely as if he had stripped it from her arm himself. It had been like a gong had gone off in him; one level of the ancient curse removed and one less level of power for him to recover.

Fists tight he strode around the room. The faint taste of the ancient silver still lingered on the air. After almost losing the woman to him, they now must be aware of their danger. If it had come off her wrist had they locked it up, then? Could that be it?

He shoved behind the small cash register counter and found the safe in a cubbyhole in the house's inner wall. It was a safe intended to protect the shop's goods from the usual depredations of the common criminals who might live in this backwater of central British Columbia. A backwater town in a backwater country.

He set the thief body free to ply the combination lock and dreamed of the power that would come with success. An old foe vanquished. Power returned. The long handle of the safe turned with a low thunk and he pulled the foot-high door open releasing a gust of silver-and-stone-scented air.

His eyes burned. His nose watered as he hauled a stack of black velvet trays out to inspect. Some cursed person had placed jet stones in the top tray. He set it aside to examine ornate silver necklaces. Earrings with cabochon emeralds. A silver pendant fashioned like doors, with silver filigreed trees over an ancient glass window. He stroked the exquisite piece. Someone had labored hard over this.

Quickly he rifled through the trays. It had to be here. It had to, yet all of these pieces were marvelous—but new. Not what he wanted at all!

Stymied, he stood. He strode around the room fighting the desire to smash the glass counters, sweep down the displays, ram a fist through the large windows to make the women pay. By all the hounds of hell and the infernal flame that burned within him, the bracelet was his! He *would* make them pay.

On impulse he pulled a bag from under the counter and poured the safe contents into it.

A movement of air, a whiff of roses. He spun around as a woman with moon-pale skin and wild curls pushed through the beaded curtain.

"I've called the police," she yelled as he mowed her down, smashed into a glass display case and leapt for the front door. The sound of glass shattering followed him as he yanked at the door. The lock tore through the sash sending a bell wildly ringing and he was out and across the porch, down the stairs and gone, loping up the street.

A fool. He'd been a fool to do that, but for the bracelet he would do anything.

The breeze off the lake shifted direction. From the north it came, carrying the scent of peach and cherry orchards and a hint of ancient silver. He kept going, following the trace northward on the long runner's legs and stopped once he had crossed the small creek called Trepanier. The town spread behind him, suburban houses strung along the lakeshore that curved gently southward toward the heart of the old town of Peachland. Ahead stood a large, three-story, L-shaped building of apartments surrounded by gardens.

Redolent of myrrh and frankincense, the scent of power billowed out at him. He stood there, the water running beneath the bridge, the man's blood running in his veins and satisfaction running in his ancient brain.

Here. The bracelet was here, pouring its magic out a condominium window. That meant one of the women had done the foolhardy thing and placed the bracelet on her wrist. His bracelet. He would deal with her.

In the distance came the scream of police sirens echoing over the lake. Time to get off the street and make his plans.

CHAPTER 1

THE CLOCK ON CHLOE MAIN'S BEDSIDE TABLE said two in the morning when her phone burred in her ear and dragged her out of a luscious dream of... The dream vanished as she bolted upright in bed, her long braid catching on the darn bracelet on her arm. She almost tore the hair out of her head, so that by the time she fumbled the phone up she was solidly awake.

"Hello?" she asked, scrubbing at her eyes to avoid the sleep that wanted to descend again. The white cotton sheets and duvet were warm and inviting.

"Chloe, it's Lila. There's been a break-in at the store. The police are here. Can you come?"

At the shakiness in Lila's voice, Chloe's skin went cold. All possibility of returning to sleep disappeared as she swung out of bed onto the cool hardwood of the shadowed room. "Are you okay?" She didn't bother waiting for a reply. "I'll be there in ten. Five even. Just let me get clothes on."

She hung up and swung around the room with its wide queen-sized bed and its old fashioned dresser beside the sliding glass door opening out to the condo patio. The floor-length sheer curtains billowed from the breeze through the narrow opening she'd left open for fresh air. Underwear first. The good thing was that her trusty caftan tunics and her braided hair meant she was pretty low maintenance. A midnight blue tunic and leggings and cool water palmed over her face. She grabbed an amethyst crystal off her livingroom shelves, a cream colored shawl, then took the stairs down to the basement. There she aimed her silver Camry out onto the road and followed the headlights the half mile down the beach to *This and That: Jewelry and Unsung Treasures.* Nothing moved on the street as she pulled into the curb at the front of the store behind a marked Royal Canadian Mounted Police patrol car and a large SUV.

Compared to the other sleep-darkened houses the red and white house was an opal ablaze with light. She pushed through the gate and ran up the steps and inside, the bell above the door tinkling. She stopped. Leastwise she was stopped by a constable blocking her way and someone examining the broken front door latch.

"Excuse me, Ma'am, you can't come through here." The cop was tall, young, still baby-faced and wasn't that a comment on her ripe old age of thirty four. He had eyes the color of azurite, and onyx-colored hair, but she'd be darned if she was going to let him get in her way.

"Like heck I can't. Lila Weber called me. Is she all right?"

She went to march across the shop to the beaded doorway into the back of the house, but he caught her arm. "If you're a friend of Ms. Weber's why don't you go around the side of the house? She's being interviewed in the kitchen."

She read the guy's face, then scanned the room. An officer was busy photographing the area behind the counter and the guy she'd almost run over when she burst inside was back examining the door. Crime scene. This was a crime scene she was standing in. Her chill went deeper. She tugged the shawl tighter around her shoulders and stepped outside, to take a deep breath, then ran around the side of the house to the backyard. Light blazed from the kitchen, exposing another officer busily doing something to the house's back door. She eased past and into the sunny kitchen that didn't quite feel so sunny at this time of the night.

The room was a lovely one, built almost like a summer kitchen with bright windows in a long row over counters that ran most of the length of the room. The walls were white, but the cupboards were yellow. Bright spots of turquoise ceramics on the counter and on the wall made the place feel like a summer day in the tropics—except for the woman huddled at the table.

The nook sat at one end of the room, with bench seating around three sides and a lone chair on the fourth. At the moment Lila was seated forlornly on the nook bench across from a uniformed police officer. Lila was the owner of the house and one of Chloe's partners in *This and That,* but at this moment she looked nothing like the together business woman she usually was. Her head of long auburn curls had gone wild around her head and her hazel eyes had gone palest green. In the absence of her silver rings she twisted her fingers and her flawless skin was almost as pale as the room's walls.

"Lila! My God. Are you all right?" She pushed past the uniformed police officer who sat in the chair and slid into the nook bench beside Lila to give her a hug. Under normal circumstances Lila might be the most composed person in the world, but at the moment everything about her shouted scared. Even her aura was off kilter and tarnished.

Small shudders ran through Lila's body and Chloe quickly stripped the shawl off and draped it around Lila's satin-pajama covered shoulders, then slung her arm around her friend and pulled her into a hug. "It's okay. We'll get through this. We will."

"She was just telling me what happened," said the officer—another youngster, with the same cookie-cutter sternness.

Lila nodded and wiped at her eyes. "I'm sorry. I feel like such a ninny. I was asleep but something woke me. I came down stairs for a drink of juice, but then I heard something from the shop. I don't know what I thought it was, but for some reason I grabbed the phone and went into the store. He scared the heck out of me when he shoved past for the door."

Shivering, she pulled the shawl tighter around her pearl-pink pajamas.

"How about I make us a cup of tea?" Without waiting for an answer, Chloe pushed free of the table and put the kettle on to boil on the gas range. She found a good Indian loose leaf tea that she added to the water and some chai spices that smelled pleasantly of cardamom and pepper. When everything was boiling, she added sugar and milk and then strained the result into a teapot. Carrying the pot and three mugs, she went back to the table to play mother and pour the tea.

The heat of the spicy tea helped cut her own chill and Lila's trembling seemed to lessen. Chloe faced the officer. "You have questions for me?"

"Just a few. I've already taken Ms. Weber's preliminary statement. There'll be some detectives who will probably want to ask more tomorrow."

Chloe met Lila's eyes and they both sighed. They'd both had enough to do with police for a lifetime over the past few days when their friend and *This and That's* star employee, Kylee Jensen, had been abducted and held prisoner. It seemed to have something to do with the bracelet Chloe now wore. She covered the incriminating bracelet with her hand and nodded. "What do you need to know now?"

Lila shook her head. "I'm so sorry I wasn't more help. It was dark and I really didn't get a good look at him. There was just a flash of lighter-colored hair and then he was gone. The way he ran away I'd say he was younger, though."

The officer made a note of it and then looked up. "I was asking Ms. Weber for an estimate of the value of the stolen goods."

"Stolen?" Chloe turned to Lila. "You said a break-in..." The image of the officer photographing the space behind the store's counter suddenly filtered in. "Oh my God. The safe! But things were in there to be protected!"

Lila shook her head, her eyes welling with tears. "I knew we were getting more high-priced inventory and with Reggie's design's too, I knew we needed to improve our security. I just hadn't gotten around to it what with everything happening with Kylee and the bracelet."

Chloe's gut felt like she had just swallowed a granite boulder. "There was a lot in there," she said, considering. "Reggie had finished her samples for the Milan show and so they were all in there, too. They were one-of-a-kind pieces. I had a stones in there that I thought were going to work for my crystal therapy." She looked at the officer and swallowed. "I'm going to need to think about it, but off the top of my head I'd say the value of the goods was probably at least twenty to twenty-five thousand dollars. I can pull together a complete list for you." And kick herself as she itemized each piece.

"With descriptions, please. We'll be wanting to check the local pawn shops of course. And any photographs would be helpful as well."

"Of course." She caught Lila's ice cold hand and squeezed it knowing that her hand was probably just as cold. She felt frozen, numb except where she held onto her mug.

By the time the police left it was going on five in the morning and the summer sun was rising over the mountains on the other side of the lake. Nerves still frothing so there was no way she could sleep, Chloe sent Lila upstairs for a shower and set to making breakfast. Apparently the detectives would come to ask their questions later this morning.

In the quiet of the kitchen she sliced fresh apricots and peaches and washed fresh cherries, all from local orchards. Then she toasted English muffins, pulled out the almond butter and homemade Saskatoon jelly and carried a tray with the food and a fresh carafe of coffee out through the debris of the store, trying not to look at it. On the front patio she sank down on the wicker couch with its tangerine and turquoise pillows and looked out at the lake.

Okanagan Lake ran eighty-plus miles north-south in south central British Columbia and was the kingpin of a string of long narrow lakes that drained into Washington State. Okanagan Lake was deep and the home of the mythical Ogopogo lake monster, but mostly it was a summer playground for boaters and kayakers and people who came to visit in their recreational vehicles. But this sunny July morning it was just a quiet silver lake, the breeze barely placing a ripple on the fine surface.

The still water rustled along the fine gravel beach across Beach Avenue belying the disturbance she felt at the store. She'd felt a premonition of bad things to come when she'd put the bracelet on, but who knew it would be this?

She held it up to admire in the morning light. The bracelet was a mysterious piece. It had come to *This and That* in a box of odds and ends from an estate sale and Kylee, after digging it out of the mass of jewelry, had put it on. From there things had gotten weird with the estate sale agent murdered; Kylee's abduction at the hands of her neighbor Tom Beaton; and a string of men who had claimed that they had been possessed by aliens. One of them had committed suicide from guilt at what he'd done. The others were dealing with the aftermath and suffering mental breakdowns.

She poured herself a cup of coffee and sipped it while waiting for Lila. Of course whether all these happenings had to do with the bracelet was a matter of some debate.

The bracelet itself was intriguing. Apparently an antique, for its silver showed signs of wear, it was comprised of a series of seven small doors, each linked to the other by delicate silver chains so they formed a cuff that that was cleverly closed by a small ornate key that fit through a lovely scrolled keyhole. The trouble was, apparently once you had the bracelet on, it didn't want to come off again. That had happened to Kylee, until the piece had fallen off in bed almost as if the bracelet itself decided when it should come off. Now it was here to stay on Chloe's wrist.

Each of the seven doors was unique. One was an arched silver door with grapevines twined around it. Another had a tiny gargoyle face for a knocker. Still others had hinges that looked like something out of an elfish kingdom, while another had leaf-shaped hinges. One of them looked like a classic Dutch door with separate upper and lower doors sections. Another was solidly square with raised lintels and a Fatima hand door knocker. The last, her favorite, was what looked like a wooden door bound with iron strapping and large iron knobs—at least it felt that way when she ran her fingers over it. It reminded her of something you might see in North Africa. Some of the doors even had tiny ornate locks and chains hanging from them so they were as secure as the bracelet apparently was on her wrist. Apparently that was more secure than the shop safe.

Sighing, she looked out at the lake.

Along the paved walkway that ran along the beach, the few early morning joggers slapped their feet on the pavement as they loped past wearing spandex. Their pooches did a doggie jog beside them. From uphill came the low drone of early morning traffic. She breathed in air heavy with warm lake water and the promising scent of fresh baking from the bakery café down the street.

Peachland was a good town. It was a small town that still had its 'old timers,' but it was being dragged kicking and screaming into becoming a destination for vacationers. With that came subdivisions to support all the people who were moving into the area for the country lifestyle. Up the hillsides from the lake many of the old orchards had already been torn down and replaced by houses.

"And isn't that just a depressing thought to start the day with." She reached into her pocket and pulled out the amethyst crystal. She'd forgotten to give it to Lila. The stone was known to protect against burglars and ward off violence and danger. Too little, too late, it seemed. She stuck the stone back in her pocket and sipped her cup of coffee. The caffeine wasn't going to help her nerves any.

The bell over the shop's front door dinged quietly and Lila stepped out onto the porch, her curls a damp mass around her shoulders. She'd dressed in a pair of navy Capri pants that showed off her long legs, and a sleeveless lavender top that skimmed her body, but the lack of sleep showed even through her carefully applied makeup. There were bags under her eyes and she wore a haunted look along with her usual many artful silver rings. Sinking into her throne-backed wicker chair, she closed her eyes.

"I swear every muscle in my body aches and he didn't do anything to me other than knock me over."

"Fear can do that. It tightens all the muscles. So does shock, and you've had one."

The early sun illuminated Lila's once well-known beautiful face and brought the copper out in her hair. "Maybe they should market it as an alternative to isometric exercise. I might do yoga, but I feel like I've been through a war. I'm going to feel this for a while." Her lips curved, but then she sighed. "I called Reggie. She's coming right over. Thank goodness one of us has had a full night's sleep."

Any appetite Chloe might have had evaporated. "I was the one who convinced her to put her designs in the safe. They'd have likely been left alone if they'd been in her shop."

"That, my friend, is a silly thing to say. How were you to know someone would break in?"

What could she say? Out on the water a V of Canada geese were playing chicken with a lone yellow kayak. The wind was picking up some and a small shiver ran up her back. The familiar sense of foreboding settled on her shoulders. No good was going to come of this. Over the years she'd learned to listen to her feelings.

Her hand closed over the stupid bracelet that had caused for so much trouble for Kylee.

"You think it might have something to do with the bracelet?" Lila asked.

Chloe turned to her and realized that Lila had been watching her and the way her fingers seemed drawn to the slim band of silver. Chloe shrugged. "Who knows? Probably not. I mean the bracelet wasn't in the store so there'd be no reason to break in here, would there?"

Lila looked thoughtful, but nodded.

A clatter came from inside the house. Through the windows Lila had opened after the police were finished, the beaded curtain clacked and then, "Holy shit!" Footsteps hurried across the hardwood and the bell dinged above the door as Reggie pushed out onto the porch. She sagged onto the wicker loveseat, shoving her black Cleopatra hair out of her face. "What the hell happened?"

"We had a two a.m. shopper. I surprised him in the store," Lila said, her skin paling even in the warmth of the sunshine.

"The place looks like a disaster," Reggie said, looking back at the door. She wore her usual camo fatigue pants and a black tank top, a look that belied her actual kindness. "The lock's torn right out of the door frame."

Chloe nodded. "Another thing to take care of. How about I get a pen and paper so we can make a list?" She heaved herself up out of the chair knowing she was really just being a coward delaying telling Reggie about the safe and the fate of all of her custom pieces. She went through the shop and retrieved paper and pen from the kitchen and returned in time to hear Lila telling the bad news.

"The safe was open. The thief took everything."

Chloe stood just inside the door as the muscles tensed across Reggie's shoulders. Then they sagged. "You're kidding, right?"

Lila shook her head as Chloe stepped onto the white-painted porch. The scent of the red and white petunias and baby's breath in the hanging copper pots along the porch rail was almost enough to make her nauseous. She collapsed in her chair again and sighed. "I'm so sorry. I was only trying to help."

Reggie frowned. "What are you talking about?"

"The fact that it was me who convinced you to put your pieces in the safe. It's my fault they were stolen."

"Well that's just plain stupid, isn't it? The crook could have broken into my shop as well. In fact, I need to check that. I guess I also need to let the designer know about our little setback and get busy trying to reproduce what we've lost." Reggie nodded. "Write it down. Contact Milan designers. And make a note of seed pearls. If I'm going to re-do some of those pieces. I have an idea to take them over the top to downright gorgeous."

Feeling a tad overwhelmed at her old friend's graciousness. Chloe dutifully acted as scribe as they brainstormed temporary closure signage, getting the front door repaired and the security system updated along with a myriad of other tasks. They decided to use the opportunity to repaint and restain the store. Then

Reggie excused herself to check on her workshop in the back and Lila stretched and stood up.

"I think I have an appointment with a broom to get rid of the glass, and you my dear need to be as good to yourself as you were to me. Go home. Take a shower and get a bit of rest. I'll call when the police arrive."

Chloe stood, prepared to argue that Lila had been through enough, but Lila stopped her with a hug. "Who else would be here within five minutes in the middle of the night? You are one heck of a good business partner and one wonderful friend. Thank you. I don't know what I would have done without you."

In truth both Kylee, who lived up the hill, and Reggie who lived in West Kelowna would probably both have responded almost as quickly, but Lila's first thought had been to call *her*. She hugged Lila back and read the fortitude on Lila's face. She needed time alone to get herself put back together. Maybe they both did after the long night.

Chloe left Lila to clean up and headed out to her car.

CHAPTER 2

"Seems like we've been here before," Jas Stone said as he pulled the unmarked police sedan into the curb in front of the big, old, red and white heritage house. The traffic on Peachland's Beach Avenue was fairly mild for only a few days after the Canada Day celebration that had brought hordes of people to the parade and party. A lot of those people would be vacationing in the area, but this morning the usually popular beach was surprisingly empty. Maybe it was a result of the big "Closed for Restoration" sign on a sandwich board in front of the store. Knowing a small town like Peachland, there probably wasn't an inhabitant of the town who didn't know the place had been robbed the night before. The sign probably contributed to the fact there was a parking spot open right in front of *This and That*.

"Like returning to the scene of a crime," Danny said.

Jas turned the ignition off and glanced at his partner. Corporal Danny Forester was looking up at the house with an uncertain expression. He wore his usual khakis and a blue polo shirt. He ran his hands through his thatch of red hair. If anything the motion managed to make his hair look worse.

The guy was still coming down from a bad bout of something that had him AWOL from work and spouting weird stuff about having been possessed by an alien. Thankfully he'd had the smarts not to mention the latter point to the brass at the West Kelowna RCMP detachment, so he had been allowed back on active duty with only a reprimand on file. That and the Commanding Officer had asked Jas to keep an eye on him.

"Figure they'll be happy to see us?" Jas asked, thinking of the long-haired beauty he'd partnered with on the search for Kylee Jensen. Chloe had been her name. Chloe Main, but that was about all he knew. They'd both been focused on finding her friend. The last time he'd been here had been here was only a few days ago to take Kylee's official statement.

"If I was them, I think I'd rather not have us dropping in. I mean the abduction and now this? In Peachland? A domestic violence case, maybe. Public mischief or kids drinking. We hardly ever get a break-in, and now this."

"Welcome to the big city," Jas said to the community-at-large as he climbed out of the car and followed Danny to the house. It was odd, but the place looked, well, bruised today. Like a domestic violence victim who was trying to hide her scars. Maybe it was the fact the front door was off and there were two workmen removing the front door jam, but the place had the sense of being pushed off its foundations.

Danny stepped past the workmen, into the shop with Jas on his heels—broken display case, glass swept into a corner. Fingerprint powder on the cash register counter and around the door. "The owners around?" Danny asked. "Lila Weber?"

"In back," said one of the workmen and nodded toward the hall beyond a beaded curtain.

"Kitchen, most likely," Danny said and led Jas down the dimly lit hallway.

"Hey," Danny said as he entered the kitchen. "Guess who."

There were three women there. Tall, auburn-haired Lila Weber was on the phone at the counter. As usual she looked cool, collected, and as lovely as the minor celebrity she once was. According to Danny, a Google search for Lila Weber turned up that she had been the lead in a favorite cult film about a mythical hero who fell in love with goddess. She'd never done any acting after playing the goddess and either by choice or circumstance had fallen back into obscurity. But boy did she still have cheekbones.

She nodded the two of them to the table where Chloe sat along with another woman who looked like a cross between an action hero and Cleopatra. But it was Chloe who held his attention. She was dressed simply enough in a loose-fitting yellow tunic that set off the tan of her skin and the hip-length column of her braided dark brown hair. But it was her eyes that held him. When she looked up at him, their deep blue seemed to turn intense lavender. An optical illusion, of course, but it was seductive as hell, especially with her lush mouth.

Totally unprofessional, dude. He stopped himself and let Danny take the lead. Keep an eye on the guy and all that. That was where his attention was needed.

Chloe slid out from behind the table and extended a hand. "Detective Forester, isn't it?. And Stone." She seemed to frown as she briefly glanced in his direction, then turned her attention to Danny again. "We've just been working on the list of what was stolen and trying to come up with a more accurate estimate. Unfortunately I might have underestimated things a bit when I gave a figure to the officer last night."

She looked back at the table. "This is Reggie Lewis, our jewelry designer—Regulus Designs. I think you met the other day. Remember that name because she is going to be famous. Reggie, these are Detectives Forester and Stone. They arrested Tom Beaton." Beaton was the man who had abducted Kylee Jensen. Oddly, he also claimed he'd been possessed by aliens—when he was lucid at all. He was currently being held in the Kelowna Regional Hospital psychiatric ward for observation.

The black-haired woman colored briefly as Jas shook her hand. "It's Corporal actually. For both of us. Detective is used on Municipal police forces, or on television. Not for the Mounties."

He caught an unhappy flicker across the Chloe woman's face, so she obviously resented being corrected. Reggie motioned to the seating. "Did you want to interview us here?"

Lila, having just hung up the phone, joined them.

Danny glanced at Jas. "How about if we start with Ms. Weber?"

"Together. Sure." There was no way in hell he was letting Danny Forester conduct an interview alone given the short time since his AWOL period. The guy still couldn't fully explain where he'd been or what he'd done, just that he remembered being at the scene of the hit and run of an estate agent, and then he'd come to Peachland and started watching the women at *This and That*. It was creepy as hell that they were back here, and Jas wasn't taking any chances.

"How about on the back patio," Lila said and Danny nodded.

"You might want to take some water," Chloe offered.

Danny accepted, but Jas made it a rule not to take anything from either victims or suspects. As he stepped outside, he glanced back at the two women at the table. Chloe was watching. There was almost laughter in her eyes.

Fifteen minutes later he was beginning to figure out why she'd been laughing.

At the rear of the house the smallish backyard was half taken up with a raised flagstone area that served as a patio. Like the front porch of the house, there was an expensive looking set of wicker patio furniture complete with brightly colored cushions.

The whole effect was one of pool-side lounging, the only trouble being that there was no pool and no breeze either. With no shade over the patio he was frying his ass off here in his standard-operating procedure summer weight sports jacket. He *could* take it off, of course, but he was already sweating like the proverbial pig. Danny, meanwhile, looked like he was just getting comfortable, seated on one of the wicker chairs as he eased Lila Weber into her recollection of the night before.

Jas had preferred to remain standing. Let the interviewee and interviewer develop rapport. He could always jump in if Danny went off the deep end or missed something. He found his mind wandering, wondered whether Chloe Main used this patio to get that tan of hers. She really did have great almost violet eyes in creamy, sun-kissed skin and what looked like a mane of hair judging by the thickness of her braid. A man could lose himself in those eyes and get tangled in that hair. Too bad she hid her shape in those hippy–style caftans. She'd been wearing something similar when they'd searched for Kylee Jensen together.

And that was not what he was supposed to be focused on. He yanked himself back to the interview.

Thirty minutes into the interview that felt closer to an hour, the dark-haired Lewis woman stepped out of the house, nodded and let herself into the small workshop—jeweler's workshop, probably. Made sense. Then workshop fans started pouring more hot air out onto the patio and he seriously thought about shooting them out. If not for the paperwork involved in the firing of a service revolver, he might have.

Instead he shifted position and lasted another fifteen minutes by which time he was pretty sure his underwear was sodden.

For the third time Danny was taking Lila Weber through her description of the suspect. He'd tried a straightforward cognitive interview, and had gone on to more probing questions, all to no avail. Now he seemed bent and determined to use the questionable practice of having her imagine she was standing outside the store and seeing the suspect running toward her.

Lila shook her head. "That's the weird thing. I don't see anything. It's like one of those blurs on TV when someone moves really fast. Like the Flash or something. I don't get *anything* clearly and I'm usually really good a noticing details."

Danny sighed and looked up at Jas. How the hell did the guy stay as cool as he looked in this heat? Jas felt like his skin was frying and yet ol' Danny–boy's redhead skin seemed just fine.

"I 'm going to ask a few questions about whether there might be any connection to the Kylee Jensen case," Forester said.

Jas opened his mouth to stop the interview right there, but what the hell. If Danny wanted to waste his time on that kind of question, it gave him a chance to get out of this heat.

"Tell you what. Why don't you finish off here and I'll head inside and get Ms. Main's statement," he offered. Better to be accused of leaving his partner than of condoning this line of questioning.

He didn't wait for a reply, because he really was dying here. He let himself inside and the back door clicked shut behind him. He sighed at the coolness, just as the amethyst-eyed beauty stepped into the kitchen from the hall.

For a moment he didn't know what to say. She stood there in the sunny white and yellow kitchen with its brushed stainless fixtures, looking almost as shocked at his presence.

"Uh. Sorry. Water. Uh... I needed water. It's damn hot out there."

And by the glint in her eyes she knew perfectly well it was—in fact she'd likely been laughing at him the whole time he'd been out there! Just what did she have against the police. No, make that what did she have against him? She *had* been less than talkative the night of the search. His momentary pique faded at the light in those eyes and the faint scent of something dark and floral she wore. From somewhere in the recesses of his memory, the word freesia came to mind, like an incense stick trailing smoke into the room. Interesting, just as his reaction was. It had been a while since someone got him interested.

"The water's in the fridge," Chloe said, and moved into the room, her numerous necklaces clicking together as she shifted to the counter and opened a drawer. She pulled out a long narrow box with a colorful picture of what looked like a many-armed man with an elephant's head. Hindu god, though the name escaped him. A whiff of sweetness and spice made him almost take a step back. God preserve him, it *was* incense.

With long, deft fingers she pulled out a stick and replaced the box in the drawer, before lighting the incense stick with a barbeque lighter. A long thread of sickly sweet smoke poured from the tip of the stick and the bracelet around her wrist caught in the sunlight through the windows. Then she looked at him again, her brows arched above those eyes. "The water's there—or would you prefer tap water? There're glasses in that cupboard." She nodded to the cupboard beside the fridge.

"Uh. Yeah. Thanks." He pushed off from the door, feeling like he was shoving though deep water. He should know, he'd spent an earlier part of his career on an RCMP deep-water rescue team. But this wasn't like him—at all.

The woman—Chloe—the name suited her somehow—turned to leave.

"Your friend out there mentioned a few things that I'd like to ask you about."

Chloe paused, questions filling her gaze. "Ask away, I suppose. What would you like to know?"

He fished in his jacket pocket for his notebook. "Ms. Weber indicated that you were responsible for locking up the previous day. Is that correct?"

"Of course. I was minding the store because Kylee was away for the day." Her hand strayed to the silver bracelet she wore—the same one there'd been all sorts of talk about as being the reason for Kylee Jensen's abduction. A lot of claptrap if you asked him.

"Tell me about it."

She sighed and turned back to him, the incense stick purling a trail of smoke into the air. "I went through my usual procedures of course. I cashed out and then I pulled the most valuable displays and a few other things for the safe. I locked them up and that was that. I thought you wanted the list of what was taken. It's on the counter right beside you. I've made two copies so that there's one for the insurance as well."

He noted her comments in his notebook and looked back at her. "You mentioned other things for the safe. Like what?"

Shaking her head, she looked down at her hands. A momentary expression of guilt crossed her face. "There were Reggie's sample pieces and some of my crystals—the ones that looked most suitable for my healing practice."

Jas frowned and raised his brows in question. "Healing practice?"

She met his regard. "Yes. Healing. With crystals. They have certain resonances within them that act on the human aura to calm and purify. I'm in the final stages of opening my own healing clinic."

"Uh—huh ." With a straight face he made a show of writing 'crystals??????' in his notebook and glanced back at Chloe.

Apparently his face hadn't been as straight as he figured, because her lips were pressed into a less than happy line. Not exactly what he'd been going for when he'd decided to interview her. He needed to diffuse the situation, but *come on*, healing crystals?

He flipped his notebook closed and considered a moment. Well in for a penny... his mom always said. When she wasn't busy spending their last penny on some-or-other fortune teller.

"I see you're still wearing the bracelet. Don't tell me *you* can't get it off now?" he tried a smile. A laugh together would ease the tension in the room.

But the woman's face went still and guarded. Her one hand closed over the bracelet in question."Now why would you mention that? It's a whole lot of hokum, isn't it?" she asked softly.

The incense in her hand trailed smoke signal challenges across the gap between them. What could he say? His first inclination was to say yes, but his single mother raised him not to go out of his way to offend people.

"Well. Hokum might be a pretty strong word. I think I'll go with strange. Or odd." Or unfounded or, like healing crystals, stretching the bounds of credibility.

Her gaze narrowed as if she read his real feelings. "I can see that you don't believe in much, Detective Stone."

"Corporal. Corporal Stone."

"Of course. Because detective is on TV or municipal police." She quoted his words back at him and there was a miniscule shake of her head as if she thought use of his correct title was minutia. "Now unless you have some additional questions for me, I really should get back to cleaning up the store. We've a lot to do before we can open for business again."

She ducked out the door, her soft footfall rapidly fading. Damnation, he *did* have a question or two more for her. The guilty expression was hiding something. He grabbed a bottle of water from the fridge and followed her, pushing through the clacking curtain of beads.

She'd stuck the incense stick in a small brass holder and set it before a small bronze Buddha figure on a shelf behind the ancient-looking cash register. She glanced at him briefly, but carried on with her work, sweeping the glass up into a bin, taking down the jewel-toned scarves and folding them into a box. She righted a mannequin that had been knocked over, removed the array of necklaces from its headless neck and brushed off its black velvet covering. She left the tall shallow earring display alone—those glass cupboards hadn't apparently been touched by the perp, but the glass display counters she emptied out and placed each item in a small silk bag, then shifted around the room, sweeping everything out. She had a graceful way of moving, as if she listened to music and he wondered what kind of music it would be. Something with sitars and chanting, probably.

Totally not his thing, even though her cream top shifted over her and gave tantalizing glimpses of the curves of her body. This was no girl-woman. Chloe Main was most definitely a woman.

While she worked he tried to stay out of her way, but then she slid behind the cash register counter and pulled out two trays of stones, one purple and one black, and began sorting through them. She looked up as if she'd first noticed him. "Is there something else?" All business.

He really should just go. Forester would be a much better interviewer for this woman, given that so much about her just set him off. Let Forester interview her and then the two of them could get out of this madhouse of women who claimed that a bracelet was grounds for kidnapping and that crystals were the perfect thing for healing. The whole story about the bracelet was just so farfetched. And all the talk about possession was another ridiculous leap farther, even if Forester seemed to believe it, too. The Beaton character—well he'd clearly been off his rocker when he took Kylee. Psychotic breakdown or something, that was all. The shrinks would figure out what was going on.

"Uh, yeah." He followed her to the counter while she picked out four small stones of each color. Shaking the stones like dice, she went to each corner of the room and placed one stone of each color carefully together on the floor or window sill.

When she returned, she turned a look on him like it was a dare. "Crystals. Jet and amethyst for protection," she said and waited. "I don't want there to be any more break-ins."

As if a few stones around the room would do any good.

He pulled out his notebook again and met her dare.

CHAPTER 3

"In cases like this, when someone opened a combination safe, I have a few follow up questions," said Corporal Stone. "Can you tell me who beyond yourself and Ms. Weber had the combination?"

He stood across the glass store counter from Chloe, his previously crisp white shirt satisfyingly sodden, but he gave off a scent of heated male, dark earth and leather that was surprisingly not unpleasant. She took a step back. His powerful red aura sent a shock through hers every time he stepped anywhere near her, like now. What was it about this man that sent all her alarm bells ringing even though the word she'd dubbed him with when she first met him was, well, Honorable? But the red aura didn't feel honorable. Not at all. It meant he was a powerfully sensual being even if there was a certain dusty gray to it that spoke of guardedness. She swallowed at the animal power of him. Maybe he was the problem, more than the bracelet that had seemed to send a shock through her when he entered the room. His black hair still looked decidedly perfect even though his black gaze looked less than certain at the moment.

Uncertainty was good, wasn't it?

Yes. Her work here was done. She'd brought the good detective—make that corporal—down a notch. Served him right for being a bit of an ass in his attitude.

She looked down at the crystals she'd buried her fingers in and realized that her hands were shaking and she'd forgotten what he'd asked. "Hold on." She held up a finger for him and tried to ignore his presence as she took deep, incense-scented breaths to steady herself. She could positively feel him start to fume. Then she opened her eyes and smiled sweetly at him. If there was one thing she knew from having a brother like Brett, it was how to infuriate a man. "Okay. You were asking?"

Make him say it again. Why was it was so darned gratifying to watch him squirm? She was being a very bad woman doing this to him, but damn, he deserved it.

"As I said. I wanted to know who besides yourself has the safe combination?" The typical cop reserve seemed to descend over him. His notebook was held ready for her answer and that was both good and a shame because it totally shut down the tingle she'd been getting off of him.

What was wrong with her? She didn't want to be attracted to this guy. This cop.

"Well Lila and I are about it. There's Kylee, too. But she's away until tomorrow."

His pen nib scratched across the notebook. He looked up at her. "And where is Ms. Jensen?"

"My brother took her down to Radium Hot Springs for a few days. After the abduction she was kind of shaken." Another scritch-scritch note.

"And where were you last night, Ms. Main?"

What the... "Me? I was at home in bed, of course. Until Lila called me and asked me to come over. I got here as fast as I could—within five minutes—well maybe ten."

It was a cop looking back at her with that steady dark inspection, not a man she was teasing. Almost as if he thought she was part of this whole thing.

"I—I just live down the beach. I have a condo so all it took was throwing on some clothes and I was here in a flash."

"Your address?"

She gave it to him and looked down at the bracelet. Silly thing might have given her a jolt when he first walked in, but it didn't seem to have any effect at all on him. He was looking at her like she was a suspect.

"Can you think of anyone else who would know that you had suddenly decided to place all those additional valuables in the safe?"

His gaze never left her. What did he want? Couldn't he tell she was dying inside because she'd made Reggie lose everything— all her designs. "No. No, I can't. There's nothing I can say other than I was responsible. I talked Reggie into putting her designs in the safe for safekeeping and all I've done is get her into this predicament." Dammit, her eyes were watering and all she wanted was for this man—this cop—to let her be.

"You're feeling pretty guilty about that," he said.

She looked up in surprise. "Wouldn't you? Do you know how many hours in that oven of a workshop she spent to design and create those pieces. They were beautiful. Glorious, and they were going to walk down the runways of Milan. Do you know what that would do for her career? And I wrecked it!"

The good corporal snapped his notebook closed and slipped it back in his pocket. He seemed to assess her and he shook his head. "This is going to sound pretty stupid, but do you think there's any connection between this theft and the bracelet?"

Where the heck that question came from she didn't know, but she looked down at the bracelet on her wrist and made a show of studying each of the links in turn. It let her put herself together when she thought he was going to go in for the jugular and confirm that she was responsible. Was he trying to be kind by changing the subject? She just needed him to leave, and the only way she could think of to get him to do that was by being everything he seemed to hate. "Well...It is a lot to take in, and it doesn't really seem to make a lot of sense, but from the moment I put the bracelet on I got this sense of impending doom. And fear. It's really quite threatening. I think it was telling me this was going to happen." She deliberately looked up at him with her most dead pan, moon-unit expression and pulled out some patter from 1970's reruns. "But I mean, that's really far out, isn't it?"

The guy turned stone-still and his eyes went flat. That nice warm aura pulled back and for a moment she could breathe. And think. He was looking almost sick to his probably nice rock-hard stomach, but then his eyes narrowed, his jaw worked and his skin returned to its normal sun-darkened tan. He pursed his infuriatingly kissable lips and rubbed his five o'clock shadow. "Okay. I think maybe I deserved that. I take it my bias about psychic stuff shows?"

"A little bit," she bit back a smile, because he really had been a jerk about her crystals.

"You're not really a psychic, are you?"

His eyes were jet black and made her think of the protective forces of the stones she'd just used around the store. She didn't like that she thought of him that way.

"I guess that depends on what you consider a psychic. Do I tell fortunes? No. Do I think there's something more to the world than what we experience with our usual five senses? Most definitely."

She raised her chin at him, daring him to make some inappropriate comment.

"So just what do you base that opinion on, then? A hunch? A feeling? Maybe the way the wind blows, or maybe once an owl hooted outside your window and coincidentally an elderly neighbor died?"

Apparently he didn't turn away from a dare anymore than she did; it didn't expose a finer side of this fine looking specimen of a man. A darn shame, that.

She steeled herself, reached out and grabbed his wrist, feeling the bright jolt of his body's energy like a small lightning strike in her chest. "Feel that? That's what I base my 'psychic nature' on—the fact that we're all comprised of neurons firing and cells fissioning and so on. That releases a lot of energy. I can feel it. We all can if we pay a little attention."

"I don't feel a damn thing." None too gently he jerked his hand away, but there was something there. Confusion, maybe in the way he looked at her. "Look. I came in here to interview you, not get into some pissing match about whether it's reasonable to believe in stuff like telepathy, reincarnation and our future written in the stars. I came in to ask you about the robbery and whether you're concerned for you and your friends' safety. Not whether the bracelet is psychically connected to aliens or something." He hooked his fingers around 'psychically connected' as if that would soften the insult. "There's still the possibility that there's some weirdo out there who figures that the fact you're wearing the bracelet makes you fair game for whatever weirdness he's into. He could have broken in here looking for it. I'm sure you and your friends don't want anything to happen."

As if that was her cue, Lila pushed in through the beaded curtain, Danny at her back. "You were getting kinda loud and it looks like we've got a car-full heading this way." She nodded out the window at a small pack of fashionista-types walking along the beachfront promenade toward *This and That's* front gate from a brand new iridescent white Audi. They stopped when they saw the sign.

"Do you want to go out and explain to them, or should I?" Then she stopped and gave Chloe and the good Corporal the once over. "Is everything all right here?"

Chloe cast a glance at the Corporal, who stood so sternly here before her. When he'd reacted to her he'd looked the epitome of the brave protector—stern jaw and flashing gaze. But in the face of Lila and Corporal Forester's intrusion his certainty was fading. For someone so definitively male, it was actually kind of charming; as if it softened that blazing red aura and cleared some of the dirty gray overtones. She no longer felt his presence like an attack against her. There was pressure, sure, but more like the pressure that holds tectonic plates together.

Odd, that thought. She sighed. The whole day was looking like it was going to be a mess.

"Everything's fine, Lila. Corporal Stone's just checking on a few things to make sure we're all safe. I told him we are. Right?

And as for me, don't worry. I don't need any help from you, Corporal. Nothing at all."

§

In the dimly lit jewelry shop, the two women stood like bookends on the silence that followed Chloe Main's absolute put down. Then Chloe excused herself and went outside to hurry down the stairs to the women who were standing around the sandwich board looking upset. She looked animated and friendly, not at all the guarded woman he'd interviewed, so something was definitely going on. Hmm. He glanced over at Danny who was watching him.

"So you finished the interview?"

Danny scrubbed his fingers through his mat of red hair. "Sure did. Ms. Weber was very helpful. How'd it go in here?"

Jas shrugged noncommittally. Not much more he could say unless he wanted to start talking about fire and water.

After ten years as a cop, being told you basically were good for nothing, cut kinda deep. Chloe had made it clear that the only thing that was going to come out of her mouth were more of the none-too-veiled insults at his lack of belief in her New Age mumbo jumbo, while Lila Weber looked like some vengeful goddess in lavender the way she was looking at him. No question, if you took on one of these women, you took on the whole pack.

Definitely not his plan.

"All right then. I guess we'll leave you to your own devices."

They thanked the Weber woman and went outside into the pleasant shade of the front porch and down the stairs into sunshine, passing Chloe and the women still clustered around her.

"You see," she said. "The police are just leaving. We really need a chance to get the shop back in shape before opening, but I understand your need what with the wedding coming up. Is there any way you could come back tomorrow? We could try setting up some displays on the patio for you?"

Jas paused at the car to see what the women would say. There was a low murmur and then, "You mean a private party?"

Chloe considered a moment and then nodded. "I guess I do. If you're willing to be a guinea pig for us."

"Deal!" said a young woman who seemed to be at the heart of the group.

Chloe smiled and it really was a beautiful smile the way it lit up her eyes. Then she caught him looking at her and the light faded. He didn't like that and slid into the driver seat and closed the door.

Chloe Main was the exact opposite of most people who believed in psychic nonsense. Sure some cops believed, but they weren't the norm and mostly kept it to themselves. Most of the believers lived life on the fringe. Questionable lives. But Chloe Main seemed far from that. Lovely. Practical. Proud. A good business woman. Grounded, except for her beliefs. He just didn't get her.

But finding out more about her hadn't exactly worked. All he'd done was alienate her more and raise more questions. And why should he care, anyway? She was some damned New Ager and he'd had enough of that to last a lifetime when he was a kid. His mom and all her cronies with their tarot cards and their astrology and their palm reading—they couldn't make a decision without consulting those damned card readers and she'd even tried to stop him from entering policing, telling him he'd lose himself if he did.

Just how did a grown man 'lose himself'? He shook himself and found Danny frowning at him.

"So just what went on in there," Danny asked.

"Like I said, I was just talking to Chloe—Ms. Main—about her part in this thing. You know she and the Weber woman are the only ones with the safe combination. Well, them and Kylee Jensen who happens to be out of town. And Chloe Main was also the one who suggested to the designer that she put her showpieces in the safe. How's that for a nice set up if there was one? Oh yeah. And we talked about the bracelet, but as you heard she isn't worried." He kept his voice noncommittal, though a part of his innards twisted uncomfortably. Just what was he doing? Trying to cast suspicion on her? Or was it just that he was pissed at how she'd bested him in their conversation. But at the same time he had a niggling feeling that something was wrong. Where it came from he had no idea. He glanced at his partner and started the car.

He pulled out from the curb and pulled a U-turn, heading them back toward West Kelowna. Beach Avenue seemed to have picked up traffic and there was a crowd at the neighborhood bakery/café all lounging in spandex after a walk or a run. Summer people mostly, he'd bet. Through the open window he inhaled the scent of fresh cookies and espresso.

Any way he looked at it he was done with this place. So done.

"Yeah. I guess we are." Danny said, looking sideways at him.

Jas had to think a moment and realized he'd spoken his thoughts aloud. Hopefully not all of them.

" I think it's kind of interesting that Lila Weber has so little description of the man in her store, " Danny said. "It's damn weird the way she describes it, don't you think?"

"Not really. There're lots of witnesses who can't describe a suspect."

Danny shook his head. "Not like this. Usually they remember something or they come up with something. They have this need to give us something even if it's wrong. But Lila Weber—it was more like something erased her memory. Reminds me of how I don't remember everything from when I—you know."

Oh God, not the possession thing, again. This was just feeding Forester's own delusions. "I really don't see where one case has got anything to do with the other. Lila Weber is probably just a poor witness, and as for the other case, we caught Tom Beaton."

"But Kylee Jensen said she believed the Tom who abducted her had an entirely different personality than normal."

Jas had to hold himself back as he gripped the steering wheel. "It's called a psychotic breakdown or something. We'll leave it to the head doctors to sort that out. Either way, we've got reports to make and paperwork to do on this case. " He wished the hell Forester would quit trying to link the two.

Thankfully, Forester just closed his mouth and looked out the window as Jas steered the car up the long, steep slope of Drought Hill. The view over the lake was spectacular, as usual, the water almost the color of those stones of Chloe's, the dark hills like the burnished sweep of her hair.

"Penny," Forester asked as the road flattened and curved between the pine covered hills toward West Kelowna and the detachment.

Jasper shook himself, trying to rid himself of the image of the laughter in Chloe's lavender eyes. "You'd have wasted your penny."

CHAPTER 4

The sun had already risen the next morning when Chloe stumbled out of bed and to the kitchen of her third floor condo. The room was painted the palest of blues to capture the blue light off the water. With its white cupboards and marble counters, the room radiated a cool clear light that helped her wipe the uneasy sleep out of her head and prepare her for the magnificent view out her kitchen window. Having been raised in Peachland in the house overlooking the lake that Kylee Jensen currently rented, it would be easy to become jaded with the view: miles of blue water stretching out from virtually her front doorway. But the kitchen paint job helped bring the lake view inside so each time she entered the kitchen the energy of the lake found her. It refreshed and innervated like a long cool drink of water.

This morning even the view wasn't quite so refreshing. She couldn't remember the dreams last night, but her body still carried a disturbing heaviness to her limbs as if she was trapped inside her body. She had this horrible sense of impending doom and her wrist was still tender from the burning sensation around her right wrist where the bracelet lay. She had woken to that searing pain this morning, but there were no marks to see. She leaned on the counter a moment, willing the negative sensations out with her exhaled breath. It was all just a particularly vivid nightmare.

She fished a bag of organic, fair-trade coffee beans out of the cupboard, ground them and filled the espresso maker, and clicked the machine on, then turned to the truly important task at hand.

"Yes, you. I see you there. I haven't forgotten." Clyde, the big old Siamese blue point cat she'd rescued as a kitten from a barn up on Trepanier Creek Road, head-butted her leg. There was no mistaking Clyde's intentions, whereas the man she had fallen asleep thinking of had just left her confused. She pulled open the tiny tin of organic cat food and doled out a quarter of the tin. Clyde was up on his hind legs beside her, his paws stretching up over the edge of the counter until she let him lick the spoon. Then she set the bowl down for him.

"There, you spoiled old thing. Just so you know, you need to start exercising or we're going to have to cut your tinned food down to barely a taste at each meal. You're starting to get downright chubby."

Clyde just chewed a little faster as he hoovered his food. He obviously wasn't taking any chances that she might start him on a diet now.

Pulling her lamb-patterned cotton pajamas around her she peered out the window at the ultra-calm lake and went back to the espresso machine. She carefully went through the motions of making a perfect cup. Years ago, during the time her parents liked to call her lost years, she'd spent time in San Francisco and learned the barista skills there. It hadn't been a pretty scene as an almost-runaway, and she'd made some really bad choices before she hooked up with some people who not only taught her about the healing properties of stones and chakra readings, but had also given her a job in their café. There, amid carob and New Age music, she'd learned how to make the perfect cup of organic, responsible trade coffee. She was still giving into her addiction, to this day.

The machine burbled and belched as she steamed milk and poured it into the cup with a lovely flourish that left a fleur-de-lis on the top. Carrying her mug, she went out onto her patio and sank into her chair. The pots of bamboo she had along one wall of the patio rustled in the breeze and placed lovely shadows against the building's wood siding. She had an herb garden growing in small pots by the glass railing, along with a burgeoning pot of cacti that she always pulled in close to the windows for protection during the winter. It was lovely and peaceful and filled with the sounds of the wind and water and the small temple bells she had hung from strings attached to a small overhang.

Like at Lila's, she found so much energy just by staring out at the lake. There had to be a ley line running down the Okanagan Valley, because this place always filled her up more than any place else. Some of the places of power she'd visited like Stonehenge, and a Neolithic village in Portugal had supposedly been built at nodes where the earth's power lines met. It had felt the same as this.

"And if you don't believe in them, Corporal Jasper Stone, I don't really care." She patted her lap and Clyde leapt up beside her. He was actually too big for her lap, so he sat beside her and draped his upper body over her thighs. "He's one of the most obtuse men I've ever met, Clyde. Or maybe not obtuse, because he's smart enough to pick up on the fact I felt guilty about Reggie's stuff being stolen. He's just so willfully blind."

That was it. The man seemed to be the kind that would turn his back on facts just because they didn't fit with the rules he set for the world. "I don't like that in a man, Clyde, so why am I thinking about him?"

She stroked Clyde's lovely gray-blue fur and his purr hummed through her thighs. He was a far cry from the shaking little kitten that had turned up in the old barn on the Elkhart Winery lands. Then he'd been so wild and fierce no one could get near him. Brett, knowing Chloe's way with animals, had called her up to help his boss, because they wanted to tear the old barn down to put in the new tasting room. She'd gone up to the barn with a bag of cat treats and a borrowed cat-carry box, but it turned out she didn't need the treats. The warrior kitten had smelled her outstretched hand and it was like he decided something. He'd walked right out from between some hay bales and had allowed her to pick him up.

"You chose me, didn't you, little man?" Clyde gave a sleepy chirrup and looked up at her with adoring, half-mast, sapphire-blue eyes. And it was a love that would last til death did them part.

Not like 'love' with men, if there really was such a thing. No, there was. Kylee and Brett showed it in spades. It was her that would never experience love—all the mistakes she'd made in life pretty much ensured it.

To rid herself of the old regret, she thought about the private jewelry party she'd agreed to yesterday. Lila had had some misgivings, but with some convincing she'd seen the potential that providing private parties could have. She sipped her coffee while watching the summer people on the lake, the flotilla of Canada geese floating past, and far out on the lake, a lone sailboat catching the breeze. If private parties worked for jewelry sales, she wondered if it might be something they could do with an exclusive list of their most regular customers. And then there was the potential it might have with the healing stones. She could envision small groups of like-minded women doing meditation exercises and then she would assist each of them to reach that sacred place of calm.

As she thought, she grabbed the end of her braid, undid the purple cord that kept the ends bound together and worked open the strands with her fingers. The breeze spread her heavy hair around her shoulders, but it didn't help the tight feeling in her chest that had plagued her all night. She felt restless and unsettled. Working out the details of private parties just made it worse. That wasn't like her. Usually sitting here was meditative, her way to wake up and start the day.

Her hand found the links of the silver bracelet and she slid the links around to study each one. It really was a charming piece of jewelry. It made no sense that it had disturbed her sleep as it had.

She placed her palm above the metal and opened herself mentally, while she inhaled the heat and sun-warmed water of the morning.

Heat and stunted straggling trees torn by hard winds. A sense of dust and death and endings and grief.

She jerked her palm away. What the heck? Was that real or imagination? Her hand felt hot, just like her wrist had, but when she turned it over there were small red marks on her palm that almost perfectly matched the links of the small metal doors. At least she thought they did, but they faded away almost as quickly as she'd spotted them. Something weird, but then when had the bracelet been anything but weird. Did what she'd seen mean the bracelet came from the desert? They suspected that already, given what they'd found out about the bracelet's previous owner, a now-deceased British Colonel, George Bristol who had served in Egypt. Maybe it was all the power of suggestion.

"And now you sound exactly like a certain police Corporal."

Time to get her butt in gear and get some exercise. She eased Clyde off her lap and stood up just as someone rang the doorbell to her condo. No one had asked to be buzzed in, so it had to be one of her neighbors. She shoved her hair back behind her ears wishing she hadn't unbraided it, and went to the door.

Her neighbor from down the hall, Allan Green stood there, clasping a brown paper bag and looking far too bright and ready to face the day. He was a slim, forty-something, slightly-effeminate ex-school teacher that had somehow parlayed his teaching into a career writing textbooks. He was now retired from his non-fiction and was trying his hand at writing children's books. He was almost literally vibrating the way he was bouncing up and down in his rainbow-colored trainers and black running gear. He kept glancing furtively up and down the hall as if expecting an attacker. Chloe followed his gaze, but there was no one there.

"Are you okay, Chloe? Have you heard?" Allan worriedly swiped at a wisp of fawn-colored hair that had fallen across his forehead.

"I'm sorry? Have I heard what? Do you want to come in?"Conscious of her lamb covered pajamas, she stepped aside to allow Allan inside and led him into the livingroom.

It was a good room, with high ceilings, of warm wood browns and greens with a lovely blue-green-brown weaving which reminded her of a forest creek hung on the wall above the fireplace. She motioned Allan to the brown micro-suede sofa and sank down across from him in the matching chair.

"Can I get you something? A coffee? I'm going to make myself another." Or maybe she wouldn't. She really needed to get out there for her walk.

Allan shook his head and grasped Chloe's hands. Behind him, shelves ran along one wall holding displays of various crystals she'd collected over the years, her pride being a magnificent amethyst thunder egg that was almost a foot across and a single rutilated quartz crystal that stood almost eighteen inches high. They'd cost her a fortune, but they kept her place filled with energy and balance.

"I heard about what happened to your store the other night," Allan said. "It's the talk of the town. That and the attack on your shopkeeper. How could someone like Tom Beaton do something like that, I ask you. Anyway, when I heard about the break-in here this morning, I had to check on you. You must be so unsettled."

Chloe pulled her hands loose and frowned. Allan was good people, but mightily in love with gossip, too. "I'm sorry. I'm not following. What break-in here are you talking about?"

Allan leaned forward, too clearly enjoying his role as bearer of bad news, but his knuckles were white on the bag he clutched in his lap. "Why Ginger and Harry Singh, of course. They got home this morning after spending the past few days up in Vernon to avoid the Canada Day press. Their place had been broken into and all of their lovely jewelry stolen."

Chloe sat back in her seat for a moment unsettled by the memory of walking into *This and That* and the violation she'd felt. Ginger and Harry owned the condo next to hers, at the lakeward end of the building. "Really. That is a surprise. And no one saw anything? Not even with all the security around here?" Another twinge of ill-ease ran through her. Just what was going on in Peachland? It was like they were having a crime wave.

Allan shook his head, his wide eyes showing his fascination with the subject. "Apparently not. There are still so many people around the condos what with the celebration this week and friends visiting tenants. I suppose unless they find fingerprints the police won't do much of anything."

Exactly like the store. "Maybe the security cameras will show something."

Allan brightened. "That's right. I'd forgotten about them. I'm sure they'll catch the guy, won't they? But in the meantime I'm going to move my jewelry to my safety deposit box. Given it's Sunday, do you think I could put my things in your safe until the banks open tomorrow?"

Chloe frowned, eyeing Allan's brown paper bag. A man had jewelry? A watch. The cufflinks from his wedding and a couple of tie pins was about all her father had had in his life. Allan's bag suddenly looked bulkier than she'd noticed before. She had a small safe similar to the one at the store that she had purchased because some of her healing stones were quite expensive. "Of course. As long as there isn't too much. I don't have a lot of room."

"It's just a few things, really. If you can." The brown paper rattled and Clyde joined them in the livingroom. He went to Allan to sniff the bag hopefully, then sat there intently watching as Allan pulled out small silk bag after small silk bag.

"I used to teach overseas. For some reason I kept buying jewelry. Then my mom died and left me hers. I haven't had it appraised in years."

Chloe felt her jaw dropping as Allan continued to pile the small silk bags on the arm of the sofa. "What is all this stuff?"

"Well... there's a pearl necklace or two," he motioned at two of the larger bags. "Oh and a sapphire necklace that is just way too ornate to wear anywhere—not that I would. I don't know what I was thinking when I bought that, other than it was pretty and would probably hold its value. And there are rings and a pair or two of diamond cufflinks. That sort of thing."

Chloe eyed the stack of bags. That didn't explain half of what she was seeing. She shook her head. "I'm sorry, but my little safe can't handle even half of this. How about you pick out, say, the five or six most valuable pieces and I'll lock them up. The rest you're going to have to stand guard over, I'm afraid."

Allan looked disappointed, but he quickly selected the bags and handed them to Chloe. "Here. These ones." The others he stuffed back in the brown sack. Then he stood. "Don't let me keep you from your coffee. Oh, and here. Can you sign this receipt?" He scribbled a few lines on a paper he pulled from his pocket and handed it to Chloe.

> *I, the undersigned, agree that I have assumed custody of 5 pieces of jewelry from Allan Green and will hold those pieces safe until they are returned to Allan Green.*
> *Sapphire necklace*
> *Diamond studs, 1 carat*
> *Diamond studs 2 carat*
> *18- inch Tahitian pearl necklace and earrings*
> *Diamond ring 2 carat.*

"My God, Allan. This must be worth a fortune. Are you sure you trust me?"

He shrugged. "Who else have I got?"

"Isn't there anyone else in town you could leave all this with? Maybe in Kelowna?"

When Allan shook his head, Chloe stood up and led him back into her office, which was the second bedroom of the apartment. In the general calmness of her home, it was also her disaster area: stacked papers were piled on virtually every flat surface and reference books were stacked on the shelves and the floor.

"Sorry about the mess. It's the business. I'm just about ready to hang out my shingle and the paperwork has been madness. Also, Brett and I have been dealing with our parent's estate, and then all this stuff with Kylee."

She shook her head and went to the small safe on the floor of what should have been the room's closet. Instead it was filled with shelving and upright file cabinets. She worked the combination lock and opened the safe door. "Here. Hand me those bags." She carefully opened each one and checked inside before placing it on the carefully wrapped rough diamond, amethyst, opals and pearls she had in the safe. "If you're going to have me sign a receipt I guess I should make sure the items match."

She signed the receipt, set a time for Allan to retrieve his things the next morning, and Chloe let him out of the apartment. Through the floor-to-ceiling windows she could see out onto her patio and to the lake beyond. Well, she'd lounged around long enough. It *really* was time to do something more energetic. Maybe not a walk though.

Stripped out of her p.j.s she pulled on her indigo one-piece swimsuit and a grabbed her bathing cap, goggles, and a towel. She threw a long t-shirt on over top and, with a "bye, buddy" to Clyde, headed out the door for the complex pool.

The condo complex she lived in was the first and most likely the last in Peachland. It had drawn much criticism because the development had taken out a much-revered old campground, and in the process the developer had mown down an entire grove of willow trees much like the huge old tree on her parent's property. They'd been beautiful trees and she'd felt like a traitor buying into the place. But it was the only thing she could afford that was close to the water and yet let her have the privacy she needed to rebalance herself. When her parents had passed, she and Brett had talked about her possibly moving back into the family home, but frankly along with all the good stuff of the last ten years, there were some very hard memories of her teen years, too. The place had been full of those memories and she didn't need them unbalancing her, even if she hadn't yet brought herself to a place where she could sell the old homestead.

The condo complex took up the entire area of the original campground. It was a huge, L-shaped structure built supposedly to ensure that most everyone had a view of the lake except for the poor souls who looked out onto the highway. In between the two wings of the L lay a lovely garden with walkways. In the center was a huge, elevated deck and pool area so that you could lie in the sun and still enjoy a view of the lake.

Thankfully, at this time of day no children were allowed in the pool. A few of the residents had chaises claimed with towels and one elderly woman paddled with a flotation belt, but otherwise the turquoise water was empty. She stripped off the t-shirt, quickly rebraided her hip-length hair and wound it around her head before fighting it into her bathing cap. She slipped into the water. Warmed by the sun, it was like settling into bathwater.

"Well, Mr. Bracelet, I hope you like chlorine, because you are about to get wet." She fitted her goggles in place, took a breath and started swimming.

It was always strange the way she never really wanted to go swim, and yet when she did it was like she fell in love with her body all over again. The long reach and pull of shoulder muscle, the kick of her legs. The feel of her trapezoids stretching and working with each stroke. She reached the far end of the pool, did a swimmer's turn and kept going. As a kid she'd loved swimming. As a runaway in California she'd eschewed the water because it just reminded her of who and what she'd been. Now she was okay with it, because with thirty-four years you began to have at least some perspective.

She kept going, keeping count until she'd finished her usual two kilometers. She came up for air and lifted her goggles. Still not many people here. But she felt good. Really good, as a matter of fact. Even good enough to swim a bit more. She settled her goggles in place and kept going.

§

That was how Jas first saw her. He and Forester pulled the brown unmarked police car in to the sidewalk edge in front of the three story concrete condo. The place was huge and more reminiscent of something you might see on the coast. It also reminded him of the time-share condo communities he'd seen in Cancun and Puerto Vallarta, except that instead of palm trees it had blue spruce and juniper.

"Looks nice enough," he said.

Forester shook his head. "There's been nothing but problems with it. Easterners bought in as investments, but never live here, so they rent the apartments out and the renters bring in the problems for the owners who do live on site. There's been a churn of residents through the place. At least that's what I've heard. The uniformed guys are out here regularly."

"So why aren't they dealing with this, too?" Jasper asked, spotting the trim figure of a woman in a dark blue bathing suit and cap on the pool deck. Sunlight glistened off her body as she stretched out her arms above her head. Then she dove in, clean as a fish and set out in a distance-covering powerful stroke.

"I think it's the value of the goods taken. They're estimating it as close to a hundred thou."

"Uh huh," Jas said, his attention on the pool. The swimmer had one sweet stroke and she kicked like she had an outboard motor for legs. Someone visiting? Or one of the troublemaker renters Forester had mentioned.

"Stone? You with me?"

"Huh? What?" He pulled his attention away as she did a neat swimmer's turn and drove off, back the way she'd come. It must get frustrating as hell when you can barely do a dozen strokes before you have to turn again. He shook himself to get the dazzle of water and woman out of his eyes and looked at his partner. "You were saying?"

"The value of the goods stolen here was about a hundred thou."

Jas whistled. "You don't see that every day."

"Not in this neck of the woods and not all in jewelry, that's for certain."

Forester led the way down the path that aimed for the main doors and rang the apartment. They were buzzed inside, where security cameras faced them from a discreet spot in the corner. "We'll have to get the tapes if the uniforms haven't already done that." He nodded to the camera.

Forester noted it in his notebook, while Jasper examined the door for signs of forced entry into the building. Unfortunately there were a lot of them, which sort of demonstrated the problems with rental tenants. He'd seen it before in his prior posting in Surrey.

The building smelled better than most rental places did, that was certain, and someone had forked out big bucks for the elaborate artificial flower arrangement that sat on a podium in the center of the building's common entry. It was filled with exotic looking blooms of orange and red and yellow that were reflected in broad mirrors on one beige wall behind a beige couch. With the unrelenting beige carpet, the colorful flowers were a blessed relief.

A silent elevator took them to the third floor where they faced a hellishly long beige corridor lined with black doors that disappeared into the distance in both directions. If he didn't know better he'd think they'd entered his mother's version of purgatory, where whatever door you opened you found your own personal hell.

"This way," Forester said, and headed down the hallway in the direction of the lake. At least aside from the weird shit to do with the Jensen woman, Forester seemed to be himself again. He was even clear sighted this morning as if a few good nights of sleep and a change of clothes really could remake the man. A good thing, given the detachment commander was watching. Not that Jas would spill the beans about his partner's apparent interest in things occult at the moment, but if he thought police work was being compromised, well, that was a different story. So far so good.

Apartment 321 had a solid looking black door just like all the others—so the developer hadn't spared expense there. The door was opened by a tiny gray-haired South Asian woman, but tiny only insofar as she was small boned and built like she was made of wire and muscle instead of flesh and blood. She wore an expensive-looking mushroom-colored knit trouser and top set with a pale pink shawl around her shoulders that might have come from Chloe Main's shop.

"Mrs. Singh?" he enquired.

"That's right. You must be the police detectives that I was told about." She opened the door wider. "Do come inside, please."

She led them into the livingroom. It was, well, white. Floor-to-ceiling windows lit a room of white leather couches and chairs, white Berber carpet on hardwood, and white walls. The only thing that wasn't washed out of color, was a man with naturally golden South Asian skin and salt and pepper hair wearing a neon-orange polo shirt with khakis. He stood when they entered the room.

"Harry Singh," he said holding out his hand. "You've met my wife, Ginger." He nodded down at his diminutive wife, his profile displaying his great hooked nose, like an eagle. "Thank you so much for coming."

"Mr. and Mrs. Singh, I'm Corporal Jas Stone and this is my partner, Corporal Daniel Forester. We've been advised of your break-in and we wanted to take your statement and then perhaps have a look around—if that's okay?" Jas said.

"Certainly. Certainly, though I'm not certain there is more we can tell you that we did not tell the men in uniform," Harry Singh said. He motioned them to the couch.

Jasper let Forester settle there, then stepped back to observe. It was always better to have one officer do the questioning while the other observed. It allowed them to pick up on any inconsistent body language and also identify follow-up questions that were needed. Forester and he had had it down to an art form—up until Danny disappeared. Thankfully it seemed his partner hadn't totally lost his shtick since the weird-ass breakdown. In cases like this you had to be careful that something like insurance fraud wasn't going on.

He stood carefully out of the line of sight of the couple who began to answer Danny's questions about their trip away. They'd decided to visit friends in Vernon rather than face the Canada Day crowds here and had packed up and left on Friday morning to avoid the worst of the traffic. They had left Ginger's jewelry in her jewelry case in the bedroom. When they arrived home at seven a.m. this morning—they were expecting guests to arrive from Calgary today—they'd found the jewelry cabinet open and everything gone. Nothing else in the house was taken.

Jasper kept his ears on the conversation. Yada yada yada. Forester was doing his usual thorough job. The apartment, for all its stark modernity, really was quite nice. Set on the lakeward corner of the building, its broad windows gave out onto a sunlit patio that overlooked the inner courtyard, but you could also see northeastward out at the deep blue of the lake. Nice, but it was the courtyard that had his attention. The woman he'd spotted was still swimming—long even strokes down the center of the pool, lapping the other swimmers that joined her. At each end there was a quick flip of body, a flash of tanned thigh and then another line of perfect strokes to the other end of the pool, and flip again.

He just might have to come hang out here to meet her.

He pulled his attention back when Forester spoke his name. "Sorry. What was that?"

Danny looked up at him, his brown scrutiny questioning just where his partner's attention had been. "I was suggesting that maybe Mrs. Singh could show you the jewelry case and you could check out the doors and windows. Forensics was in this morning, but we might as well take a look while we wait for their report."

Jasper nodded, gave a last backwards glance to the mermaid in the pool and dutifully followed Mrs. Singh into the master bedroom. This room at least had color in it, but it was still done in weird modern furniture that seemed built entirely too close to the ground. A red duvet covered the bed and red and gold tapestries covered the headboard. It was like the room was a weird combination of Arabian Nights meets the Swedish chef from the Muppets.

"It is there. The jewelry." Mrs. Singh pointed out a mirror on the wall.

Frowning, he followed her over and was surprised when the whole mirror swung out to expose a spacious, black-velvet covered interior.

"This was where it was—my wedding necklaces and bracelets. My mother's special things. Things that Harry has bought me over the years. There were diamonds earrings Harry bought me for our anniversary, and a ruby necklace of my mother's. Both were very valuable and priceless in memories. You know?" She gave him a little head-waggle, but emotion filled her expression.

Clearly her loss was far more than the value of the things.

"We'll do everything in our power to get your things back." He looked over the mirrored cabinet without touching it. "This is the only place you had jewelry? The only thing that was touched?"

"There were a few small things—rings and such—in the bathroom on a ring holder. They were taken also. But my husband collects rare coins and those collections were untouched as were some valuable statues in the livingroom. I don't understand this. It is like they were very angry with me." She crossed her arms over her chest protectively.

"From what you've told me I don't think this is focused on you at all. It's a simple break and enter looking for something easily sold. I don't think you have anything to be afraid of."

Her overfull eyes gradually cleared of their fear. "You think so?"

He tried on his best RCMP deep voice. "I do, Ma'am. Now perhaps you can take me around to check the doors and windows?"

She did, not that there were many to check. The apartment was basically the one large master bedroom, ensuite and a great room concept living-dining and kitchen with an extra bedroom in back. He examined the window closures and the sliding glass doors from the bedroom out onto the patio. Out the window he caught a glimpse of the mermaid still swimming those long effortless strokes. Who the heck was she?

The expansive patio was filled with the sun's heat, but the Singhs had used the space to create an outdoor garden of bamboo and tall grasses that dappled the pavement with shade.

"I've never seen such huge balconies," he said as he bent to check the sliding door into the livingroom. It looked okay, but there might be a slight scratch on the frame next to the locking mechanism. He leaned in for a closer look.

"Actually, there are only four condominiums with patios this large. They're all on this floor at this end of the building close to the lake. The others are all much smaller."

He stood up from the doorway and went to the patio edge to stare along the front of the building. It looked like a solid wall of concrete with regular indentations for shadowed balconies.

The Singhs might have a great patio full of light, but the vast majority of people didn't. The patios looked crammed together across the face of the building with only short walls to separate one from the next. These extended across the building until another wall blocked the view into the Singh's domain. If he leaned out, he could see into the neighbor's small deck. An expensive-looking bike leaned against the wall and a bathing suit dried on the back of a chaise. He pulled back and glanced down into the courtyard where the mermaid was doing some kind of backstroke that sent her sailing down the pool even though she didn't look like she was moving. He dragged his attention back to the building configuration and then turned back to Mrs. Singh.

"So let me see if I've got this straight. You left for the weekend and left your jewelry here. It was gone when you got home. You had locked up your doors and windows. You don't have a security system. Is that about it?"

She nodded. The sunlight caught the angles of her face and made him realize what an attractive woman she was. She must have been a stunner when she was young. Funny how you missed that as a younger man.

"Do you wear your jewelry a lot, Mrs. Singh?"

She frowned. "I suppose so. Not the elaborate things, of course—my marriage jewelry. Those were—well, part of my dowry." She colored slightly as if embarrassed. "But the rest, yes. Why have it if you do not wear it? Diamond earrings go with everything. So do gold bangles." That head waggle again. A cultural thing, but charming.

He nodded and led the way back into the apartment where Forester had just closed his notebook. "Finished?" he asked.

"I think I've seen everything I need to see. Thank you for your time, Mr. and Mrs. Singh. We'll let you know if we find anything. Now I believe the uniformed officers asked you to prepare a list of the jewelry with descriptions, so that we can watch for it. Have you got that for us?"

"Right here," Forester waved a sheaf of papers that looked like it also included photos. "They were prepared and had everything documented for their insurance."

They took their leave and headed down the hallway.

"They got in through the patio," Jas said. "I'll lay money on it. There're marks on the door and any second story man could get onto the patio by crossing from the other apartments. They're all barely separated by privacy walls."

Forester nodded thoughtfully. "So an inside job, then. Should be easy enough to check who's living in the apartments in that side of the building."

"So we've got a plan, then."

The elevator dinged fortuitously as they reached it and the doors slid open to reveal a slim figure in a t-shirt, toweling mile-long hair. Below the hem of the t-shirt another mile long length of slim tanned legs just about stole Jas's breath before they ended in a pair of simple flip-flops and ten blue-painted toenails.

Mermaid.

Chloe Main.

Even soaking wet she was beautiful.

Fuck.

CHAPTER 5

CHLOE STARED DUMBLY OUT AT THE TWO POLICE OFFICERS and almost let the elevator doors slide shut in front of her. Corporal Forester of the russet hair was the first to move, leaping to get a shoulder into the sliding doors. When they were fully open again he grinned.

"Well, fancy meeting you here, Ms. Main. I didn't know this was where you lived."

She managed to pull her awareness away from the tall dark presence in the hallway, who had instantly transformed her luxurious feeling of completion at finishing her swim, into one of mortification at being seen like this by that—that idiot.

No makeup, hair a mess, half naked. *Quite the way to impress, Main.* Not that she needed to impress this man.

"Corporal Forester." She purposely ignored the tall detective with him. "Let me guess. You're here to investigate another break and enter and theft of jewelry. Seems we've got a crime spree going on in Peachland." She grinned. Let the big handsome ignoramus think she was psychic. At this moment offense was the best defense. She let the towel fall from her hair—most likely a rat's nest, but there was nothing she could do about that—down to shield her legs. She wasn't the kind of person who went around flaunting her body, though she wasn't shy either, but for some reason this *particular guy* made her feel naked.

Forester smiled back at her, but Stone just quirked an eyebrow.

"Okay. I'll bite. How'd you hear?" Forester asked.

She shrugged. "I could tell you my sources are outta this world." She watched for the dismissive flicker in Stone's face, but it didn't happen. "But that would be a lie. Would you believe apartment telegraph? Me and the condo owners at this end of the building—we've been here the longest and we're sort of on our own out here—we keep each other posted on what's going on."

The elevator call button buzzed. And she raised a brow at the two officers. "Let me get out of your way. I'm dripping all over the floor and I'm sure you've got more important places to be."

Dammit, would Stone just quit looking at her! The way he did it was like he was drinking her in. Herve had looked at her something like that a long time ago and that had got her nothing but trouble. Nope. Not going there, even though all the little hairs on her body seemed to stand at attention in his presence. A flush of heat ran over her skin. Man-oh-man. If she didn't know better she'd think she was attracted to him.

Clutching her towel around her hips, she eased past them, waved goodbye and hurried down the corridor. The heat of his regard following her made her want to run, but instead she slowed herself down and let some sashay into her stride. Yup, I'm a woman, Corporal Jasper Stone, and I hope you like what you see, because you, boyo, ain't getting any.

When the elevator door dinged again she chanced a glance back. The hallway was empty. She turned and almost ran to her apartment, fumbled the key in the lock and slammed the door behind her.

What the hell was wrong with her? What was with the hip-swinging walk away? What was with feeling drawn to someone who so clearly had no respect for her and what she believed in?

It had to just be that he was incredibly good looking. She was just succumbing to lust. It *had* to be, because she didn't want to think about the alternative.

There was no way she was going to be attracted to someone so wrong for her. Besides, she didn't know him well enough to be attracted to him. It *was* lust. Only lust, and she knew better than to give in to that. She'd done that before and it had been a disaster. Worse, it had almost destroyed her.

The bad memory destroyed the heat in her flesh and she shivered in the cool apartment. She found Clyde happily sprawled in the rejuvenating sunlight. He opened a sleepy lapis lazuli-colored eye when she patted him. Then she went into the bathroom for a shower.

That didn't help either. In fact her skin felt tender and the water and soap too... too... too damned sensual for words. Okay, this just plain had to stop. She toweled off, braided her hair and pulled on Lycra shorts and a body-skimming cranberry-colored smock, then headed out the door again.

If there was anyone who could help her make sense of this, it would be Lila. Besides, being busy would keep her mind off things. With the store out of commission there was painting to be done and there was also the private party coming in.

The walk down Beach Avenue did her good. The breeze off the glittering lake was cooling at the same time the sun baked the pavement. The incessant hum of boat motors was almost blocked out by the sounds of children's laughter. She stopped to watch a mother and two children at the water's edge. The mom was pointing out a mallard duck mama and her hurrying bevy of eight ducklings. Mom and chicks. The kids were trying to lure the ducklings in with pieces of cookies cast upon the water.

She sighed even while the scene made her smile. She liked kids, always had, but they just didn't seem to be in the cards for her. The men she seemed to attract weren't the kind of men who'd be good fathers. She'd just been a tool to help them find release, that was all.

It all sounded so tawdry and depressing that she set off almost running. By the time she reached the store she was sweating. Of course the 'closed' sign sat in the front window, so she went around the house through the tall side gate and found herself on the patio. The sun had filled it so that the brick patio radiated heat, though not as bad as yesterday. The patio furniture that she and Lila had picked out together sat fallow. Contrary to all those people on the beach, it was just one of those July days when it was too hot to be sitting in the sun. They were going to need cold drinks and the sun umbrella up if they were going to hold the private showing here.

Reggie's studio door was open, the oscillating fan blowing madly into the dark interior, so Reggie was back in creation-crazy mode for Regulus Designs to recover her stolen designs. She had some big fashion shows overseas that she was getting ready for and when Reggie was on a tear you just had to stand back, but be available with sustenance and liquids. The poor woman had just finished one of those pushes and now she was being forced through it again—all because her 'friend' had 'helped' and offered to let Reggie keep her stuff in the safe.

Chloe turned back to the house. She was pretty sure Kylee wouldn't be in, given she and Brett would have just arrived back. After seeing her and Brett together it was pretty official that the two of them were off the market. Heck, the way they looked at each other, while they were away they were probably off picking out silverware patterns or something. A far cry from the wild man her brother had once been with the ladies.

She knocked on the back door, then opened it and let herself in. "Lila?"

"In here." Her friend's voice reached her from elsewhere in the house. It sounded like she was in the back bedroom that served as her yoga studio, the same room she was going to sublet to Chloe to use for her crystal healing. She trailed down the hall following the sound of soft classical music. The Appalachian Suite or something that reminded her of spring.

Lila's yoga studio always made her think of growth and new beginnings. It might be the calming energy of the Buddha figure in the corner, but it was more likely simply a result of all the plants in the room. There were spider-plants in various macramé hanging baskets, ferns with huge sprays of leaves filling the corners, and even a philodendron that had grown up and across the curtain rods. It threatened to take over the entire room. The floor, which was usually filled with Lila's yoga mat, was empty, and at the side of the room in an overstuffed armchair that was the room's only seating, sat Lila. She was seated sideways in the chair, her long tanned legs shown off by a pair of faded red shorts. A plain white t-shirt, tied at the waist completed the ensemble. Her hair was pulled back in a tangled ponytail, loose curls escaping around her face. She wore no makeup, but that only showed off her natural beauty.

She studied Chloe a moment, frowned, set down the book she'd been reading and removed the empty sandwich plate that had rested on her belly. "You caught me in my grubbies. Good thing you're my friend or I might have to kill you. If I see a camera, I will."

Chloe held up her empty hands as proof she held no such offending contraption.

Lila stood and stretched, her five-foot-eleven frame towering over Chloe's five-foot-seven. "So. I've got a hankering for a tall glass of lemonade and you're just the excuse to get me out of this chair and going to the fridge. You interested?"

Chloe nodded and followed her friend back to the kitchen, which was one of Chloe's favorite rooms in the house. The bank of windows over the work counter filled the room with light and illuminated the yellow cabinetry and chrome appliances. The room's best feature was a wonderful alcove of Spanish tiles that held the gas range and free-standing range hood.

"I got a phone call this morning that you might be interested in. Allyson McVay's coming for a visit." Lila retrieved two tumblers out of the cupboard, pitcher of lemonade, and something green from the fridge.

"Where's she coming from?' Chloe asked. Allyson was an old friend of Lila's from college. She'd gone overseas as a fledging photographer right out of school and had somehow maneuvered it into a career.

"India I think. Maybe Bangladesh." Lila shook her head and she set the pitcher and glasses down on the table and motioned to Chloe. "I can't keep track. She said she'd phone when she hits Kelowna. Now come sit. Let's talk."

Chloe settled behind the table thinking of all the things they needed to talk about regarding the store.

"We need to talk about the bracelet," Lila said.

The bracelet? The bracelet. Of course. In all the muss, fuss and confusion of the break-in she'd almost totally forgotten about the thing. She held up her wrist to admire its lovely silver links.

"Chloe?"

She shook herself and realized she'd gotten lost there a moment. What was the matter with her? She wasn't the kind of person to daydream.

She met Lila's gaze, but her narrow-eyed consideration made Chloe look away.

"Not the bracelet, then, I'd say by the way you're behaving." Lila busied herself tearing the green leaves apart releasing the herbal scent of mint. She stuffed a few in each glass and poured two tall glasses over the leaves. The refreshing mint and lemon combined to make Chloe's mouth water.

She sighed and tasted the drink. "Mmmm. Good." She looked up at Lila who shook her head.

"Stalling," Lila sing-songed. "Someone has something they don't want to talk about."

"Gees Louise, can't I have a moment to gather my thoughts?" Chloe stuck out her tongue and then ducked when Lila threatened to throw a wadded up napkin at her.

"Okay. Okay. What can I say? I'm confused. My brain feels like it's just spent the night and the morning in a rock polisher. All of my brain cells have been worn away."

Lila took a sip of her drink. "So what's got those pebbles of yours grinding away?"

Okay. Here goes. "I guess it all goes back to a conversation I had yesterday." Her fingers wrapped around the bracelet. It was light. She hardly knew it was on, until she paid attention to it, like now. Then it seemed to gain in weight or presence or *something* until she swore she could feel it humming and she could barely concentrate. Also like now.

"It was that police detective—Stone or whatever it was." Jasper Stone. She remembered all too well because it fit his coal black hair and his sooty eyelashes. Damn. "An absolutely infuriating man if I've ever met one. He actually had the bad manners to tell me to my face that what I do is a bunch of hooey and that all this talk about the bracelet is the same thing again."

She shook her head and Lila raised her arched brown brows. "So you don't think it was very professional of him."

"No I don't. And it makes me wonder whether these cops are going to do a proper investigation of Kylee's case, not to mention of the break in. I mean she could have been killed! So could you have been."

"But she wasn't and neither was I."

"Damn it all, Lila, why are you sitting here being so reasonable and siding with them when we don't know if that man is going to come after Kylee again?"

"Well, actually, that's easy to answer. I'm not worried about Kylee because it's you who has the bracelet on. You, I'm worried about, now, and more so because at this moment you really don't seem to be yourself."

Lila's calm voice shut Chloe down. Lila was right. She wasn't acting anywhere near normal. "Is it that obvious?"

"You don't usually get so upset by one little comment, even if it's made by a good looking cop."

"He's not that good looking."

Lila burst out laughing. "Me thinks the lady doth protest too much. Oh, Chloe, I didn't think I'd ever see the day when a man could get under your skin like this from one tiny little conversation."

"It wasn't one conversation," she mumbled and took another sip of the exceedingly good lemonade.

"You've talked to him since then? My, that fellow works fast, but then I thought there might be some chemistry happening between you two. There's something that happens to people… something about the eyes, I think. It's a lot like reading when people *really* want to buy a piece of jewelry. I see it in the store all the time and yesterday you and Mr. Handsome Detective both happened to have the same glazed expression like you didn't know what was happening." She caught Chloe's hand. "It's okay, sweetie. I've got your back, but we really do need to do something about this bracelet."

She went thoughtful as she stroked the exquisite small doors. "It seems awfully strange that Kylee put it on and met someone she seems to think is her soul mate—no offense to Brett, I'm glad for them—and then you put the pesky thing on and get all befuddled by a man. A cop, yet." Lila's cool fingers laced hers.

"Chloe I need you with me, here, regardless of the confusion you might feel. We've got a mess to clean up in the shop and there's the small matter of the jewelry party you agreed to. You've got a good head on your shoulders and yes, you might believe in things that not everyone does, but you've always come at it logically, with clear assessments and insights. Yes, you might come to conclusions sooner than the rest of us do, and based on things the rest of us might not sense, but I've always put that down to you being really good with people. Intuitive. So I'm going to ask you a favor. You with me so far?"

Chloe nodded, surprised and a little more than pleased by the confidence Lila expressed. It was a far cry from what she was feeling right now.

"What I'm going to ask you is dangerous and I want you to think hard before you agree to anything. I know you told Corporal Stone you weren't afraid but, bottom line, I'm afraid for you. I don't know what it is that's after the bracelet, but after what Kylee went through and the break-in at the store I think we'd be fools to think things are just going to blow over. I know the break-in might not have been anything to do with the bracelet, but you never know. I'd really rather know my favorite people are safe. I think we are at a place where we have two choices: we can cut the bracelet off—Reggie says she can do it without destroying it;

or we can try to keep learning about the bracelet and figure out what the heck's going on. There's something unnatural about it, I think you'll agree, and I can't help but think that you're the best person to help us figure out what that is. So my question is how do you feel about using that intuition of yours to help us understand what the bracelet is?"

Lila's hazel expression was earnest, as if she actually thought Chloe would consider letting the bracelet be cut off her wrist. She pulled her hand back and considered the miniature doors, each so ornately created it was like she should be able to open them. What would wait on the other side? Another world? Another dimension? Fantastic adventures, certainly. The door with its iron strapping in particular caught her attention. It looked like something you might see in an Arabian Nights fortress, not that she'd ever been to the Middle East, but it could be. She could picture the door opening onto a hall of mosaic stone walls and floors and ceiling, a distant window filling the stones with light. Crystal fountains sprayed in the center of a lapis-lazuli-blue pool and glowing chalcedony and sapphire and onyx formed intricate vine patterns over everything else. Calmness, faith, and the stone that increased the power of both. The maker of such loveliness was truly an artist in stone and understood exactly what he did. The scent of summer heat and damp earth came on a breeze through the hall's window.

"Chloe? You with me, here, girlfriend?"

Chloe jerked back into the present. Lila had her hands over Chloe's, concern placing amber flecks in her hazel eyes.

"You looked like you were a million miles away."

Chloe eased her hands free because it had *felt* like she was a million miles away. Almost like she was in that ancient hall. She'd smelled something and it wasn't the mint and lemon that pervaded the kitchen. She pulled her hands onto her lap and continued to rub the silver to hide the chill she felt. "Of course I'll help in whatever way I can, but I'm not sure I'll be much good to you at the moment." She frowned. "I, uh, seem a little befuddled and I can't figure out why. That cop is about the last guy I'm interested in. I mean, really, we'd fight all the time and he'd never respect me and I could never trust him to not be laughing at me behind my back. I mean why would I even consider something like that?"

"But you've thought about it."

Chloe was going to protest, but who was she kidding. She sighed. "He looks at me and it makes me angry and ridiculously hot and bothered at the same time. How's that for an evil combination?" And afraid. Let's not forget very, very afraid.

A quirky grin lifted the sides of Lila's mouth. "Enough to make for some interesting times."

Chloe shook her head. "I swore off interesting times a long time ago. I did that and I don't ever want to do it again. It took too many years to put myself back together and get here." She looked at her glass for something to do, because just thinking about the time she's come to think of as her dangerous years made her stomach tight and small, but the glass was empty. "So are you still sure you're okay with me using your yoga room for my healing?"

Lila hefted the lemonade pitcher and offered to fill her glass, but Chloe waved her off.

"I've told you before that I think it fits beautifully with the store. The plants will do better for the company and wasn't it you who told me that being around the plants creates a resonance between the stones and them. A healthy one like you'd find in nature? All I need is a place to do my exercises in the morning and if you're prepared to use the chair that's there and one of those mobile masseuse tables, then everything will work just fine."

"Okay then." Chloe scooted across the bench seat and stood. "That's settled. I think I'm going to put an ad up online and I'll do up a little flyer we can have on the counter in the shop. I've got some ideas for the design, maybe a play on the *This and That* logo, if that's all right by you. And now that I've got my marching orders I'm going to pull out some of the jewelry in preparation for the party this afternoon and then go home and meditate on this bracelet. I'll let you know what I find out."

"And the man?" Lila asked, all feigned innocence.

"Sorry, Lila. That's one Stone I'm going to leave unturned."

She let herself out the back door to the sunshine and to the sound of Lila's laughter.

CHAPTER 6

T̲ʜᴇ ᴅᴀʏ ᴀꜰᴛᴇʀ ᴛʜᴇ ᴍᴇʀᴍᴀɪᴅ ɪɴᴄɪᴅᴇɴᴛ, ᴀs Jᴀs ʜᴀᴅ come to think of it, at five p.m. he found himself again standing in the neatly manicured grounds of the Willowview Terrace where Chloe lived. It was late in the afternoon, when most people would likely be home after a day at work and he planned to canvass the residents who lived near the Singhs. Forester had opted to stay back at the detachment to continue the criminal record cross checks on the Willowview Terrace residents.

He looked up at the building and inhaled the scent of hamburgers done on the grill and barbecued chicken. Dinnertime. People might not be happy that he interrupted them, but at least they'd be home. He sighed at the task. He didn't want to think about the number of apartments in only the one wing of the building; it could easily take him more than one evening. Frankly, canvassing the neighbors was most likely a wild goose chase anyway. With the break-in having occurred so close to Canada Day, there'd likely have been countless strangers around, or the people would have been away themselves. But police work was all about doing the grunt-work and every now and again you caught a break. Hopefully he would tonight, too.

He passed the pool—regretfully unoccupied today—and headed for the building's main door. He was going to ask the Singhs to buzz him in, but someone had used a brick to block the door open. So much for building security. That was what happened when you got renters. Someone was having a get-together and couldn't be bothered to answer their call buzzer so they ruined it for everyone and the building got trashed. He went inside, careful to toss the brick into a bush and close the door behind him.

Where to start. If the suspect had come across the balconies as he suspected, then starting on the third floor made sense. It would be a lot harder to climb up the building and then cross the balconies, given the glass railings left next to nothing for a climber to cling to.

He rode the elevator up to the third floor and damned if his palms weren't sweating. He felt as uneasy as a suspect in an interrogation room and yet it was him doing the questioning. It made no sense at all, and yet it did, because he just might happen to run into Chloe Main again.

"Idiot." He shook his head. Why else would he volunteer for this duty? He hated canvassing and usually they got the uniformed guys to do it. Even Forester had looked at him askance when he'd headed out the door, but the man was still hurting too much from his own come-down to make a comment.

He started with the apartment to the left of the elevator, figuring he'd go up one side of the hall and back down the other. Then he'd continue down the other direction to where the Singh apartment lay.

And the direction Chloe Main had left the elevator.

Putting off the inevitable, or saving the best for last, he just wasn't sure.

He knocked on the black door and heard footsteps inside. "Who is it?" asked a male voice through the door.

"Kelowna RCMP. We're canvassing about a break-in. I'd like to ask you a couple of questions."

The door clicked open and he faced an accountant type. Well maybe not accountant. The guy was slim, without the muscle mass you expect in the twenty-something male, but he had a bit more swagger. Maybe high tech, or as much high tech as you got in Kelowna.

"Can I see some ID?" techy guy asked.

"Corporal Jasper Stone," he said, producing his badge.

When the guy finished looking, Jas put the wallet away and took out his notebook. "A break-and-enter occurred in the building two nights ago. We're not certain of the time. We're interviewing the building occupants regarding whether they saw anything suspicious."

Ten minutes later Jas excused himself and headed to the next door. He'd learned nothing from Mr. Tech, AKA Michael Corliss, except that the guy had apparently paid far too much for an apartment in what he'd thought was a prestige building, but now the place was filled with low-lifes and how come the police hadn't been out here canvassing when someone keyed the side of his five-year-old Honda Accord. Ten minutes for one interview and there were thirty apartments on the floor. It was going to be one hell of a long evening.

§

It was as exciting as heck and there was a part of her that just didn't want to believe she was finally going to do this. With the late evening filling her windows Chloe puttered around her apartment, carefully selecting the stones she was taking with her to the first healing appointment at the *This and That.* She carefully wrapped an alabaster crystal, because her client had told her she was dealing with a lot of stress. The delicate white crystal was good for tension, headaches and the lack of concentration and sore joints that came with age. Her client, Marcia Oldstrum, had a tough job as the publisher of the oldest newspaper in the Okanagan. Trying to stay afloat in these difficult times of the Internet couldn't be easy, and yet she'd made the family of small newspapers that were published in each of the three largest Okanagan communities as necessary to life in the valley as breathing.

She wrapped the alabaster in fine cotton flannel, placed it in a silk bag, and packed it in her doctor's bag sandwiched in between an amethyst crystal that was wonderful for headaches, an Australian amulet stone that was a restorative, and the onyx beads that would help multiply the effects of the other stones. She had her incense, blankets, an amber necklace, and her masseuses table. Even a docking station for her phone so that she could make sure there was soothing music.

"I think I'm done, little buddy. What do you think?"

Clyde raised his big blue-gray head from where he lounged on the couch hoping to be noticed. His blue consideration was noncommittal. Anything that took her away from home and him, was never his favorite thing.

She snapped the doctor's bag closed in satisfaction. She was as ready as she'd ever been and she could barely believe it. In celebration, she went into her kitchen and poured herself a glass of Elkhart Winery's excellent Viognier and went out onto her patio. The sky had faded toward black, but at this time of year the fine clouds still held the sunset's blush against the deepening azure. Sinking onto her throne chair she put her feet up and hummed a few bars of she didn't know what, but it was peaceful sounding. Something she'd heard before. Clyde came wandering out and leapt up into her lap, kneaded her thighs and settled. The low rumble of his purr filled her hand.

It had been a good couple of days. The outdoor jewelry party had gone off without a hitch; *This and That* had outfitted the bridal party. The value of the sales had been enough that Chloe had suggested they distribute some flyers to local bridal boutiques. It was the kind of thing that bride and bridesmaids might appreciate as a low key afternoon together. This time Lila had pulled together some tiny cucumber and shrimp open-faced sandwiches and some lovely lemon-coconut squares from the bakery. They'd served mint lemonade and cranberry tea and spread the delicacies out on tables amid the jewelry. A light breeze had come up off the lake. Overall it had been a nice escape from the depressing interior of the shop.

Chloe sighed and sipped her wine.

Out on the lake, the water had turned black, broken only by the running lights of the few boats not already at anchor. Down at the lakeshore a few families were packing up their propane hibachis, music and laughter wafted over from the still existing camp ground just beyond the apartment complex's garden. There were still stately old willows and poplars on the campground. She wondered how long it would be before that property sold out, too. The owners, Wilf and Rebecca, weren't getting any younger.

Well, tomorrow she would officially start her own separate business and she just hoped she enjoyed it as long as Wilf and Rebecca. She'd only been talking about opening a crystal healing center since she was eighteen and newly off the San Francisco streets. There were times she still couldn't believe she'd abandoned everything she knew and loved up here to head out alone to see the world. She'd ended up in the city by the bay. Maybe she was just channeling the age of the flower child, but it had been a much bleaker existence that she'd found. But something good had come of it—she'd been helped by the commune-church of New-Agers who'd taken her in off the street after everything bad had turned even worse. They'd taught her a lot of things that a certain corporal would call woo-woo, but that had been all too real to her. Like how to read a palm, about organic farming in the city, and healing stones and chakras. It had been as if her eyes were suddenly opened to things she'd always sensed and felt, but had never known what they were called.

She sipped her wine and set the glass down on the table beside her, her fingers finding the silver links around her wrist. In the warmth of the evening they were amazingly cool, the perfect ornamentation of each door like Braille beneath her fingers. Who would make such a thing, taking such pride and care in the minute details? She drew in a deep breath and, with that question in mind, opened herself.

The dim light over the water, the reds in the sky all seemed to swirl and eddy before her, like the deep recesses of a fire opal. Iridescence appeared over the view like light on labradorite, rustle of the bamboo in the breeze came from behind her almost as if something crept there watching. She shivered. What was it about this bracelet that had her nerves jangling and Lila so concerned? Aside from its unique form, it was just another bunch of silver like every other piece that they had in the store.

"But you're special, aren't you? Kylee always seemed to think so, and now I can sort of understand how protective she was of you." She reached for her glass, but the glass wasn't there.

What the…?

The scent of lake water faded and was replaced by a sense of heated earth. The breeze was different, too. Thicker somehow. Yes. Sand particles lightly peppered her skin, and out beyond her patio the sounds of cars from the highway had faded, too. Were those hoof beats she heard? Bringing warning? She stood up, suddenly sure it *was* a warning. Clyde tumbled off her lap and gave her a dirty look before retreating to the apartment.

Something bad was going to happen unless—unless she did *something—and on the dusty road outside, the one she feared had found her. They were coming. They were coming. They were pounding at her door.* She stumbled away from her chair and knocked the table. The crash of breaking glass stopped her. Her wine glass. It was there.

And out on the lake the running lights ran north and south and the breeze brought the scent of sun-warmed water. From inside the apartment came the sound of knocking at her door.

What? Who? She abandoned the broken glass and went inside nursing one heck of a headache and the hair-raising feeling that for a moment there, she'd been somewhere else. Vision? Maybe. Something beyond that? Crazy talk.

But it had all been so real. And the panic she'd felt…

She went to the door. "Who is it?" she asked and peered through the peep hole.

Holy Mother of God, could the night get any more confusing? Or worse? Definitely worse, because standing impatiently in the hallway was none other than the man she'd been trying to put out of her mind for the past two days.

She yanked the door open. "What?" She caught herself. No need to be a total bitch. "What can I do for you, Corporal Stone?" When she really wanted to ask what the hell he was doing knocking on her door at all at this time of night. She checked her watch. Eleven p.m.

"Uh, I'm very sorry about the time, but there was a report of a break-in. I'm trying to canvass the neighbors to see if anyone saw anything." He met her gaze, but then looked away to the wall. By the way he was talking, his teeth were clenched.

"I, uh, heard." Not her best opening. "The Singhs, right. Ginger and Harry?"

"You know them?"

She looked down the hall. Empty of everything except his scent of warm earth and leather. "Well sure. Of course. Apartment telegraph, remember? They're next door. What do you need to know?" Okay. She was getting herself back. She could be cool with this. Cool as ice and just as crystal.

"We believe the theft occurred two nights ago. Did you happen to notice anyone strange around then?" he deadpanned, totally in police mode.

"Really? You want to ask me that at this hour?" Her brain felt like it was coming loose, this whole situation was so strange and she really just wanted to retreat back into her apartment and clear her head of whatever had happened on the patio. That and clean up the broken glass.

"Please," he said. "What did you happen to see or hear?"

The poor guy looked like he was running on automatic and no longer was thinking about what he'd asked. He'd be a perfect victim for a joke, but she wasn't really into battling an unarmed man. "How many apartments have you been at so far?"

That stopped what she could see was a shtick he'd used too many times. He looked at her and really seemed to see her. Then he sighed and all the muscles in his jaw relaxed so he almost seemed to smile. "Let me guess. You were out until all hours cleaning up the shop. Sorry to disturb your evening."

He went to turn away and for a moment she felt sorry for him. What an awful job. His hair was tousled from running his fingers through it and his five o'clock shadow had gone about half past eleven. His jet black eyes were deep-set with the same fatigue that seemed to weight his shoulders and leaden his clean leather scent. She'd lay money down that not a soul in the apartment block had even thought of offering him a chance to sit down or even a glass of water.

"Actually I was home around midnight, but I didn't see or hear a thing. Listen," she bit her lip. "You look like you've been through the ringer. Do you want a cup of coffee or something? I mean if you're going to keep knocking on people's doors..."

When he glanced back at her as if he didn't believe her offer, she shrugged. It didn't mean a thing. It was the kind of thing one human being did for another, if you were a good person. Which she tried to be. She might not like the guy, but she could be kind. It was a matter of being in balance, and anything that would help her balance right now was a good thing.

His throat worked and then he nodded. "That would be nice."

Nice and noncommittal, but he turned back and slogged his way past her and into the apartment.

The weird stuff from the patio set aside to consider later, she closed the door and followed him into her kitchen where he'd stopped and was studying his surroundings.

"What would you like? I have coffee or tea or water or wine. I make a mean espresso. Or latte." Suddenly more than a tad nervous, she nodded sideways at the espresso maker that filled up a huge chunk of the counter.

He turned around to look at her and holy-moly, he seemed to fill up the room and it wasn't a small kitchen. His eyes had gone smoky and his scent of sun-warmed earth seemed to permeate the room and weaken her knees.

"What do you recommend?" His dark brows rose and his lips seemed to quirk in the corners.

She liked that about him—the secret smile. It wasn't a smirk. More like the way an unpolished gem hid its power. She could see beyond it. Heck, she could *feel* his red aura pulse like a tattoo against her breast and hers seemed to pulse right back in response. If he could just keep his opinions about her work to himself she might actually like him.

His brows arched higher and the small smile broadened. "So... a recommendation?"

Crap. What was she thinking? She looked away to the fridge, the coffee maker—anywhere but at him. "The coffee's very good. The water's free and the wine comes from my brother's winery. I was having a glass on the patio when you knocked at the door."

He checked his watch. "Then maybe I'll have a glass of wine. It's too late to keep knocking on people's doors, so I guess I'm off the clock." He grinned and suddenly she really wasn't sure she'd made the right decision inviting him into her home. He was standing too close to her even across the room and his essence was so eminently, intrinsically male.

"Wine it is." She turned away so she could breathe again and pulled two goblets out of the cupboard and the wine from the fridge. "You go make yourself comfortable. I'll bring it in."

Just let him leave the kitchen, please. She was no longer the kind of woman who threw herself at men, but there was something about this one and that was just so—*wrong*. Someone like him could never accept her for who she was.

Maybe—maybe what she was feeling was just lust. That was a natural chemical reaction of the body. But she didn't do little rolls in the hay, even if it might recharge her, just like she recharged crystals in sunshine. Just a matter of balance.

The trouble was, her hands were shaking as she poured the wine and she could feel his ruddy aura brushing against hers like a cat, even from the other room.

"Who's this big guy?" His deep voice seemed to shiver against her skin.

Carrying the two goblets, she found him next to her shelves of crystals displayed in the dimly lit livingroom. Clyde threaded around his ankles.

"Now that is strange. Clyde loves my friends but he never does that to anyone but me."

"Ol' Clyde even likes to have his tail pulled." He stroked the cat from front to back, actually lifting his back legs slightly off the ground.

Chloe was about to protest, but Clyde pressed into Corporal Stone's leg and asked for more. The good Corporal obliged until Chloe offered him the glass.

"Cheers," he said and tinked the edge of her glass with his. "To a much better end to the evening than I'd foreseen." He gave her that million watt grin again and turned back to study her display of crystals.

"Just what had you envisioned?" she asked seating herself on the arm of a chair.

"The drive home. A beer. Leftovers or maybe takeout picked up on the way. This is much nicer. A fine wine, by the way. These are interesting." He motioned to her collection. "Pretty impressive the size of some of them."

"The reticulated quartz is about ten pounds. It can be found in Australia and the U.S., but this one I happened to bring back from Brazil."

"Brazil, huh? You've been, then?" He went closer and bent to look at it. Stray light from the kitchen brought out the red-gold inclusions so that it looked embedded with fine gold needles.

"Yes. I spent a few weeks there on a buying trip with Lila. Why?"

He shrugged and grinned over his shoulder. "It's just a place I've always wanted to visit—the Amazon and all. What's inside it?"

"Those are rutile quartz entrapments inside it. Pretty huh?" She kept waiting for the dig, the cutting remark, but so far so good.

"What's it good for?" he asked, still looking at the huge single crystal.

"Pardon me?" Oh no. Here it came—the ridicule.

"I wondered why you have it. It's beautiful and all, but you talked about crystal healing. Why this?" He turned back to her and he seemed almost impressed—almost *interested*.

Trust him? More like test him. She took a deep breath. "Well, if you really want to know, Corporal Stone, this kind of quartz is good for the lungs. It reduces coughing, helps with bronchitis, and combats inflammation. It also has a calming effect. It stimulates self healing and discovery of the truth. I find it helps me keep my apartment as a calm sacred place." And right about now she could really use some of that calming. Her flesh felt like it was vibrating and it wasn't a vibration she was used to.

She waited for his expression to change, and for disdain to reshape his mouth, but it didn't happen. Instead he turned back and seemed to study the crystal. "I've never seen a crystal so big outside of a museum—not that I've made a practice of looking."

He straightened and scanned the room before looking back at her. "This is really nice. Not what I expected at all."

Pondering that a moment, Chloe took a sip of her wine, nice and acidic on her tongue. "So... what? You were expecting tie dye and macramé?"

"Nah. Well. Maybe—I don't know. I mean it's a surprise that you live here, is all. I know I took down your address, but I just didn't associate you with these apartments or maybe with this one."

Before she could respond he held up his hand. "Joking. Really. I wondered where you lived. I just hadn't figured you lived in one of the prime pieces of real estate in the complex." He stepped away from the display toward her. "Listen, could we start over. I'm off the clock, so forget the Corporal Stone. Could you just call me Jas? My friends do."

He'd wondered where she lived? He wanted her as a friend? A flush ran through her skin and she was scared it might show, so she turned toward the patio. "All right Jas, let me give you the grand tour. Pardon the broken glass. I knocked the my glass off the table when I ran for the door."

She took a gulp of wine and led him out into the fresh air wanting to fan herself as she stood by the rail looking out at the lake. How the heck did he make her feel all flushed like that? Thankfully there was a breeze and she raised her face to it, let it play in the stray curls around her cheeks. The air smelled of cool water and pine and heated granite hills. Warm earth and leather settled around her and she inhaled. Her skin warmed and she rubbed her wrist, fingering the bracelet. When she chanced a glance sideways he was watching her.

CHAPTER 7

Chloe Main really was a most lovely woman—unexpectedly so. In the past he might have written her off because of her interests, but something about her said she was so much more. The night breeze caught at the fine fringe of hairs around her exquisite face. Her lips were damp with wine and her heavy-lidded eyes were open. That horrible braid seemed like a prison for the miraculous hair she'd been toweling when she came up from the pool. He could imagine its softness in his hands and the way it would flow around her tanned body like a curtain. It reached her lower back braided, so how long would it be when loose? It was a puzzle he wanted the answer to.

"So just how long have you been growing your hair?" he asked and looked out at the water. The breeze had picked up and raised light waves that hissed in the gravel. The boats were all gone and so were the families and the groups of teens who usually hung out by the water until the beach closed at eleven. It was like they were alone in the world with only the rustle of her bamboo and the bamboo from the Singh's patio around them in the warm air.

"This?" Her hands almost seemed nervous as it touched her braid. "Oh, I guess I quit cutting it when I came home at eighteen. It's a hassle sometimes, but most of the time it's just me." She shrugged. "I guess it's sort of like wearing a badge. It sets you apart, but it's who you are. How long have you been an RCMP member?"

"About thirteen years now. I came later to the game. I was twenty-five when most of the other recruits were right out of college."

She shook her head. "Wow. You really are an old man," she deadpanned waiting for his reaction to her jab.

"And right now I feel like it." With regret, he checked his watch. "Yikes. Where did the time go. Don't you have to get up early in the morning?"

She sighed and looked over at his wrist. "Wow. Eleven-thirty and I was just getting ready to settle into a long chat." He could feel her regard like a warm stroke on his skin. No way. He was letting his imagination run away, and that wasn't a good thing. Imagination was what kept children up at night after a scary movie. It was what could get a cop killed because he was too busy paying attention to imaginary foes than the reality around him. Or it killed his partner.

He drained his wine glass and headed unsteadily for the kitchen. The last thing he needed was to revisit those old painful places. Maybe that was why the OIC of the detachment had paired him and Forester together—they were both damaged goods and maybe together they couldn't hurt anyone else.

He set the wine glass down and headed for the door. Chloe caught up to him there. "I'm sorry I didn't have any information to help you with your case, but I'll keep my ears open. If I hear anything I'll let you know."

She stood so close beside him he could inhale her light natural incense and this scent he could almost wish would get caught in his clothing, in his nose, in his brain. He'd been stupid to stop and have the glass of wine, but on the other hand it had shown him something he hadn't expected. *That he wanted to lean in and inhale her, maybe hold her shoulders as he tasted her lips?* He stuck his hands in his pockets and managed a smile that hopefully hid what he was feeling.

"This was nice. Nice to see your apartment and what makes you tick." *To see her, you idiot.* On impulse he caught her hand and felt a surge of heat. Way to go, Stone. This was one stupid idea. "The bracelet," he said trying for an explanation. "You're still wearing it."

"Well, yeah." She grinned up at him. "It's going to take more than some scary story about imaginary aliens to make me take it off. Besides, Lila's asked me to do a little research for her."

"Research? Well, keep me informed if you find out anything interesting. It might help our investigation." The way her smile broadened he suddenly realized what he was saying. That kind of research...

Her smile increased almost as if she'd heard his thoughts, and aside from being somewhat embarrassed, he realized he really liked her. Would really like to lean in for that kiss, but she was a witness in two investigations now, and not a very good one given her interest in esoteric bits of knowledge. She was not just some girl he'd gone out on a date with.

He released her hand and stepped out the door, nodded and started away, but then stopped.

"Chloe," he said turning back to her. "If you ever get scared, call me."

He turned away listening for the door to close behind him. It didn't happen for an awfully long time.

§

The next morning Chloe was up earlier than normal because she hadn't slept well the night before. Heck, if she was going to toss and turn, she might as well be up and away. She threw off her cream-colored, recycled-cotton sheets and opened the pale curtains to look out at the lake. Restless waves seemed to mirror what she felt. The wind was up and change was coming and not just in the weather. A light haze covered the bright blue sky giving it an iridescent moonstone gray color. The clouds often meant heavier weather following behind. But the sun still rose like a great burning eye over the mountains and there were already sailboats out on the lake running before the wind. The bamboo on her patio rustled uneasily.

Yup. Just like she felt. At first it was just a matter of not being able to turn off her mind. Emotions that she had held in check for a very long time seemed to have torn loose in a maelstrom—all tied up with the scent of leather. He liked her, at least she thought he did. He'd almost kissed her, at least the tension between them had felt like it.

Of maybe it was all her imagination because hadn't he said that was her problem?

"Darn it Main, you're letting a man get into your head. That is no way to get ready for a healing." In her lamb p.j.s she padded out to the livingroom, then sank down into a lotus position and half-closed her eyes. Meditation had always been a good way to deal with unsettled conditions.

She focused on a spot on the Oriental carpet that reminded her of a peacock's eye and breathed in slowly, feeling the air rush coolly past the tip of her nose. She held it a moment, then let it slide out, focused on the transition to warmth on her skin. Another deep breath and the tension melted out of her shoulders.

She never should have invited him in last night. He'd actually been leaving and she'd called him back.

No. She pulled her focus back to her breathing, to the spot on the carpet. Breathe in. Exhale and empty her lungs. Again.

All the hairs on her body had been like metal filings and Jas had been her magnetic lodestone. Her skin had actually tingled when he was in the apartment.

Not. What. You. Are. Supposed. To. Be. Thinking about.

Warm breath through her nose as she exhaled. Cool air sucked in. A brief relaxing. Hold and usually all the tension would melt right out of her in the space of four or five breaths. She could sit here focused on her breathing and just *be*. At peace.

A hint of warm earth weaseled into her nose and she wanted to scratch it right out of there. Her skin itched.

"Damn it!" She leapt up. Meditation wasn't going to work with both her mind and body conspiring against her.

She marched back to her bedroom, changed into her swimsuit, grabbed a towel and shoved her mess of hair into a bathing cap. Usually she took the time to massage conditioner into it, but she'd deal with the tangles later.

She hurried down the hall and pushed through a fire door, surprising a tenant at the first apartment. She hadn't seen before him before. Another renter, probably. This one was young, with longish hair down to his shoulders and an ornate dragon tattoo winding up one arm. He wore a worn gray t-shirt and jeans and carried what looked like a messenger bag over his shoulder. Probably heading off to work at some tech firm or something. There were a few of those in Kelowna.

"Morning," she said as she passed him.

"Yeah. Uh, hi."

At the elevator she stabbed the button. Thankfully the car was there and the doors slid open. Glancing back the way she'd come, she stepped inside. Funny. The guy was just standing there. But then maybe he hadn't seen an older woman in a bathing suit before.

She looked down at herself. She wasn't bad. Come on.

Two kilometers of front crawl later she still hadn't found that Zen resting place. She toweled off on the pool deck but the breeze had picked up until the morning wasn't that pleasant. She had gooseflesh and made a hurried retreat back to her apartment. A hot shower and a half hour spent untangling her hair before she gave up and swiftly braided it. There were times when she actually considered cutting it off, but that would be like removing a chakra. The breeze would dry it on her way to the shop.

She dressed in leggings and a new top she'd purchased for exactly this occasion. It was pale cream Indian cotton, woven in the finest sheer fabric, but three layers together made it decent to wear with only a bra underneath. The middle layer had been dotted with tiny crystals in the same color that seemed to somehow catch the light and shimmer, while the top layer had tiny seed pearls scattered across the bodice. The whole effect was of light skimming her body and it was a perfect combination to heighten her awareness of energy forces in the world. What a perfect way to start her business. With earrings and necklaces of rutilated quartz and shimmering blue sodalite for calm, in addition to her protective jet necklace, she could feel her discomfort fading.

While she waited for her espresso machine to heat up, she busied herself with her tincture of amethyst. First she cleansed the crystal she had chosen which was a deep lavender color. She ran it under the tap to remove any impurities and visualized any impurities running out of the stone and down the drain. Sending out her gratitude to the earth for giving up this fine stone to her, she also sent out her intent to make healing water. When the stone felt ready, she carried it in her palms out to her patio and set it on her table—cleansed of spilled wine and glass the night before—and left it for the wind and sun to dry and feed it power.

Fifteen minutes later she aligned the crystal along the ley line that ran north-south along the lake, and directed its point toward a small pitcher of purified water. She bowed her head and sent a blessing into the crystal, then stepped away. She left it for an hour as she made herself a chai latte—no coffee for her when performing a healing, but she steamed the milk for a rich froth. Then she drank it with a piece of toast and organic honey standing looking out the window.

There were whitecaps on the lake and southward there were tall thunderclouds gathering at the end of the lake. Not exactly auspicious, and her skin felt prickly. After fifteen minutes she poured a mouthful of the amethyst water into a glass and tried it. A momentary surge of lightheadedness washed over her and a sizzle of energy buzzed in her chest. It was all a good sign that the tincture was working. She just needed to let the power continue to accumulate in the fluid a while longer.

She sat down in the sheltered corner that held her throne chair and considered what had happened the last time she'd sat there. It had been very strange the way suddenly the damp breeze had disappeared and she could have sworn she was no longer seeing the Okanagan Valley. What she *was* seeing, she wasn't sure.

The bracelet gleamed dully on her wrist, the patina of age effectively removing the shimmer of silver. The miniature door details continued to fascinate her. A hint of dust and incense filled her nostrils and she frowned and jerked upright as a rush of energy flooded through her body and settled deep down in her core. She stood up and looked at the chair.

That was twice she'd had strange sensations sitting there. It wasn't nice. Not nice at all.

Her fingers worried the bracelet and she frowned. She hated to say it, but the strange occurrences seemed to come from the darn thing.

"From you," she said, tapping the bracelet with her fingernail like she was admonishing Clyde. And here she was talking to an inanimate object—exactly the kind of thing that Jas would hate.

She needed to get out of here and get to the store. It had almost been two hours since she set the crystal out with the water. The tincture would have enough power.

She brought the pitcher and the amethyst crystal back inside and set them together on the counter, then went to her cupboard of supplies and brought out a small bottle of expensive brandy. A thimbleful in the pitcher would "fix" the vibrations so that the water would keep. She poured eight ounces of the resultant elixir into a pretty rock crystal flask and placed it in her doctor's bag. She was ready to go.

A last pat on Clyde's head and she headed out the door and down the hall. There was no one around until she left the buildings complex gardens and found herself walking against a strange hot wind blowing down the lakeshore. She inhaled, but it wasn't desert she smelled. There was no dust peppering her flesh like there has been last night until Jas interrupted. This carried the scent of juniper and pine. Familiar, though she didn't think she'd ever been anywhere they grew together other than a short time spent on the Greek islands. The breeze increased until it sleeked her top against her, picked up her braid and almost tore the masseuse table in its case out of her grasp. Almost as if it was trying to stop her from reaching the shop.

Silly thought. She stumbled up the steps of *This and That,* and inside the bell over the door ding-a-linged her arrival. Kylee, back from her holidays, looked around from painting lavender-gray paint onto the walls above the dark oak wainscoting. She was a little bit of a thing with a shock of shoulder-length blond hair, large eyes and a pixyish way of moving that reminded everyone of Audrey Hepburn. She put down her paintbrush and grinned.

"I don't believe this. I go away for a few days and you guys try to wreck the place and now you expect me to pick up the pieces."

Chloe spread her hands. "Don't blame me. I was just an innocent bystander. But it made sense to take the opportunity and refresh the store. So we paint and restain the wood and floor. The place'll be spectacular. Just you wait."

"Sure. Sure. Sure. It just wasn't what I was expecting to come back to. But hey, Lila was telling me about your brainstorm of private parties. I gather the first one went well."

"Very. I'm thinking we need to get flyers out to the bridal shops."

Kylee nodded. "Maybe high schools too. For Prom." The wheels were already turning in Kylee's brain which wasn't a surprise given *capable* was the word Chloe had picked up from Kylee at their first meeting. The woman was smart and a real asset to the shop. At the rate she was adding to the shop, they were going to have to offer her a partnership.

"Is Lila around?" Chloe asked.

Kylee waved toward the beaded curtain and Chloe pushed on through and down the hall to the kitchen.

"Lila?" she called.

There was no response from the house, so she dumped her bag and table by the counter and went out back. Reggie's workshop door was open and the wind had dropped enough that she could hear voices.

"Knock-knock," she called and stuck her head inside. It smelled of hot metal, burned wood and sweat. "Mind if I come in?" Lila and Reggie were seated at one end of the shop.

"Hey, girlfriend!" Clad in her cargo pants and singlet, Reggie sat astride a stool in front of her workbench that was strewn with small plastic bags filled with semiprecious stones salvaged from estate sale jewelry. Her long Cleopatra hair was tied back in a pony tail with a piece of what looked like silver wire. "What brings you to my humble abode? You decide to do the right thing and have that bracelet cut off?"

Chloe's hand clamped over said bracelet. "Now why would I want to do that? That'd be like—like throwing away my crystals and depending on the police to solve things." She grinned and stepped inside, past the counter that ran the length of the walls. Across from her a matching counter held various kilns, grinders and sinks needed in the jewelry-making business. A set of smudged windows filled the wall beyond Reggie's workbench.

"Hold it right there," Reggie said and held up her hands in a picture frame. "That has got to be one of the most beautiful tops I've ever seen you wear. I swear you positively glow. Has something changed for you?" Her eyes narrowed.

"Seriously?" Chloe crossed her arms, choosing to ignore the secondary question. "Since last night getting the bracelet off *has* crossed my mind, but I'm going to see this through."

Lila rose from her place on another stool. "What happened last night?" She dragged Chloe over to a third stool so they sat knee to knee in the dimly lit workroom. This close the auras of her friends were like a gentle wash of power over her. It had always been like this with the three of them, like they were three pieces of a single crystal long lost to each other but now brought together.

She sighed, not quite sure where to start. "After you, uh, asked me for that favor, last night I sat out on my patio and decided to concentrate on the bracelet to see what happened." She shook her head, remembering, her skin chilling as she told them about the sense of displacement and otherness. When she was finished telling them about breaking her wine glass and going to answer the door, she found them both looking at her.

"Decidedly weird," Reggie said shaking her head, her long dangly earrings of bells gently tinkling.

"I guess what I want to know, is what it means to you, Chloe? You're the sensitive one. What does it say to you?" Lila asked.

There was such hope in Lila's eyes, and worry—as if Chloe held all the answers they needed.

But she didn't. She closed her eyes, blocking out the hope and the urgent need that came through Lila's aura. "All I have is confusing impressions—not even images. Just dust and dry and horses and maybe juniper and cypress. How do I make sense of that?"

Inhaling she looked back at her friends. "I'm sorry. I didn't get much sleep last night."

"But it's a start, Chloe. Things might get clearer as time passes. You've just barely put the bracelet on," Lila said.

"On the other hand, it might just be Chloe's mind taking artistic license with the research you and Kylee did into the bracelet's provenance. Did you ever hear back from the British Colonel's son about his notes?" Reggie asked.

Lila shook her head, her mass of auburn curls catching the light like the hornblende inclusions in falcon's eye stones. "Sorry. I've been a little preoccupied. I'm still waiting to hear from Allyson. She said she'd be here in the next day or so. Of course she hasn't called to update her plans. She never does. Darn woman has been the bane of her parents' existence, since she ran off with a band when she was just sixteen. We laughed about it in college, but being on the receiving end sort of gives you a different perspective."

Chloe cringed. She'd done the same to her parents, though she'd been seventeen and had finished school before she left.

"If there's anything I can do to help," she said, grabbing her friend's hand. This time, when she looked at Lila, she realized that she had dark circles under her eyes and small worry lines fanning out from their corners. Her college friend's arrival alone wouldn't do that to her. It had to be the break-in and the bracelet and the things that kept happening. But just like always, Lila kept her worries to herself. "Is everything going okay with the renovations of the shop?"

"Everything's fine," Lila said. "Things always work out. The insurance adjuster was out today and it looks like they're going to pay out."

She smiled, but it wasn't her normal easy smile. So something was going on that Lila was holding within herself. Chloe frowned. Whatever it was, it had Lila worried, but this wasn't the place and time to discuss it.

Reggie looked back and forth between them. "So it sounds like there's a lot of surprise visitors decorating our lives right now. Just who was it that disturbed your little experiment last night, Chloe?"

"No one. Someone canvassing." Chloe shrugged. She might have come here hoping to talk to Lila, but Reggie? She might be a good friend, but she wasn't exactly good at keeping a secret...

"Canvassing about what? That late at night? That's kind of strange, don't you think?" Reggie glanced at Lila, who nodded.

A glance in Lila's direction revealed what had happened. Chloe closed her eyes. "You told her, didn't you?"

"She didn't have to. I happened to look out of the workshop, here, and spotted you and the good Detective in the kitchen the other day. There was enough heat I could have run my kiln, even though I couldn't hear the soundtrack. So Detective Stone found an excuse to visit you?"

"It wasn't like that. There was a break-in at the condo and he was canvassing for witnesses."

"And you saw something," Lila asked, leaning back against the counter and obviously enjoying this.

"No. I didn't. The poor guy looked exhausted and he was just finishing for the night."

"Saved the best for last, did he?" Reggie chortled.

"No. He simply arrived at my door and realized the time and said that was it for the night." Or had he? He *did* have her address.

"So you took a poor, tired man into your apartment?" Reggie raised her brows.

"Yeah. I did. Sometimes my good nature has me doing stupid things without thinking."

"It's the sensitive in her. Her heart and body know, but her mind hasn't caught up yet," Reggie joked with Lila.

"No wonder she didn't pick up more from the bracelet."

"So what did you do?" Reggie put on her avid girlfriend voice. "I mean you've got hunky Mr. Policeman alone and all." Another lascivious lift of her brows.

"Would you guys stop it! Nothing happened. Nothing at all. We talked, that's all. I behaved myself and Jas was a perfect gentleman. We had a glass of wine and then he had to go because we both had to work in the morning. That's it. And if you think I'm going to sit here and let you make up stories about Jas and me, well." She stood up. "I'm not sticking around. I have a room to set up and a client to get ready for."

"She calls him Jas, did you hear? She calls the good Corporal, Jas."

Dammit she was giggling and Reggie giggling always meant trouble.

"You—you are no longer my friend." She wagged her finger under Reggie's nose and then Lila burst out laughing. "And you are on notice, Lila."

Their laughter burning her cheeks, she turned on her heel and marched back toward the house. So much for girlfriends. She was going to have to figure this thing with Jas out, alone.

CHAPTER 8

Willowview Terrace looked a lot different than it had the night before. Then, the moonlight had filled the garden and there had been a sweet scent of flowers that had reminded him of floral incense and the shadows that hid in Chloe's dark hair. Now it was a place of sunlight, but a brisk breeze ripped at the lake and the pool so there were no sunbathers. No mermaid swimming, either, but then Chloe had said she had an appointment today. She'd be at the shop. Probably working on the renovations and repairs. Maybe he could slide by on the pretext of updating them on the break-in and the Jensen abduction case. Forester was out talking to the psychiatrist at the hospital to determine whether they could even try to question Beaton again. The man had been under sedation since the night he abducted Kylee Jensen.

"You are one sick man, using someone's misfortune as an excuse to flirt with a woman." He'd seen other officers do it enough. The ones who hung around the emergency room to pick up a cute ER nurse. The ones who cultivated the court clerks. Even the guys that picked up the babe waitress at the local RCMP restaurant hangout. It was one of the perks of wearing the uniform. Women were drawn to them. Not that he was in uniform anymore, but the RCMP rank could still get him as many women as he wanted.

Not that he wanted any.

"Yeah, right." He headed for the Willowview Terrace front door again, but this time the thing was closed and locked. The brick, however, had been fished out of the bushes and sat in the corner by the glass door. He shook his head. Some people would never learn. He buzzed the Singh apartment and waited, hoping someone would pick up and let him in. In the meantime the place looked almost deserted. Just garden plantings and a few starlings and robins. A bit of color under a bush by the raised pool deck caught his eye.

Just a plastic bag caught in the wind, probably. He looked back to the door, still waiting for someone to pick up, but there was something about that bag. The way it sat there, it wasn't like it was snagged on a branch—it was like it was full. Someone's rotten lunch?

Oh what the hell. The Singhs weren't answering anyway. Crossing to the bushes and the bag, he took out a pen and used the tip to carefully pull the bag open.

"Holy shit."

Carefully he stepped back onto the pavement and fished out his phone. He punched a number and waited. "Hey. It's Stone. I think I've got a break in that break-in case. I just found a bag in the bushes at Willowview Terrace and I don't know much about jewelry, but it looks like it might be the Singh haul. I just wanted you to know before I call Ident to come check the scene for evidence. Talk to you, partner." He hung up, dialed again and called in Ident, and took a few photos with his cell, even though he knew Ident would do a much better job. Then he sighed and took out his notebook to describe the scene and how he'd come to be here.

Of course he left out the part about wanting to flirt with a certain woman.

Three hours later the Ident officer was done and the bag with jewelry was carefully sealed in an evidence bag for transport back to the detachment. There, Jas could check the contents against the list of stolen items. He checked his watch. Almost noon. He could take his lunch break and maybe take a certain lady for a bite to eat. Simply an act of payback for her kindness the night before. He headed toward his unmarked blue car.

"Hey! You! You're a cop, right?"

A man, about five-foot-nine with bleach-tipped black hair threaded through the paths toward him from the back of the L-shaped complex. He was about thirty five and wore an expensive-looking suit. Stockbroker, maybe. Or financial planner. The kind that couldn't quite make it in the big city, but was about being the big fish in a small town like Peachland.

"Corporal Jasper Stone. Can I help you?"

The guy ran his hands through his hair and shook his head. His brown gaze had that 'why me' deer in a headlight look Jas had come to associate with victimization.

"Calm down, Sir. What's the problem?"

"I've been robbed. At least I think I have. My girlfriend's stuff is gone." The guy looked shaky.

"Sir, what's your name?"

"Rick—Richard. Richard Zeiss."

"Richard, you look like you need to sit down. How about we go to your apartment and then you tell me your story and I can look around. That sound okay?"

Richard's dazed look cleared at the simple plan. "Sure. Yeah. Come on."

He started back across the courtyard while Jas sighed and called it in to the detachment. Then he followed Zeiss.

The apartment sat in the rear arm of the L-shaped building, closer to the highway and directly overlooking the gardens unlike how Chloe's place looked out on the lake. Richard Zeiss led him up the stairs to the second floor of the building and inside an apartment that faced the lake. Even though the building was concrete he could feel the rumble of the highway that ran behind the apartments. The apartments at the rear of the place must be noisy as hell. How the developer ever thought he could sell those places...

Zeiss led him inside—into winter. The place was a fucking freezer after the heat outside and the air conditioner was still churning. Zeiss placed his keys on a small table beside the door. Then, shoulders slumped, he motioned Jas into the living area. The place was done up like something out of a magazine, except a magazine could use camera angles to give a sense of spaciousness. Not so with this place. Unlike Chloe's condo on the third floor there were no high ceilings, but like her apartment there were hardwood floors and lots of floor-to-ceiling glass to bring the outdoors inside. Beyond the complex gardens and pool, there was still a lake view which probably meant this place was worth a pretty penny. The insides were all done up in overlarge, low-slung black leather, and a large home entertainment console. A rack under the wall-mounted TV was full of every kind of video game device Jas could think of. Okay, maybe the magazine would be something like Today's Gamer.

Richard poured himself a drink, plunked down on the couch and sprawled there looking like a petulant kid. "Aren't you going to ask me some questions?" He slurped back what looked like scotch or rye whiskey.

Jas sank down opposite the man and pulled out his notebook. "Why don't you just tell me your story? Everything you can remember."

Richard took another long pull of his drink and nodded. His gaze skittered around the room past artwork that looked like it was purchased the same time the furniture was. Showroom specials. Nothing personal about the space except maybe the video games and the stack of car magazines on the floor beside the couch. "All right. Here goes. I was out last night on a date if you must know, and when I got home I was tired and I just fell into bed. This morning I got up and was dressing for work and I reached for my tie pin and it wasn't where I always leave it."

He shook his head and inhaled more of the booze so the level in the glass was going down past the refill stage. Not good if the guy was planning to drive to work afterwards.

"Anyway, I went looking, thinking maybe I'd been weird and put the pin away yesterday after work, but I looked in my drawer and it wasn't there. It wasn't anywhere. And then I noticed that my girlfriend's jewelry was gone. She'd left it here for safekeeping while they were painting her apartment. It was a ziplock baggie with a bunch of silk bags inside. I had it in a drawer in my dresser." He shook his head. "She's gonna kill me."

"Does your girlfriend have a key to your place? Is there any chance she might have come by and reclaimed her things?"

"No. Absolutely not."

No hesitation at all which gave it more credence.

"It's gone. Just gone. Someone had to have broken in."

Jas stood up and scanned the apartment. There was a fortune in electronics. If someone was breaking in, why just take the jewelry? "Perhaps you can show me where things should be and I can take a look at the doors and windows?"

Richard hiked himself out of the couch like he'd rather stay where he was. He trudged into the next room.

The bedroom didn't quite fit the image Jas had formed of the man based on the livingroom area. There, the room was clean and polished and ready for the world to see. Here, an overarching odor of dirty laundry pervaded the room and an ensuite bathroom leaked the smell of must and soapy water into the air-conditioned air. The bed was a tangle of black sheets and duvet—he didn't want to think what forensics would find if they shone a black light on it. What looked like an expensive highboy dresser sat against one wall. Bare laminate floor. Walls devoid of any art.

Richard pointed at a chest of drawers. "Julie's stuff was in there. Top drawer."

Jas pulled on a set of disposable gloves and opened the top drawer. A tangle of sock bundles and underwear filled the space from top to bottom. He ran his hands under the clothing. Nothing there. He shoved the drawer closed. "You're sure the bag was in there? You couldn't have put it in another drawer?"

"Look, man. I'm not some idiot. I know where I put them. They were in the top drawer. Julie put them there."

Jas nodded. "Mind if I take a look?"

The guy rolled his eyes, but nodded and Jas made quick work of checking the other drawers. Nice cashmere sweaters. A bunch of well-worn t-shirts. When he was done he turned to the window over the head of the bed. This room didn't have the sliding glass door to the patio like the Singh's, but he checked the locking mechanism anyway. The window was locked up tight.

He led the way out of the bedroom and over to the sliding doors to the patio, let himself out and looked down the side of the building. The patio had nowhere near the spacious living space that the Singh's or Chloe enjoyed. The patio from the third floor apartment placed the outdoor area in partial shade. There was room for a small patio set, but Zeiss had only a couple of cheap plastic chairs and a side table. An empty glass similar to what he'd been drinking from inside suggested how he used the space. No plants. No cat. No sign of life, and when Jas looked sideways out from the patio, it was to an endless line of similar patios separated only by low decorative walls. The next patio over had a wicker chaise and a mass of potted plants all in riotous bloom, so somebody there cared.

He pulled back and checked the patio door's locking mechanism. More scratches. Whoever it was really wasn't taking a lot of time to make this hard on investigators. He straightened and went inside to where Zeiss had obviously refreshed his drink. High points of color had formed on his cheeks and Jas would bet that that was pretty much how he turned up for work a lot of the time.

"okay, Mr. Zeiss. I'll need to get your girlfriend's name and contact information. In the meantime I want you to prepare a list of everything taken and get it to me tomorrow. Here's my card. I'm going to have Ident come to see if they can lift any prints so I'd appreciate it if you didn't touch the patio, the patio door or anything in the bedroom."

"What about work? I can't hang around here all day."

"You have homeowners insurance?"

Zeiss nodded. "What's that have to do with anything?"

"Let's just say that a claim is going to require a police file number. If you want me to open a file, you'll stick around here and not make things difficult. Besides, you're in no state to drive to work."

"You can't talk to me like that! I'm a tax payer. I pay your wages." Color had bloomed in Zeiss's face.

If someone would only pay him for every time that line was tried on him. He grinned. "Try me. What kind of vehicle do you drive, Mr. Zeiss?"

Zeiss puffed himself up. "A custom paint job brown BMW 533i Gran Tourismo. Why."

"Plate number?"

The guy told him.

Jas eyed him and flipped his notebook shut. "I suggest you do what I said, Mr. Zeiss. I'm going to be notifying the West Kelowna detachment to be watching for your car. They'll pull you over and demand a breathalyzer test. So the ball's in your court."

He let himself out and worked his neck as he strode down the hall. Dealing with assholes always made him tense.

Outside, he called it in, then advised dispatch he was doing follow-up on a case and then taking lunch. When he put his car in gear it was almost like it knew where he was headed before he did.

§

Thankfully, setting up the healing room for Chloe's late morning appointment helped her settle her frazzled nerves and get over her 'sort-of' mortification over her friends thinking she had a thing for a certain Corporal. That was so not happening. So what if Jas's—no, Corporal Stone's aura and hers seemed to mesh together like crystals growing out of the same node. So he'd had a glass of wine on her patio last night. He'd been tired and she'd been kind and offered, that was all.

The healing room was almost ready and her client, Marcia Oldstrum, should be here any moment. The masseuse table was set up on a diagonal so that it followed the flow of the ley lines down the core of the valley. She had set up small cones of onyx in the corners of the room as a means to reinforce the power of the crystals and had her phone and docking station playing soft piano and natural forest music. Lila's many plants gave the room a green glow as if you were in a lush jungle. They cleared the air so it smelled of green growth and damp earth. She inhaled and closed her eyes.

All it needed was a touch of leather to be positively erotic.

She jerked upright from where she'd sagged against the table. Where the heck had that come from? She shook herself and kept busy putting towels in the drier to warm and fussing over her small table of crystals complete with her flask of amethyst water. Just let Marcia get here and she could get busy. Busy was good as a distraction.

But to really have the crystals work their best, she needed to be centered. Otherwise her very presence could unfocus their healing. Plunking down in Lila's reading chair, she cradled her hands in her lap, closed her eyes and took a deep breath, then focused on the heat of the breath as it left her nose. In, and there was the slight tickle of cool air in her nostrils. Out again. And again, with each breath sending calmness into her jangled nerves and calmness and healing into the room.

A soft knock at the door brought her eyes open.

"Your appointment's here, Chloe." Kylee smiled in at her, her blond hair tousled and cute over her gamine features. Even in cut-offs and denim shirt with paint freckles on her skin she was adorable.

"Thanks. You look like Daisy Duke in those shorts."

Kylee grimaced. "Not exactly what I was going for but it works for painting and Brett approves."

Chloe chuckled and followed her toward the shop. "He'd have to be a blind man if he didn't."

"Say, while we're closed down would it be possible to borrow one of your books on crystals. I want to be able to tell people more about the healing properties of the stones they buy. Maybe do up little cards for them about how to keep the stones—what did you call it—charged?"

"Not a bad idea. Let's talk more about this later, okay."

Kylee nodded as they came into the shop. Marcia Oldstrum was seated out on the porch.

"We should probably talk some about that, as well." Kylee nodded at Chloe's wrist and at first she didn't understand.

"The bracelet? Sure." But she did a quick retreat to the front door and outside for her customer. "Marcia, welcome. Thank you for being willing to try crystal healing and for putting up with our sorry state of construction." Chloe shook her hand and was almost swept away by the sharp stab of Marcia's aura. It felt brittle and yellow-brown and muddy with stress and fatigue.

She was a small woman of about fifty who seemed to be eaten away from within. She was thin, with narrow features, sunken cheeks and eyes that glittered like moss agates. Her red hair was a not-quite natural looking cinnabar color, but it went with her pale skin. Even in the heat of an Okanagan sunny day she wore a navy pantsuit, white blouse and jacket. And her aura seemed to vibrate painfully against Chloe's. It was that which had led to her talking to Marcia about crystal healing in the first place.

"I've got everything set up, so why don't you come with me?" She led Marcia down the hall and into the side hall that led to the healing room. There, she handed Marcia a dressing gown. "I'd like you to get out of your outer clothes and put the robe on, then come on in here and I'll be waiting." She motioned to the room.

After Marcia closeted herself in the bathroom to change, Chloe retrieved warm flannel sheets from the dyer and spread them on the masseuse table. When Marcia climbed onto the table, she wrapped the sheets tightly around her.

"Feel good?"

"Toasty."

"That's what I was going for. Is this music okay, because I want it to be relaxing, not annoying."

Marcia shook her head. "It's fine. I feel all snug and warm and comfy."

"Good. So I want you to do some relaxation breathing with me for a few moments and then we'll move on to the crystal work, okay?"

Marcia nodded again. She already had her eyes closed, but there was still a tightness around her mouth and eyes that spoke of tension.

"Here's what I want you to do." She explained about the breathing and focusing on the rush of air over the tip of the nose. Gradually Marcia's breathing rate slowed and all the ragged energy in her aura seemed to smooth. Good.

The woman's aura was a mess and clearly needed cleaning. In particular, the vortex of the fifth chakra that drew power into the throat was wobbly and sulfur colored. She drew in her own breath and matched Marcia's breathing rhythm, then caught Marcia's shoulders and sent her own energy into the woman, focusing on the fifth charka. The wobble steadied, the chakra took on a clearer yellow hue.

"I'm going to apply the crystals now." She loosened the warm sheets around Marcia's neck and placed her amethyst crystal there, then lay her alabaster piece beside it. In the best of all worlds she would have alabaster to place around the amethyst to focus the energy downward, but this would do for a start.

She stepped back from the table to let the crystal do its work. "We're going to leave the crystal on there for fifteen minutes. Just focus on your breathing, and if you happen to fall asleep, that's okay." She retrieved another warm sheet, laid it over Marcia and stepped away, setting a timer so that someone like Marcia could benefit from the sound of time winding down. It would be hard enough for someone wound so tightly to stay still for so long.

Chloe settled in the chair and closed her eyes again, focusing on the energy fields in the room, the flow of power through the earth and through her into Marcia. At fourteen minutes she stood and went to the table. Marcia still breathed steadily, but it was the calm breath of honest slumber so Chloe almost felt bad waking her. But the time was up and the fifth chakra had regained a balance over her body. The muddy color of her aura had healed somewhat, too. Now the clean yellow shone through.

The timer softly buzzed and Chloe stabbed it off and gently removed the crystals. The amethyst felt heavy and darkened, so it had acted as storage for all the stress Marcia had been feeling.

"Marcia!" she called softly and the moss agate eyes flashed open. "How do you feel?"

Marcia shifted inside her cocoon of blankets. "Good. Maybe even better than that. I fell asleep, didn't I?"

"You did. The breathing helps you relax and your body took over. That's a good thing. It shows that you were truly relaxed." Chloe stripped off the top blanket and helped Marcia sit up, the other warmed sheets still around her shoulders. "Take a few minutes and just sit and enjoy how you feel. The crystals helped to rebalance you. Here. This is amethyst water. I want you to drink it all down."

"What's in it?" Marcia asked, accepting the flask.

"Purified water and energy and a bit of brandy to help hold the energy in place."

The newspaper publisher looked at her strangely and sipped the water. "It doesn't taste like anything at all. I can barely taste the brandy."

"And that's a good thing, isn't it? Now drink up."

Marcia did, and color seemed to creep into her wan features. She frowned, but that gradually changed into a small smile.

"Okay now?" Chloe asked as the music continued its lulling tinkle behind them.

Marcia nodded.

"Then I want you take the sheets with you and change in the bathroom. Leave the sheet there and I'll meet you out front in the shop, okay?"

Marcia agreed and shuffled into the Lila's guest bathroom while Chloe tidied up the healing room. It had gone well. Very well in fact for a first session. Of course that didn't mean there'd be more sessions. Marcia Oldstrum wouldn't waste her time on anything she didn't feel was working.

The shop was empty except for an open can of paint and Kylee with her paint brush. "So how'd it go?"

Chloe worked her shoulders and thought a moment. "Good. Really good as a matter of fact. Even I feel refreshed and ready for anything." A set of footsteps down the hall and Marcia pushed through the beaded curtain, looking like a different woman. Her hair no longer looked quite like straw and her skin had a luster. She came directly to Chloe.

"Thank you." She caught Chloe's hands. "I haven't felt this good in a very long time. The headache is gone and my neck isn't so stiff. Even my shoulder isn't giving me any problems and my doctor says it's arthritic."

"I'm glad it helped. I thought it would. Now you can maybe help spread the word."

"Spread the word! I'm going to be singing your praises. Listen I know you offered to do this for free as a loss leader, but I want to pay you. I really thought I was going to take time off work for a while, but now I don't have to."

Chloe shook her head. "No. Free was our agreement. And as for staying at work, did you ever think a little work-life balance might be in order?"

"Hah! Now you sound like my ex-husband. Nope, I'm an old work horse. Put me out to pasture and I'll still be trying to walk the furrows." She checked her watch and headed for the door. "Gotta go. Another meeting, but can you schedule me in for next week, please? Oh, and I figured you'd refuse payment so I left you something on your table." With a grin she was out the door like a whirlwind and gone.

"Wow. I can certainly see how she got to be head of her own newspaper chain," Kylee said. "Let me catch my breath a moment."

"She is a force, all right." She turned back to Kylee. "So let me put my things away and I'll come out here and help you paint."

"In that top?"

Chloe looked down at herself. "Well. Maybe a quick trip home first." She headed back to the healing room where she found a crisp fifty dollar bill laying on the table. She flicked off the music and sank into the chair for a minute, trying to quell her mounting excitement. If Marcia Oldstrum thought that highly of the treatment, there was a lot of potential in this business. A lot.

With slightly shaky hands she folded the fifty in half and placed it in her wallet. Then she packed up the docking station and bundled the sheets for laundering. With care, she started rewrapping the crystals, sending energy into each one with thanks, when footsteps in the hallway disturbed her. She turned around. It wasn't Lila or Kylee or even Reggie because the footfall was all wrong. So was the aura.

Oh no.

From out of the shadowed hallway stepped Jas Stone.

CHAPTER 9

"Hey," Jas said. It was all he seemed to be able to come up with seeing her there. She looked beautiful, almost radiant the way her top shimmered and the muted sunlight through the window caught around her. Almost as if she shone with an inner light, which was a damn stupid thing to think, but at the moment she looked it. Almost like one of those elf queens in that Tolkien movie everyone had talked about a few years back. Just like the ordinary folk in the movie, she was out of his league and yet something inside him yearned for her.

Except Chloe Main was real and, at the moment, with her lips slightly parted in surprise—most imminently kissable. He glanced around at the spidery plants in their dusty old macramé hangers and the small piles of crystals someone—probably Chloe–had spread around the room. A black, old fashioned, doctor's bag sat open on a table and was about the only normal thing in the room, except that she was packing her stones in it, not medicine.

"So this is it, is it? The place you heal people?" He kept his hands in his pockets, but still did a mental parentheses around heal.

She must have heard it for her radiance seemed to fade. Damn. He really needed to watch that judgment.

"It is," she said primly. "And just in case you wondered, it went very well."

"Good, then." He scanned the crystals she was wrapping. "So—uh—just what did you do?"

She looked up at him. "Well. To your eyes it would have looked like I helped her feel comfortable and put some stones on her chest while I spouted some mumbo-jumbo." As if he couldn't possibly appreciate anything more than that.

The glow around her diminished further and he felt like a heel. Oh, what the hell. "Listen. All kidding aside, I came by because I thought maybe I could take you to lunch for taking pity on a poor tired cop last night. You interested?"

She gave him a sharp glance from where she was wrapping a piece of purple-colored stone with the meticulousness of a forensics team member collecting evidence. "I'm sorry. I have to help with the repainting and so on."

And the abrupt way she said it might have cut a lesser man off at the knees, but damn it he was police and he dealt with less than willing suspects most of the time. He'd seen her friendly the night before, so if he just stuck to his approach she might give him something.

She finished packing up her things, folded her table so the room was just a plant-filled space with a lone stuffed chair, and turned back to him. "You're still here."

He couldn't help but grin. "I am. If lunch doesn't work, how about a coffee?"

Shaking her head, she pushed past him. "I told you. I have to work."

He followed after her. "Well, you don't have customers. I could pick something up and bring it back. We could chat then."

The beaded curtain clacked behind her as she turned back to him. Beyond her Kylee Jensen and the tall one, Lila Weber, looked up from a conversation over the open paint cans.

"I have painting to do," Chloe said. "I do not eat in the shop even now. It's a bad habit to get into. It reflects poorly on the business when the place smells like takeout and there are crumbs everywhere."

"Hey. You're speaking ill of the food I live on." He feigned a wound to the heart which got an extreme eye roll from Chloe. She doggedly crossed the room and placed her things behind the counter. This was not going well. He was crashing and burning with the best of them, and the silly thing was he was putting himself through this mortification when he wasn't even sure he liked the woman. Sure he'd thought about her too much, but that didn't mean anything.

"What time do you expect to be finished today," he asked and hoped he didn't sound as desperate as he thought he did.

"Chloe, did this fine man ask you for lunch?" Lila asked.

"Yes." A curt reply. "I told him that I had painting to do. Kylee has done her share and should take her lunch beak now. I just need to go home and change."

Lila checked the slim silver watch on her wrist and pursed her lips. "Tell you what. Allyson's called for me to meet her flight, but I have an hour that I can give you. How about I do a bit of the painting myself and you can both go. I'm sure your session this morning depleted you and lunch would give you time to recharge."

It was almost humorous watching the horror coalesce in Chloe's expression as Lila made her offer. "Lila, no. It's not just your shop. It's mine, too, and we've got a fair amount to do to get the place open again."

"And I know how rare it is to have a handsome man come into the store and invite one of us out for lunch—unless we include your brother. So go."

Chloe didn't even acknowledge his existence, and he really should be offended. Actually he should be pissed as hell. Who turned him down like this? In recent memory, nobody. He was tall and in shape. Other women had told him he was decent to look at. Let the woman go, his brain kept saying. But another part of him wasn't prepared to walk away. Maybe it was lust. Maybe it was the challenge she presented, but he'd committed himself to lunch or coffee with her today, so he was going to stand his ground. Fortunately Lila Weber was his surprising ally.

"Well, that's settled then." He offered Chloe his arm, which she firmly rejected. Instead she grabbed her purse, positively stomped to the front door, and out into the sunshine.

He sighed, wondering if he'd ever figure her out.

"Ice cream. Try ice cream. She has a weakness."

He glanced back at Lila standing beside the counter. "She always like this?"

"I'd say only when she likes someone and is mad that she does."

"Hell of a way to show it." But ice cream it was.

§

She waited for him on the front lawn feeling vulnerable and weak in the knees. Maybe Lila was right and she was a little depleted. The sun was misty through the light caul of clouds, its power to revive dissipated. The breeze was still brisk enough it felt cool, even on a hot day, or maybe it was just her, because at the moment she felt shaky—almost shocky. Was this how it was going to be after every healing?

She'd felt so good in the healing room, as if her aura had expanded and could heal the whole world. Now she just felt small and shriveled. Great way to go out for lunch with a man who seemed to find every sensitive button she had and push it. Not to mention that ridiculous firework sparks went off in her brain whenever she was near him.

He came down the stairs with the lithe movement of a man secure in his body. Tall, rangy, cowboy way of moving so she could imagine him on a black RCMP horse with his red serge jacket and his brass buttons gleaming.

"You ever ride in the Musical Ride?" she asked. The RCMP was famous for its mounted officers on their black horses, doing military quadrilles on horseback. They toured all over the world.

"Nope. I thought about it once upon a time when I was a kid growing up in horse country on the coast. As a teenager I rode because that was where the girls were." He gave her that charming lopsided smile that sent a tremor through her aura. Or maybe it was that he'd stepped in close beside her. "So where's good. And it apparently has to serve ice cream. Lila says."

He was watching her face as she realized her friend had set her up in more ways than one. "I'll get her for this, you know."

"What are friends for?" He led her toward the gate. "The bakery, or in town?"

She hesitated.

"Town it is. There's more choice anyway."

His car was a dark blue Ford sedan that smelled—true to the clichés and his admission—of fast food. He cleared the passenger seat of papers, but otherwise the car was devoid of any sign of the man who drove it. For a moment the mystery of his background intrigued her. A police radio burbled almost out of sight under the dashboard.

She climbed in. "After lunch I have to go home and change so I can paint."

"Sounds good. I'm happy to drive you."

Damn! She was an idiot. She didn't want this guy taking her home and then back to the shop. She didn't want lunch with him, either—fat lot of good that was doing her.

He pulled out sedately into traffic and they cruised in the most relaxed manner down along the curve of the lake shore past the miniscule yacht club with its dark gray pilings, and the supervised swimming area crowded with families with young children. He pulled into the curb in the shade of some willows beside the town's cenotaph near the water.

"How about here?" He nodded at the *Blue Hills Restaurant*. It was an award winning dining room coupled with a casual terrace area where people could dine in flip-flops and have a pint of good dark beer. The food was good, but going there would be like a date.

"You sure?"

"Forester tells me they have good food and I seem to recall the other night you said you and Lila had been about to eat there before everyone realized Kylee was gone."

"You remember that?" Who would remember such an insignificant remark?

He shrugged and waggled his brow. "I remember a lot of things. Too many, possibly."

His scrutiny suggested he wanted to say something more, but instead he opened his door. "Come on. Let's have that meal you got robbed of."

Surprisingly—or maybe not—he was a cop—he was a perfect gentleman, ushering her in front of him into the terrace area of the restaurant with a light touch of his hand on the small of her back. At the table he held her chair before sinking into his own across from her.

The place was built of logs, the seating area in a series of broad steps up from the sidewalk before ending in a large spacious white table dining room with views from a second floor out to the lake. Where they were seated a half-wall provided shelter from the harsher side of the wind, but the air still moved pleasantly around them. It was redolent with the scents of barbequed burgers and pizza and beer. The place was crowded with summer people, with hastily pulled on cover-ups over their bathing suits.

"So what's good?" Jas asked, flipping open the menu that had been given to them by a waitress in black shorts and white t-shirt.

"You know, you didn't have to do this, Corporal." Keeping her voice carefully neutral because this close to him, she could again feel his aura. His might be a muddy red when she looked at it, but the occasional flashes of clarity seemed to send a reaction through her right down to her core. Heat flooded up through her and she was sure her skin flushed.

Glancing up from his menu he gave her that resolve-weakening wicked smile again. She gulped. Did the powers that be specifically issue smiles like that to hot men like him?

"It had nothing to do with have to. Well maybe it did. I don't often go through what you put me through to take a woman to lunch."

"So why do it for me?" she asked and felt like a fool. God, she felt nervous and her fingers were twitching over the bracelet as if it was a worry stone.

She hid her hands in her lap.

That got him to sit back a moment and he met her gaze. "Well... that's a hard question to answer and yet it's not. I mean look at you. That mane of hair. That face. Those violet eyes. Who wouldn't be attracted? And then there's the fact that you're damned infuriating." He shrugged. "How could any man not be attracted?"

"When you put it that way, I guess I'm flattered. And if it's any consolation, I find you infuriating too." And good looking, but she wasn't going to be admitting *that* any time soon.

But their admissions seemed to ease the tension between them. They ordered their meals—a spinach salad for her because she loved the way they included ripe pear, candied pecans and fresh organic soft goat cheese, while he, on her advice, had the barbeque burger with blue cheese with a side of fries. That business done they looked at each other. Smiled.

Awkward.

"So how's your investigation going?" she asked around a sip of iced tea that she'd ordered when they'd both passed on the excellent beer because they had to work.

"Which one?"

"Oh. Right. There are three aren't there. A regular crime wave in good ol' Peachland. First Kylee's abduction, then the burglary at the store and now the Willowview Terrace thing, too. How the heck do you keep it all straight in your head?"

"Nothing esoteric." He shrugged. "Good notes, I guess. And training. Mostly the notes. I see you're still wearing the bracelet." He nodded at her wrist.

She held it up so the sunlight caught on it and the small door of iron strapping seemed to gleam. "Well, I still can't get it undone, so I guess it's on for the duration." Unless, of course, a good session in bed would get it off, like had happened to Kylee. There *was* that. Hmm.

"You guys learn any more about it?"

What could she say? "Lila still hasn't heard anything from the Colonel's son, if that's what you're asking." Tell him about her experiment? It would test his credibility, but heck, he was the one so determined to take her to lunch. Let him have Chloe Main in all of her glory.

"I did try a little divining with it. I got something, but I'm not sure what yet." She sipped her iced tea and watched him.

The good Corporal blinked once. Twice. "You did what?"

"Divining. You see, Jas, all matter vibrates and sometimes an item picks up the vibrations of something that has happened around it. I have some sensitivities and sometimes when I'm in a meditative state, I can sense things through my aura." Oh, gods, she was laying it on thick, but it was just so much fun to watch the expression on his face—or rather him fighting his natural incredulousness. "The other night when you dropped by you caught me in the midst of such an attempt. It was strange, really. It was like the lake went away. It was nighttime and there was a hot wind and... and..."

The day darkened around her. The lake and barbequed burger scent faded and was replaced by the scent of juniper, cypress, pine, and dusty air that sent her head spinning. *Beyond courtyard walls, the high road rang with the sounds of heavy feet. They were coming. She—they needed to get out of here. Had to get out of here.* She was half out of her chair when warm hands found her arms and a surge of heat ran through her and she felt a searing burn on her wrist.

"Chloe. Chloe, what's the matter?"

At her name, she came back to herself. Colors returned and it was daylight, not nighttime. The warm scent of lake water and pine filled the air as an undertone to grilled meat. She sagged a moment into warm arms and found herself shivering. The arms came around her, comforting.

"What was that?" Jas's deep voice rumbled in his chest and she realized where she was. Who she was with. She went to push away, but he was holding on tight, one hand cupping her head to his chest.

"I—I'm not sure. It was like a vision, a memory, something, channeled through me." She tried to slow her breathing.

"Your heart's pounding," he said. "I can feel it."

And this was far too intimate, even if his arms did feel like home. She'd given in to someone else's apparent safety years ago and had sold her soul as a result. It had taken her years to regain herself so she wasn't going to trust so easily again. She pulled away. Jas released her and she avoided meeting his eyes as she reseated herself. Too many people were looking at her like she was some weirdo. Maybe she was.

He sat down across from her, his face concerned, and thankfully not dubious. "You were talking about your vision the other night and then suddenly it was like you vanished out of your eyes. They went huge and black and your skin went dead white and then you leapt to your feet and that's when I grabbed you. Sorry. Does that happen often?"

Did he think she was a medical case? Maybe someone who needed the psych ward? Heck, after that, maybe she did. Her insides still shook, she'd been so *afraid*. Terrified, really. She still was, but she shook her head. "Never before. I hope it doesn't happen again, either." She held up her hand between them and it was visibly shaking. "This is not like me, but it'll pass." She hoped.

"Maybe you really should think about getting that bracelet off if it's affecting you like that."

His face was so concerned, that she couldn't help herself. It would have been funny if she could just get her heart to stop racing and her pulse to slow. "I don't think I ever would have expected to hear such words from you, Corporal Stone. You almost sound like you believe in things like psychics."

But he didn't color and he didn't even look embarrassed. He just shook his head. "I just saw a lovely woman that I like suddenly disappear before me and become a terrified cornered animal. At least that's what it looked like."

Strange. "That's exactly what I was feeling. I was in a house—a villa courtyard or something and people were coming for me and I was deathly afraid." She met his scrutiny and there was no judgment. His need to understand what had happened seemed to morph into a need to understand her in particular—as if she was the key to a puzzle, perhaps. Or the critical piece of evidence to solve a crime. He looked like he was going to say something, but the waitress chose that moment to bring their meals.

He talked about the break and enter at the store and the thefts at her complex. Then he shared the strange turn of events where it appeared that the stolen jewelry might had been recovered in a bag left on the grounds.

"Wonderful for Ginger," she said. "If only the same thing would happen with the things taken from the store." And she couldn't shake the feeling that whatever or wherever she'd been it hadn't been wonderful. He went on to tell her about a second break-in at the condo and she tried to attend.

He had such an orderly way of telling a story, it was a pleasure to listen to. All those years giving evidence as a police officer were probably coming into to play. He had lovely long-fingered hands that were expressive as he spoke, and as she watched, his rigid police exterior seemed to ease. The muddy tinge to his aura even seemed to fade, but all his attempts to distract her couldn't erase the feeling of doom that had settled on her. The fear from the vision had crystallized so deeply inside her that she was no longer sure what was from the vision and what was her own imaginings.

"Chloe?"

She suddenly realized she hadn't been attending. Not really. She'd been off somewhere trying to understand what the heck was going on. She tried for a smile, but apparently it didn't convince him.

He called for the waitress. "Can you package this stuff up to go, please? My lady, here, isn't feeling well and I'd like to get her home."

The waitress scooped her salad before she could say anything. "You really didn't need to do that. I'm fine. Really. I am."

But his expression was still doubtful. "Chloe, you've been sitting there and you've barely touched your food. You're still white as a ghost and you didn't even rise to the bait when I said that you and your crystals are just a whole lot of hokum."

"You said that?" She managed to find some indignation, but even that was hard to drum up with fear like a huge black crystal growing inside her.

"Well, not really. But I might have just to get your attention. Chloe, something's wrong. I can tell that much. Tell me what's going on."

She shook her head. "It's nothing you'd understand." No way in heck would he.

"Try me." He reached for her hand, but she didn't dare let him touch her, because it just might give her permission to be less strong. It was only strength that had saved her before. If she wasn't powerfully strong this time, this fear was going to overtake her.

The waitress brought them the bill and the boxed-up remains of their meals, and Jas—Corporal Stone paid. She shouldn't have let him. Then he tried to catch her elbow and help her out to the car. She refused his help and stumbled, but caught herself on a table. Darn it, what was wrong with her?

At the car she climbed in and put her head back, eyes closed. "Just take me back to the store, please."

A grunt was all she got in answer, but the car started and he pulled a U-turn and headed back along the lake. He must have pulled out his phone because the next thing she knew he was talking to someone.

"Hello, Lila? This is Jas Stone. Something's wrong with Chloe, so I'm taking her home."

She opened her eyes and winced at the sunlight. "What the heck do you think you're doing? I'm fine. I'll be fine!" She reached for the phone, but he held it away from her.

"She had some kind of spell. I don't know what, but she was talking and then suddenly it was like she wasn't there and she hasn't recovered yet. No. You don't need to come. I'll take care of her—until she throws me out. She's pretty pissed I'm not letting her come back to the shop. Uh-huh. Okay. See you." He pocketed the phone again and sent a grin in her direction. "See? All taken care of."

"You won't get thrown out of my house, because I'm not letting you in."

"Suit yourself." He shrugged and sped up along Beach Avenue and over the small bridge spanning Trepanier Creek and then pulled in at the curb right in front of the Willowview.

"I feel like I almost live here, myself, what with all the time I've spent here the past few days."

"You wish," she snarled, shoved open the car door and climbed out before he could open it for her. She stood up so fast she had vertigo and had to stand there too long gulping the wind, so he came up beside her and a firm hand cupped her elbow.

She could have folded right into his warm strength right then and there, but instead she pulled away. "I don't need your help, okay. I'm a big girl. I've been on my own for a very long time." She struck out on wobbly legs into the gardens past the pool toward the front door.

"But you still live in the little town you grew up in. You're not that much on your own with all your family and friends around you."

"What do you know about being alone? You in your tight brotherhood of police. You've no idea what being really alone is like."

She reached the door and if she could just get the flipping key out of her purse she could go inside and leave him out here. She fumbled in her bag, but the keys weren't forthcoming and... darn it they had to be here somewhere. She kept digging, but nothing really came into focus, until finally a pair of strong gentle hands relieved her of her purse. Damn it, she was *not* helpless.

He fished in her purse a moment then pulled out a set of keys. "These them?"

Damn him for being so flipping competent and over-confident and compassionate in the way he was looking at her. She did not need taking care of.

But he caught her elbow again. This time it took and he guided her inside, into the elevator, up two floors, and along the hall.

She still could still block him at her apartment door. She could get inside and keep him out.

But she wouldn't. She realized it now feeling his aura wrap around her, just as she knew what a crystal would do when she held it in the palm of her hand and felt its vibrations. She was going to invite this man into her apartment, into her life, and eventually she was going to sleep with him.

CHAPTER 10

He didn't even think to let her open the door herself. He simply unlocked the door and guided her inside to the livingroom couch. Sunlight filled the room and almost seemed to light the crystals, but mainly it was a nice sunny room with warm, comfortable furniture of brown leather and brightly colored cushions. The bamboo on her patio swayed in the breeze and on the lake there were small whitecaps. He'd bet that the sailboats would be out in force closer to Kelowna.

Chloe ran her hands up over her hair. "All the wind, I must look a mess."

"You look fine. Better than fine, except you're so pale."

She looked up at him. "What are you doing here, Jas? Why me? Why now?"

He crouched down in front of her. "I'm trying to help you. Why? Because I happen to like you. And now, because I finally met you and, at this moment, I think you might need me."

Her eyes had gone deep purple and her face had an intensity as if she really could see something beyond the world around them. He didn't look away.

"I always said that I'd take care of myself. That I was the only one I really knew I could depend on. I know. I know. Lila and Reggie and now Kylee have proven that it's possible to have friends. But not men..."

Men. Her eyes closed and he got the strongest sensation that she was trying to hide—not from him so much as from herself. Something in her past that impacted how she viewed him and made trust an issue for her.

There was nothing he could say to that. Trust had to be proven.

He hiked himself up from his crouch to sit on the couch beside her and eased her into his side. She fit naturally against him, her head on his shoulder, her softness against his angular frame as if she was a piece of him that had been missing, but she was stiff. Small shudders still ran through her. Whatever had happened to her back in the restaurant was still making her afraid.

"You're shaking," he said softly into her incense-scented hair—surprisingly the scent really could grow on you. "Why don't you tell me what you're feeling right now and then maybe we can work backwards to understand what set you off?"

He stroked her back and the length of her braid, the small pearls and crystals on her top like the grains of truth you had to sift from a suspect's statement. She sighed as if her whole body exhaled and shuddered.

"I don't understand it, and I don't know why I'm afraid. At first it was like I was terrified of what was in the vision, but then it sort of set off my own fears."

"Okay," he said. "But I don't want to go back to the restaurant yet. I want you to tell me what you're feeling right now." Soothing strokes on her back and she shivered against him.

"Afraid." She gulped. "Of you." So softly he almost missed it.

Of him. He wanted to sit her up and protest his innocence, but instead he simply inhaled deeply and sighed. "Well, there it is. And it didn't hurt too much to say it, did it?" He kept his voice light, though it kinda hurt to acknowledge it. He'd sworn an oath as a police officer. The RCMP oath might not state to serve and protect, but he'd always seen those as his duties.

She nodded into his chest, then looked up at him. "I'm sorry." Her dark eyes were half-filled with tears. "It's not you, it's everyone... male."

He cupped her head with his palm and shook his head. "And that is a damn shame, Chloe Main, because the woman I see is eminently loveable. You must have left a trail of broken hearts behind."

That brought a wry smile. "Thanks, but I don't think I've let anyone get close enough to make their heart vulnerable."

Goddamn her lips were so close to his and so damn kissable. If he could kiss away her tears and her fears, he would, but that would be taking advantage. He pulled his police demeanor around him—not that he usually interviewed people who were nestled in his arms. But the long strokes down her back were having an effect. Her tension seemed to have drained out into his palm. Of course maybe it was the damn crystals lining the wall behind them.

"Was there ever a time when you weren't so afraid?"

"Once. Once upon a time in a land far away and long forgotten." Her voice had gotten fainter and, with a deep breath, she relaxed against him.

"Where was that far away land, Chloe? Where were you last unafraid?"

She smiled softly as if remembering something good. "San Francisco, of course. Everything changed in San Francisco."

Then her mouth gently parted and her breath fell even. She curled closer into him, but her arms were still crossed protectively across her chest. He wrapped his arms around her more tightly and closed his eyes as well, trying to put the facts as he knew them together.

It wasn't much. She'd alluded to San Francisco before. She'd spent time there when she was still pretty young. A runaway? Kids did manage to get down to the U.S. without their parents. She'd mentioned a commune that had taught her all her New Age stuff and that had helped save her. He'd thought when she used the word 'saved' that it had been some religousy thing. He needed to rethink that. So something had happened to her as a young woman and she'd never recovered. Sure, she'd become a strong woman in all areas of her life, except, apparently, one. The most important one in his opinion.

He pulled out his cell phone and stabbed the number for Forester. His partner picked up on the second ring.

"Forester."

"It's Stone. I just wanted to check in and let you know I'm 10-10 dealing with a personal matter in Peachland. I'll call when I'm back on duty." He glanced down at Chloe. That could be a while.

Forester was silent for a moment. "Everything okay? You sound different."

"Everything's fine." He was just speaking softly, for God's sake.

"They finished the forensic exam on Beaton. The report should be out tomorrow."

"Good to know. I'll be there tomorrow with bells on." He clicked the phone off and slid it back in his pocket only to find a violet gaze looking up at him. "Hey. You fell asleep."

And was still waking up by the look of her. She had one of those dazed, still-half-asleep looks and her body was still relaxed against him. Her eyes, gone black now, seemed locked on his, and she uncrossed her arms and reached up loop them around his neck.

And then she lifted herself up and kissed him.

§

In the night-bound courtyard he held her one last desperate time. The air was filled with the over-sweet scent of the nightbloom and with dust raised by the many soldiers and their horses waiting outside.

"Please don't do this," he begged.

But she had to. It was the only way to save him.

She pulled away and he yelled and leapt past her to the gate. A great, gray pall came between them, like the pall of a sandstorm, and she was blinded and torn away and lost. Forever lost, but when she opened her eyes...

...there was no courtyard, only four familiar walls, shelves of what looked like glowing crystals and a stranger with his arms around her.

No. Not a stranger. Jas. And she was—Chloe. And she was not lost, either. She was in her apartment. The subdued sunlight through the front windows placed masculine shadows on the angles of Jas's face. *She* wasn't lost. As a matter of fact she was miraculously found! Jas had found her and she had found him, even if she was afraid of how he might hurt her.

No. She was not afraid. That was the fear of someone else. A young girl who thought she was a woman. She *was* a woman now.

Her arms found Jas's neck and she pulled him down to her. Kissed him and was mortified and pleased at her forwardness. Softly, she tasted and tested and he answered her right back. Such light touches of lips, exploring the shapes of each other's mouths, breathing in each other's scents, the feel of their skin, cheek against cheek as he brushed back her braid and inhaled the hollow beneath her ear, before shifting back to peer into her eyes. His long fingers caught her chin and restrained her.

"Are you sure? Because if we start something, I don't think I'll be able to end it."

Don't think about what it means, what it could bring, because everything could change in an instant and the man you loved could be taken from you. She tightened her arms around his neck and kissed him again. This time deeply. She was sure. Very sure. This man had taken care of her when she'd had the attack in the restaurant. He'd been prepared to just be with her and care for her until she was better. And his aura set fire to her own.

His hands shifted up to hold her head, her face, as he answered her back and demanded more. More? Yes, there was so much more that she wanted to give.

She went up on her knees and shoved his sports jacket off his shoulders. He obliged her by stripping it off his arms. Then she grabbed his polo shirt and tugged the hem out of his waistband, then pulled it up. Tanned skin and rock hard abs underneath. Everything she could have hoped for and more.

"Chloe." He caught her face and looked deep into her eyes. "Are you sure about this?"

She nodded, never more sure in her life. She wanted to live, wanted to prove that she *was* alive, not like the woman she'd dreamed of—the one who was so afraid. But why should she be afraid of this fine man? In answer she stripped her top up over her head. Jas caught the top from her and tossed it aside, the pale jewels glittering. Then his regard grazed her skin and his aura flared the color of flame and desire. It licked around her and her own aura turned honey-dark in answer.

"Make love to me." She stood up and shimmied her spandex leggings off, so that she stood there in only lace bra and panties.

Jas stood before her and cupped her face to kiss her. Then his hands ran lightly down her shoulders, to her sides and pulled her into his chest. "My God, you're beautiful. All white light and steel."

The feel of his flesh against hers sent a flash of white light flaring through her. Was that what he was referring to? What did it mean that she was baring her barely reconstituted soul to this man?

Don't think. Just do. Be.

She helped him unbuckle his belt and he stripped off his trousers, socks and shoes, then stood there in blue boxers that set off his tan.

"I never figured you for a boxer guy," she said as she stepped into his arms.

"And I never figured you for lace panties. I could hope, but I expected white cotton."

"There's nothing that says a New Age person can't wear lace," she said blushing as she enjoyed the strength of him, the way he was so obviously aroused by her.

"And that is a very good piece of news."

Suddenly he swept her off her feet, her arms coming around his neck as if they had been that way many times before. "So which way's the bedroom. I don't fancy doing this on the rug."

"You don't need to carry me. I'm too heavy." God, he must think she was a moose.

"No, Ms. Chloe Main, you most decidedly are not. Now where are we going?"

She pointed him in the right direction, the Master bedroom down a short hallway behind the kitchen that gave onto the third large room, that gave onto her huge patio.

The floor-to-ceiling curtains were open, light streaming in to pool on the large Siamese cat lounging on the cream colored duvet. The blue walls made the room seem filled with water, the sunlight shimmering.

"Sorry, old man." He plumped her on the bed and stretched himself beside her, sweeping Clyde off the bed with one long arm. "This is a two person party, no familiars allowed."

"Familiar?" she asked as she pulled him down to kiss him.

"Isn't that what they call pets of psychics," he mumbled as he nuzzled her neck and the heat of his breath, the touch of his lips made thinking just that much more difficult.

"No."

His lips found her earlobe and her breath hitched.

"Witches have familiars," she managed.

"Aah." He lifted her braid and made a study of removing the elastic at the end, then sensually pulled her hair free of its restraint, brushing her skin with the tip of the braid, then leaning in to trace kisses where the hair had been. Her flesh sizzled and she wanted his touch. Wanted him.

She shook her head, burying her face in her pillow. "I'm not a witch and Clyde's just my cat," she gasped.

"Is he now?" He stopped and raised himself above her on his elbow. "Well, look at you. A man could get lost in those eyes of yours. Your hair could hold him prisoner. There's no way at all a man's got a hope of escaping. That sounds like a witch to me."

His fingers traced down her sides trailing small fires in her flesh, but it was the darkness in his eyes that took her breath. This man—he wanted her for more than her flesh, just as she wanted him, regardless of their differences.

"I want you," she said and pulled him down to her, immersing herself in dark earth and leather.

When they kissed it was like the licorice taste of antimony. When their tongues touched it was sweet kirsch wine. She kissed his lips, his cheeks, ran her face down his cheek, loving the masculine roughness of them. Oh God, it had been so long since she had been with anyone like him. *Anyone at all.* Did she dare do this? Open herself to him?

His head dipped and it was too late for doubts. He traced kisses down her neck to her chest and over the soft mounds of the tops of her breasts so her nipples puckered and pressed tender against their lace restraints. She wanted his hands, his mouth on them, but instead his head sought lower down, tracking down her belly to her navel and resting there a moment, before his palm found the mound down lower and pressed, gently rubbed until her back arched up into him. She heard his low chuckle.

Then he was back stretched beside her and his arms came around her and—easy as pie—he swung her astride him and peered up at her with studious dark eyes that said he would remember every inch of her flesh just as he remembered evidence. Then he sat up to embrace her, so her legs came around his waist and felt him throbbing against her.

She swallowed and looked at him, her mane of hair heavy around her shoulders. His gaze was dark, with flecks of green malachite, his flesh the warm tone of amber against his onyx-colored hair. Altogether the stone of strong warrior, lover, thinker. A heady combination, and one she was drunk on. His red aura blazed around her, all the dirty gray lost. It sent hers vibrating so the bright yellow color faded to palest chrysoberyl.

"I want you, too," he said, his voice low in his chest, so she felt it through the contact of their flesh. His strong hands ran over her face, through her hair down over her shoulders and down her back. Her bra released and he slipped it over her shoulders, loosing her heavy breasts. He tipped her face up to his. "Truly a beauty."

His palms found her breasts, so lightly she thought she might go mad with want. Then he leaned in to taste and the warmth of his mouth sent sparks flashing through her so her brain sizzled and snapped.

Courtyard in the dark and men coming for her.

She didn't want to leave. If she left it was the end of her—of them.

He leapt to protect her.

She arched in his arms as his mouth feasted upon her, as she came up on her knees to make it easier to do so, as his fingers hooked her panties and slid them down her thighs.

"Here," he said, and lifted her up so she could free her legs. He tossed the panties aside and swiftly divested himself of his boxers, then settled her back across his lap. "Where were we?"

"Someplace dangerous we might never come back from," she murmured as he swiftly smoothed on a prophylactic.

Around them, night swirled with day and the room was asea with great, blinding, swirling waves of power like she had never seen before.

"Are you ready," he asked and his voice came from somewhere far far away. In distance? In time?

It didn't matter. "Yes," she whispered.

And he lifted her up and filled her and began to move. Waves of pleasure sent heat surging through her body, like lava pouring. Thrust and pressure drove her inwards like tectonic pressure coalesced coal into diamond. She was diamond, forming. *They* were a diamond forming, stronger together than ever apart.

She opened her eyes to find his focus intently on her face as he thrust and she met him in slow pleasurable movement. Then he caught her hips and, like that, swung her up and around. Still deep inside her, he carried her to her dresser and set her down there, with her back to the mirror, her legs still akimbo around him.

He pressed into her slowly now, and heat flushed her face. What she must look like from behind, all pale skin and flaccid flesh.

"Look," he said, as if he read her mind. "Look at how beautiful you are, and he turned her head so she could see over her shoulder, see the sheen on her back, see the thrust of his hips, see the fall of her hair in a tangle that enveloped them both. "Do you see what I see? Why I want you?"

It was him she saw, dark-eyed as a god, lost in his desire and that was the most sensual thing she had ever seen. He had given himself up to the moment, to whatever it was she was prepared to give.

She tightened her legs around him and ground herself against him. Deeper he drove. With each thrust he sent fissures cracking through her. All those glittering walls she had built for protection. All the secret barriers that only she knew. One by one he found his way through them until she was naked before him and only wanting more.

She shuddered around him again and again and he smiled down at her and lifted her up, laying her on the bed again, this time rising above her, and spreading her wide. "Ready?" his eyes asked and hers answered *always*.

He drove into her and she cried out as the last of her barriers crumbled around her. She grabbed his hips and thrust up to meet him, again. Again. Flesh met and married, male entrapped in female. Energy entwined between them. Her breath came in short gasping cries. His breath was harsh and urgent with each thrust. He drove home once—twice—three times more and her head might explode or perhaps she might die. All Jas's muscles tightened and he pulled her up into his chest as the world exploded around them. There was a shout and it might have been his or hers, she couldn't say. Then he collapsed beside her on the bed.

They lay there in a tangle of arms and legs and pale white sheets while she tried to catch her breath. It had never felt like this, not when she was eighteen. Would likely never feel like this again. She raised her gaze to study his handsome face. And found his smile waiting.

"I wasn't expecting that," he said and gently pushed her hair back from her face. "It's not too often I get seduced by a beautiful woman."

She boxed his arm. "Seduced, my eye."

"What do you call it when a woman drags you home and then throws herself at you?"

Was that what had happened? She couldn't be sure. She pulled back rubbing her head. "I've never seduced anyone in my life." Except maybe in San Francisco, but that hadn't been a seduction. It had been a business transaction.

Oh God, just what had she done? Covering her face, she rolled away from him.

"Chloe?" he caught her and wouldn't let her escape. Warm arms enveloped her and imprisoned her against his chest. "What's going on in that beautiful mind of yours?"

His voice was soft as he nuzzled her ear.

Swallowing, she shook her head. No way in heck was she telling him her past. A man like him would be up and out of her bed *so* fast. Or else he'd think she did this all time. She didn't think she could stand to see the look in his eyes that the truth would bring.

"It's nothing. I guess I'm still feeling whatever happened at the restaurant."

She tugged loose and he released her like a gentleman. At the edge of the bed she sat up and looked down at herself. Naked—and she felt that way. Something had happened between her and Jas and she didn't like how vulnerable she felt, as if all the protective walls she'd built around her all these years had shattered and she was left with a pile of broken shards. Crystals. She'd never thought of them that way before. All these years she'd been collecting broken shards that could never be put back together again.

The bracelet gleamed dully on her wrist, so Reggie's theory about a roll in the hay solving that particular problem was also wrong. A warm hand rubbed her back comfortingly and she would have purred if everything else didn't press in around her. Here she was, having just made love to a man when she should be at work. She should be solving the mystery of the stupid bracelet like Lila had asked her to.

She stood up. "I'm going to take a shower."

Jas caught her wrist to stop her and forced her to look at him. Oh Gods, what a desirable man. Long limbed. Strong torso and sultry gaze than made every part of her tremble, not to mention his very clear desire to repeat everything they'd already done. She had to look away or risk losing herself in the moment again.

"Chloe, you're not that good a liar. I can see that something's happening for you and it's coming between us. Do you want that to happen?"

She shook her head, because her throat was tightening. Darn it, she liked Jas. More than liked him. But she just couldn't chance it. Sooner or later he'd learn her past and leave her, even though she wasn't that person now.

"Then tell me."

"It's nothing you need to know."

The way his lips tightened, he clearly didn't believe her, but he swung off the bed and pulled her into his chest so she could feel his heat like a caress on her body. "All right. Let's take that shower."

Catching her hand, he led her to the open door in the corner of the bedroom, then flicked on the lights to reveal the floor to ceiling tiling and glass wall of the huge shower stall. "Hmm. Did I mention that you have a very nice place here?"

Inside the shower stall he stood behind her and let her adjust the water until a hot deluge fell on their heads from the rain-spout showerhead, drenching them both. She pumped a handful of shower gel into her palm and began to soap herself off, when two other hands gently shoved hers away.

"You're doing it all wrong, Chloe. Let me show you how."

His soapy palms pulled her back against him as he ran his hands down over her sides to her hips, then up her belly to her breasts and came to rest there, softly kneading her flesh, sending flames shooting through her as he caught her nipples and squeezed. Her breath caught in her throat and her head collapsed back against him as one of his hands slid lower and between her legs. His fingers found her, would know just how much he aroused her, no matter that she shouldn't want it.

He teased her, bringing her up on her toes, as his lips found her cheek and slipped lower to nibble her shoulder. A long finger slid inside her and began to move, slowly, ever so slowly and she wanted more. Wanted what she'd had before with him.

She opened her eyes and looked sideways at him. "You make a very strong argument."

He grinned. "I was hoping you'd see things my way." His manhood throbbed between them.

She turned in his arms and ran her soapy hands down his rock hard chest. "Two can play that game, you know."

"Would it be wrong to say I hoped that would be the case?" He cocked one brow at her and she couldn't help herself. She stood on tiptoe and kissed him, then swatted him with soap in the face.

Before he could retaliate, she slid her hands down his chest, and belly, down to the dark fur and the thick shaft he promised her. Stroked him and he throbbed in her hand. Could she do this?

For him she wanted to.

She looked up at him and his gaze caught hers as she sank down to her knees. She could do this. She could. Because it was Jas.

She kissed his length and stroked the tip with her tongue, then took him smoothly into her mouth. Just as smoothly as she'd done so many years before.

She gagged and her stomach clenched and she yanked away, to the corner of the shower stall, afraid she'd be sick. "I'm sorry. I'm sorry. I shouldn't have tried this. This just isn't who I am. I'm a celibate. Okay?" Damn tears were running down her face.

He was on his knees beside her and had her in his arms. "Chloe. Chloe. It's all right."

"No," she shook her head against him. "It's not. I'm sorry." She pulled her knees up and hid her face against them.

"It's me who's sorry." His arm snaked around her shoulders as he settled against the wall beside her. "I shouldn't have pushed. I'm so sorry, Chloe." He pulled her into his lap and kissed her hair, her face, her clenched-shut eyes, her mouth. Then he rocked her as the shower poured down around them as if simple water could wash away all her past and her shame.

CHAPTER 11

Whatevertheheckwasgoingon, ithadsuddenly turned the lovely woman he'd just made love to into a basket case weeping on the shower floor. The steamy shower poured down on them, but her body had turned freezing, even her light incense scent gone, so he wrapped her tightly in his arms, hoping that would help and leaned back against the marble tiles that were still cool even under the hot water.

"Chloe? Talk to me." She was so soft in his arms, her long, drenched hair a spider web of dark across both their bodies. "Tell me what's the matter. I'm here for you. I am."

And the funny thing was, he was. As with other women, he might have taken mercurial changes as a sign to hightail it out of there and thank his lucky stars he'd gotten free But Chloe Main was different. There was a quality to her even though she believed and practiced something no reasonable man could sanely believe in. Unlike his mother, for Chloe it worked and she didn't make it into some woo-woo show. She just went quietly about her business and if people believed, well then she was there for them.

But none of her crystal healing stuff explained what had happened at the restaurant or what was happening right now. The thing at the restaurant had been damned weird. This—the way she was acting—this was more like someone who had been through hell and was currently reliving it.

"Chloe? Please talk to me. I want to help you, but I can't do that until I understand."

"There's nothing you can do." She sounded bitter and distant and oh, so alone. Just like victims he'd dealt with.

"Chloe." He kissed her forehead. "Something's happened to you. Someone did something, or forced you to do something and our being together had brought it all back to you."

She stiffened, then peered up at him, her violet eyes gone cautious as a trapped animal. "You can tell, can't you? It shows."

He stroked her hair back from her face. "In your fear, yes. It shows. People who are so afraid are often some of the strongest most impressive people I've ever met because they've been through hell and yet they're strong enough to live and come back." He kissed her forehead. "I've seen a lot Chloe. I haven't liked it. I've hated the people who cause such pain, but I've always thought we should admire the victims. They manage to go on and live another day."

She sighed and some of the tension went out of her so she leaned her head against his shoulder. "I've never thought of it that way."

"Well you should." He kissed her forehead again. Such soft skin, like silk over her swimmers' taut muscles and he could so easily become aroused again. Just what was it about Chloe Main? "What happened to you, Chloe?"

There was a moment where she stiffened, but then it was like a suspect when they lost all the fight. "I guess you might as well know. You'll eventually find out." So tired. So defeated.

She looked away to her hands clenched across her chest. Another long sigh.

"It was like this. I didn't run away when I was a teenager because my dad ruled with an iron fist, but as soon as I graduated from high school, I was gone. Don't get me wrong. My parents were great people and I miss them so much, now that they're gone, but Dad and I had a really rocky time during my teenage years. So at seventeen I left. I was going to have my great adventure and prove I could live on my own without his rules. I took all my college savings from summer jobs and headed off. You don't need to hear all my adventures, but I ended up in San Francisco and that was where my money ran out."

She went silent and so still in his arms, she might have been a statue. Her flesh was still icy cold, even with the shower's warm water. How long it would stay warm, he wondered.

"It's such a beautiful city, you know? All bright sunshine and clanging street cars and restaurants that leak the best smelling smells in the world into the streets, but it isn't that kind of place when you run out of money. I tried getting a job. I was old enough, but I had no idea that I needed a green card or a Social Security number to work in reputable places. When I realized I couldn't get one I didn't know what to do. I thought about calling home for help, but at the time I couldn't bear the thought of Dad's 'I told you so.' So I listened to the people who I met on the street." She shivered and shook her head.

"A girlfriend, Marta, let me flop at her place and introduced me to her boyfriend. He was a bad boy—I could tell the first time I saw him. Exactly the kind of guy my parents always warned me about. He wasn't tall or particularly handsome, but he had an edge of danger and he was really good to Marta. Because of our friendship he was good to me, too. He took us out for meals, snuck us into bars, and took us to parties where the booze ran freely and the drugs—well, I never would use them though Marta and Herve tried to get me to try. Then Herve started to focus on me. He'd come by when Marta wasn't there and he was so nice, loaning me money to live on, until one day he kissed me."

She went silent again, huddled in on herself like flower petals folded. It was heartbreaking to see her fighting to get this out, but he knew better than to interrupt, even though the start to her story was, sadly, too familiar. Sometimes it was cathartic for victims to tell their tale. She just needed time. So he waited for her and she turned her cheek into his chest, her eyes tightly closed as she started talking again.

"I was so stupid. I thought we were in love. I—we had sex and he told me that he loved me. We were together whenever

Marta was out and then one day he threw a party at her house and there was lots of drinking and I was drunk and the next thing I knew Herve had sold me to one of his friends. He—he—he had me right there in front of Herve and their friends. When he was done he told me to get dressed and then he dragged me out of there to his place." She swallowed. "He had a string of girls you see. Prostitutes. And I was going to be one. Except I got away and I took refuge in the Church of the New Age and they taught me about crystals and auras and so on." She shook herself and slid off his lap. "And that's that. My sordid past."

She was trying to be brisk, but her voice cracked and he loved her for her determination to be strong, even though it was probably the worst thing she could do.

He stood up, then bent to scoop her into his arms, then carried her out of the shower and snagged a towel to wrap her in. It was only a few strides to the bed. He pulled the covers back and laid her down, and sat down beside her, patting the water off of her body and out of her hair. The whole time he felt the questions in her eyes. Finally he pulled the covers up to her chin and tucked them around her.

"You should sleep," he said. "You've had one hell of a day."

Still, she said nothing, just watched him with those violet eyes that reminded him of the color of the sky just before nightfall. He sat down beside her and stroked her hair back from her face. "You haven't told anyone that story before, have you?"

No words, but the way she looked away said no.

"Thank you for telling me. It helps me to understand. It will help me to be there for you. And I will, you know. Now I'm going to go and let you sleep, but if you need anything—anything at all— just call me. I'll leave my card on your counter."

He stood and pulled on his clothes. When he turned back to her, her eyes were already closed, her skin pale against the white sheets, her long dark hair a tangled mass. His hands clenched into fists when he thought of anyone manhandling her. He just hoped she had peace wherever sleep took her, because he wasn't likely to sleep tonight.

Not when he really wanted to stay with her today, tonight and possibly forever, but duty called and he needed some space to get his head together.

The world didn't need people who would do something like that to someone like Chloe. At this moment he seriously wanted to make someone pay for how they'd hurt her.

§

The bedroom was alive with nighttime shadows when Chloe opened her eyes. She rolled over to check the glowing face of her bedside alarm. Three a.m. She'd slept the afternoon and the night away. Hard to believe. She had pretended to be asleep when Jas put her to bed—anything to be alone, to get him to leave. Thankfully he had, even though she missed the strength of his arms. And she had actually fallen asleep and slept like the dead. No dreams. No visions, nothing. Until now.

Clyde lifted his blue-eyed head from the bed beside her and meowed sleepily. She cupped his head with her palm. "I'm here big guy. Thank you for guarding me."

He head-butted her with his nose and chirruped—her favorite sound—and she buried her face in his warm soft fur for a moment and felt like crying. God, she was such a mess.

The weight of the duvet was too much and she fumbled it off and then slid herself to the edge of the bed. She felt spent, used, but it wasn't the same as when she was seventeen. She didn't feel filthy like she would never be clean. She felt replete, and with the knowledge she'd not only got, she'd given. She was—confused, because what did it mean? Her body smelled differently—of sex and of dark earth and leather? Jas. As if she wasn't just her own person anymore, she was partially Jas's.

No. She belonged to no one.

But her fingertips gave off no scent, nor did her arm. No, it was more like he was imprinted on her, like an entrapment in her flesh so he would be with her forever. Because she cared for him?

She hung her head. What had she done? She'd started it and she wasn't sure why. Always, before, she'd kept herself aloof.

What was it about Jas Stone that had loosed her inhibitions to be with him?

She felt shaken to her core. Even her aura pulsed like something was broken. Well... perhaps not broken. More like different. As if her chakras wobbled in her confusion, all but the Svadhisthana, the sweetness chakra that ruled the sexual organs. Where once it might had been the least developed of her chakras, now it glowed with bright orange energy like sunlight through amber.

She swallowed. Well, that was understandable. Just the thought of Jas's body brought an ache low down in her body that could be addressed in only one way.

Shaking her hair around her she stood up to distract herself, but the bracelet caught on the duvet. She unhooked it, but something about the metal was strange. She ran her fingers over it and it was almost as if she felt the faintest of vibrations. The small door with the iron casing in particular seemed brighter.

"You—all these problems started with you. And here I have a good time in bed and you're still firmly locked on my arm. I should have just let Reggie cut you off." But there was no way in heck that was going to happen. There were secrets within secrets in these small doors. She knew it as surely as she knew her history had ruined her for men, even good ones like Jas.

It was such a sad thought her eyes filled and she backhanded the tears away before they could fall.

It was better that he was gone. It was probably why he'd left, anyway. A good looking guy like that could get any woman he wanted. Why waste time with someone as damaged as her? If she were him, she'd still be running. Stupid tears.

Her legs felt like they belonged to someone else as she pulled on a robe of pale yellow and rose silk. She stumbled out to the kitchen and turned the lights on. The cheerful room didn't seem so cheerful this morning. Clyde, ever helpful, followed and stood hopefully by his dish.

Stabbing the espresso machine 'on' button, she leaned against the counter and met Clyde's blue eyes. "You know it's too early for breakfast. Getting up at this hour is just your mistress being more than a little crazy."

He meowed in that deep throaty, kitty roar of his. This time was good enough for breakfast, too.

"All right. But it's going to be a long time until dinner." She retrieved the open tin from the fridge, washed his plate and gave him his serving. The room filled with the happy sound of kitty slurping and she smiled.

"You're the kind of male for me, buddy. None of this drama." Clyde didn't even lift his head. Typical.

The espresso machine chugged beside her so she ground beans and tamped the coffee into the portafilter and tightened it in place. She warmed a mug under hot water, and put it under the portafilter and turned the pressure on, to force water through the grounds while she steamed milk. When the froth was thick and the coffee dark in the mug, she poured the milk in, and even made a sweet flower design on top. It was a skill she'd learned in the dark times, like a ghost still haunting her. She grabbed a spoon and stirred the design away.

Beyond the kitchen window faint light topped the mountains across the lake. She slid open the patio door and Clyde scooted out in front of her. The air was still as it often was before dawn, as if the entire world held its breath as it decided whether day would come.

The air was moist and warm from the lake. Standing there, the soft honks of Canada geese came from the flock that usually foraged along the grassy shoreline just beyond Trepanier Creek. The rush of the creek water was a constant white noise and though the air was still, the willows and pines still sighed.

Settling herself in her wicker throne chair, she put her feet up and prepared to watch in the day. She didn't often get up this early, but the start of the day was such a magical time that when she did get up, she liked to greet the sun. Besides, the sun's first rays were a powerful balm. They could revive her and maybe fill the cold barren place that seemed to have formed in her chest. Her head resting against the back of her chair and Clyde warming her lap, she watched the color of the sky change from onyx gradually fading to palest blue topaz, then tinge with citrine and pink beryl.

She sipped the rich dark latte and hoped the heat would soak into her bones. Didn't work. Maybe she'd have been better off meditating in the livingroom with her crystals, but frankly the thought of meditation scared her. It had been meditation that had started this whole thing.

She rubbed the bracelet and studied the doors and the daylight seemed to fade around her. *Darkness. A courtyard.*

She ripped herself back, released the bracelet and sat there panting. The pale yellows and pinks had intensified into amber and rose quartz that blazed in long streamers framing the mountain top. Darn it, she'd lost time in what had seemed like the briefest of instants. She'd *been* somewhere.

The fact that it was always the same place, the same time, must mean something. Was this some kind of clairvoyance thing? Or psychometrics? That was what Lila has asked her to do, wasn't it, read what she could from the bracelet. Apparently she was more attuned to the thing than she liked, but she might as well use that to their advantage. She looked up at the mountains where the light built, but there was still no sign of the rising sun. She'd do this until the sun rose. Its power would bring her back to herself. She'd feel the heat on her body.

"Clyde, if I go still for too long, I want you to use those sharp claws of yours on me, okay?" He opened one sleepy blue eye at her.

Not a lot of help there. It didn't matter. It was better to focus on the bracelet than on the pathetic state of her not-so-love life.

She took a deep breath and looked down at the bracelet doors, let herself be drawn toward the iron-bound door.

Darkness and torches and harsh words, angry words between two people in love. A man, slim and intense of eye who wanted to stand and fight, and a woman, lovely as a nymph with coils of night-dark hair who would have him hide—and live. The air smelled of burning oil and dust and their fear because there was something beyond these walls that approached. Something darker than the night that reeked of fire and ash and made her think of dark, lonely places like the space between stars. Familiar.

What?

She floated higher and looked down upon the house, brick mud walls, the courtyard and beyond, the road filled with horses and on one horse a great man rode. Who? Where was this? When?

As if her questions called him the great man looked up. He scanned the heavens and his gaze stopped. As if he saw her just as she saw him. She recognized the darkness and reached for her necklace of jet. Not there.

She tried to pull back, but his power was too much. He had her and he pulled her down to the earth, down toward the yawning maw of his eyes.

She fought, tried to rip away, but her exhaustion and doubts left her flailing, unfocussed.

Downward. Ever downwards, until a blaze of light filled her face. A cat yowled and something sharp ripped into her thigh...

The vision collapsed and she fell back in her chair. Clyde stood on her legs, his fur on end, glaring at her with dark blue eyes. The sun blazed an edge over the mountaintop and turned the lake like quicksilver. Her heart pounded so hard she swore she could hear it, but she managed a smile. "It's okay buddy. It's me. I'm here. And you did really good. Better than good. For that you get a special lunchtime meal today." She hugged him—briefly, because being hugged did not fit with Clyde's idea of dignity. Then she stroked his soft fur and Clyde, apparently satisfied that she was back and that she would keep her promise, resettled himself in her lap and began to purr.

Whoa. She looked down at her wrist and almost wished she could take the bracelet off. Something bad had happened to it or to somebody associated with it and she could only figure it was the people she'd seen in her vision. That was bad enough. Enough to take her mind totally from her sordid little life. But that wasn't the really terrible news.

No, the terrible news was that the evil in the vision didn't just remind her—it was the exact same darkness that had visited her in the guise of a man at *This and That* looking for this very bracelet.

CHAPTER 12

Jas knew that he'd been wrong to leave Chloe. He'd no more than set foot out the door of her apartment and closed the door behind him when he'd regretted his decision. Of course it was too late. He wasn't going to bang on her door. That would disturb her just when she was getting some rest and hopefully recovering from what had happened.

He drove his Tribeca into the detachment parking lot and climbed out into the already heated morning air. The West Kelowna RCMP detachment sat in the city's downtown core, cheek by jowl with the city museum and the Chamber of Commerce. The building was only a few years old and the darling of the town council because it was a showcase of environmental design: a cistern to collect rainwater, plenty of windows to use natural light and some weird-ass plant-covered roof. Chloe would probably love it. It sat sandwiched between the two southbound and the two northbound lanes of the highway which effectively had destroyed the heart of the town.

The incessant rumble of traffic and diesel stink were a constant miasma over the place. When a loaded semi geared down, all the windows in the building shook. He worked his shoulders and faced the red brick building. The sun beat down on his head and shoulders and reflected off the pavement. He wasn't looking forward to today. He'd avoided Forester yesterday and hadn't gone in to work after he left Chloe. What had happened between them had left him one moment ecstatic and the next deeply troubled. On the one hand she was all that he could ever hope for in a woman and she intrigued him like a mystery he wanted to solve. On the other there were her beliefs. He'd rejected them as a kid when his mother had espoused something similar. They didn't fit into his real world any better now.

And the way she'd seemed to have those attacks. Was she sick, perhaps mentally ill? A person who had gone through what she had might be, and yet most of the time she seemed pretty together. Like the night of Kylee Jensen's abduction. She'd been right there with him as they went door to door searching for her, and there hadn't been a hint of anything abnormal.

So what had changed other than he'd insinuated his way into her life, regardless of her consistent rejection? The only thing he could think of was all the fuss the women and Danny had made when she put on that idiot bracelet. Hell, Forester had been more concerned than any of them.

"Get a grip, Stone. A piece of jewelry does not affect a person's mind."

"Still trying to make some sense of the Jensen case, are you?" Danny Forester stepped up beside him and considered the building. "The C.O. was looking for you yesterday. I think he wanted your assessment of my mental health."

"Like I'm any judge." Jas shook his head and seriously wished he couldn't remember the utter vacancy in Chloe's face followed by the fear. Frankly, the whole thing had him pretty spooked, not least of which was the fact he cared for her. Sure, he'd had opportunity-sex before—what red-blooded guy hadn't? But this was different on so many levels.

He came back to himself and realized Forester was looking at him. "That's a hell of a thing to hear from the man who was supposed to be my keeper."

Jas scrubbed at his face and shook his head, then struck out across the parking lot. "I guess things change." He looked his partner up and down. Clean shirt and suit, a freshly shaved chin, red hair combed as neatly in place as it ever was, and a moderately handsome face that looked a hell of a lot better than his own had looked in the mirror when he shaved this morning. "You look pretty good for a change."

Forester shrugged, a cowlick of hair falling into his eyes. "Amazing what your own bed and a good night's sleep will do." But when their eyes met briefly there was that other thing between them, unspoken, but still there. Forester claimed that he'd been possessed by something—some force that was looking for the very same bracelet that was on Chloe's arm. The force that had supposedly been at the heart of Kylee Jensen's attempted abduction. Frankly, seeing what Chloe had gone through yesterday he'd found himself actually considering the possibility.

But he just couldn't go there. It was too great a stretch.

He slapped Forester's shoulder. "It's good to have you back looking like a detective instead of someone we've taken to the hospital for a psych eval."

They pushed into the institutional coolness of the circular front lobby, let themselves in through the locked security doors. and went up the stairs to their office. In a detachment of 20 members most of the heavy lifting detective work like sex crimes and murders were passed on to the much larger Kelowna Detachment. It took work to keep serious crimes in-house. Jas had taken the job, because he wanted to get out of the crazy-making environment that was Vancouver, but he'd hoped that he might slide into something more challenging in Kelowna. Instead, here he was babysitting his partner.

"You missed a busy day yesterday," Forester said, sliding into his chair behind his desk. "We got word from the shrinks that they're keeping Tom Beaton for observation. Word is, the guy's had a psychotic break, but he's starting to put things back together." He shook his head. "Poor bastard. There but for the grace of God and all that. I don't know how I managed to recover when those other poor bastards went shit-house crazy."

Jas opened his mouth, but Forester waved him away. "I know, I know sanity's all relative. We also got the Ident report on the jewelry recovered from Willowview Terrace. It is the Singh goods. Items are all there and they match the victim's descriptions perfectly. Craziest thing I've ever seen, breaking in and getting away with over a hundred large in jewelry and then just giving it back."

Jas nodded. It was strange. Just not the craziest thing he'd ever seen. Not by far after the last few days. "Any word on the stuff taken from the jewelry store? Or from the second apartment?"

"Forester shook his head. "Nada. Zip. I've been thinking, though. The M.O.s aren't exactly the same. The store break-in was first and there's been no jewelry recovered. It could be totally different perps. "

Jas shoved himself back from his desk because the events in Peachland were starting to piss him off. "In Peachland? Three break-ins and an attempted abduction in two weeks. That's gotta be some kind of record. It's gotta be the same guy at the Willowview. Exactly the same mode of entry. Nothing but the jewelry taken in either case." Standing, he began to pace. "But I'm not getting the link with the jewelry store robbery, and trying to link it to the abduction is just plain fabrication. Did Ident give any word on whether they found anything at either Willowview scenes that might help us?"

"Bupkis." Forester shrugged again. "But they're saying the guy who hit *This and That* is a real pro. Somehow he blew out the alarm wiring and he cracked that safe like the thing wasn't even locked. Not a fingerprint anywhere." He shook his head. "*That* is like Willowview. No prints, there, either."

'Bupkis.' Jas mouthed the anachronistic word. "Just where do you come up with this shit?" He said with a head shake as he turned on his heel again. Three strides and turn. Three strides and turn.

"What 's got you so worked up this morning?" Forester had leaned back in his chair, but his breakdown was assessing as he watched Jas pace.

"Nothing. You got those reports?" Jas slammed into his chair again. No way in hell was he discussing what had happened the day before. The ribbing would be bad, but worse would be the pressure to report the details. He was so not going there. Besides, Chloe had made it clear that her story was private and he would not jeopardize her privacy.

Sure. He was just nobility itself. It had nothing to do with the fact that he didn't want people to know he'd been getting laid by a very attractive witness in the Jensen case.

His computer dinged and he opened the screen. Forester had sent him what reports he'd received. Nothing there that gave them the scent of the trail. "What's this? A report from Vancouver Taxi."

"Yeah. That's the report on the limo involved in the Jensen abduction. It was leased out of Vancouver for the month by a German company. I can't pronounce the name. It's in the report."

Jas stabbed the report open and read. *Leased by the SchwarzeNacht Corporation.* "Surely to goodness we can get more than that. Who the hell were they driving and why up here?"

"I sent a query off to the company offices in Berlin yesterday. So far nothing's come back."

"Dammit." He slammed his palm down on his desktop and then realized what he'd done.

Forester was looking at him, the mildest of expressions on his face. "Wound pretty tight today, partner. Anything you want to tell me about?"

Like he was going to reveal his soul to a crazy man. He stood up. "Maybe I better go see the OIC and get that piece of business off my chest."

Forester's lips made a vague grin. "Maybe you should. Then maybe you can come back and tell me about the woman. Chloe, isn't it?"

CHAPTER 13

THE EXTERIOR OF *THIS AND THAT* GLEAMED LIKE A shiny new world compared to the dingy memories of her life the day before. The white walls shone and the red gave a gay splash of color that was a far cry from the pastels of her apartment or even the cream halls of her building where she'd just about bowled over a nice looking young man knocking on the door of her neighbor's apartment.

Somehow, after the scary vision, she'd managed to fall asleep on her patio and had woken up late. She'd barely had time for a proper shower—talk about returning to the scene of the crime—and had pulled on her favorite old cut-offs and an old blue Peachland Chamber of Commerce t-shirt that sported a silhouette of Ogopogo, Okanagan Lake's mythical lake monster. After this morning's vision she topped it all off with a necklace of jet around her neck—no way was she going anywhere without it—and she had run out the door. Her stupid hair wasn't even braided, just pulled back in a far-too-thick-to-manage ponytail. There was no way Lila wasn't going to ask about *that!*

The air carried the ubiquitous scent of suntan lotion and the lake carried its usual flotilla of power boats. Families were strewn like pebbles along the sun-heated beach. From the pleasant morning, it had turned into a scorcher that wasn't going to be nice for anyone.

Maybe if she got into the store and got busy with staining the wainscoting Lila wouldn't bother asking her about yesterday. After all, as part owner she put in a lot of extra hours, and what did it matter if she took an afternoon off every once in awhile? Of course she'd kind of left Lila and Kylee in the lurch.

She shoved her hair back off her face and went up the porch and inside. The bell dinged above her as she stepped inside to the scent of fresh paint. Kylee and Lila had done good work yesterday. It looked like one more coat of paint and they'd be done. Which meant that she had better do her part today.

Kylee looked up from where she 'd been opening another can of paint. "Chloe!" She came around the counter. "Are you all right? Lila said you weren't well. Are you sure you should be at work today?"

Kylee's hair was bright as a piece of sunshine and tousled in her petite, gamine way. She grasped Chloe's hands. "What happened? Have a chair." With her foot Kylee hooked a spindle-back chair she'd obviously been using to reach the high spots and dragged it to Chloe. "You look a little gray."

"Gee, thanks. Gray was definitely what I was going for when I got dressed this morning." She gave Kylee a hug. "I'm sorry about yesterday. I must have had a little attack of food poisoning or something." She shivered. "But I'm all right now, see?"

A pirouette to demonstrate and please let Kylee believe, but her small blond friend still had suspicion in her eyes. Chloe made a show of stowing her purse under Kylee's too-watchful perusal and then grabbed a paintbrush and poured paint into a tray.

"How about I paint the high spots and you do around the top of the wainscoting? We should be done in no time," she said, and grabbed the chair to start painting along the taped edge of the ceiling moldings. "You know, we really should talk about how we want to set up the shop. It doesn't have to go back to exactly the way it was."

She felt Kylee's considered study as she slicked the paint along the tape and then grabbed a roller to smooth the paint into the previous coat. Finally, her friend started to paint, too.

"I've already been giving layout some thought. I have some ideas, but I wasn't sure whether you and Lila would approve."

"Try me." Chloe kept her attention on the paint. It really was a good color. Neutral, but with a hint of warmth and the lavender surprisingly made most things look good.

From the other side of the room Kylee started to talk about flow—how people came into the shop and moved around it. "Right now we haven't got any logical flow. People come in, they clot around each display case, but there really isn't a anything psychological to encourage them to move in one direction or another. Instead they come in and spread out like—like—like a river delta, you know?"

"So you're suggesting that instead of letting them wander aimlessly, they should be encouraged to go in a certain direction."

"Uh huh."

"Then let's hear the details. How are you suggesting that it should be arranged?" It was a good discussion. Something that would keep her mind distracted from Jas Stone, from a certain bracelet, and from the ghosts of her own sordid past. All while her body performed the mindless task of painting.

Kylee started talking about how they could make things work better if they placed the three free-standing glass cabinet displays together in an open ended triangle. It would mean one person could deal with all the displays more easily, but there'd still be room for more, if necessary. Chloe let her talk and sighed with relief that she had changed the subject away from yesterday's 'attack.' Now if she could just get through Lila as easily, everything would be good.

"Chloe?"

"Hmm?" She looked up from using the paint roller to fill in the coat between Kylee's lower edging and what she had done along the molding. A faint mist of paint dotted her bare arms with freckles.

"What happened to you yesterday? Did it have anything to do with the bracelet?"

Chloe's hand automatically went to the offending piece of jewelry whether in protectiveness or fear, she wasn't sure. But for a moment she felt the room spin around her and it took a moment to catch her balance and steady her breathing.

"Nah. Nothing to do with it at all." But she stepped down from the chair rather than fall.

Silence behind Chloe. She turned around to find Kylee staring at her. "What? What's the problem?"

"I don't believe you." Kylee's eyes were shining as if she might start crying. "That stupid thing has been nothing but problems. I wish I'd never put it on, even though it's beautiful. I'm so sorry, Chloe. I didn't want this to happen."

The woman wore her emotions on her sleeve. "Sweetie, no one's blaming you for anything and it could be a coincidence that anything has happened since the bracelet came into our possession. I'm a big girl and, if it is this ol' bracelet, I can handle anything that it throws at me, okay?" If only she hadn't experienced the vision she might even believe that was true.

Kylee's lip quivered, but she finally swallowed and nodded. "I guess. I guess I can't force you to tell me anything. But there are greater forces in the world, you know. But then look who I'm telling."

Chloe turned back to the wall and checked her watch. "Why don't you go for lunch and let me finish up here and get things sorted out for the wainscoting. By the way, I like your idea about the display cabinets. If we keep them moveable, we can try them that way for our grand reopening."

Kylee hesitated. "Sure you'll be okay?"

Chloe rolled her eyes, "I'm a big girl. I'm quite good at taking care of myself. Now scoot."

Kylee blinked once, twice and again. "Okay, then. I just need to get something from out back and I'm out of here." She disappeared through the curtain and Chloe gave a sigh of relief.

It was quiet and she could just be in the space running the roller mindlessly over the wall until the paint was smooth.

"Hey, you. I didn't hear you come in."

Chloe spun around to face Lila and with her, Allyson McVey. Lila's longtime friend was tall and tanned with honey-blond hair in waves around her sculpted face and down over her shoulders.

"Ally! Oh my God, you're here!" Chloe grabbed her in a hug and looked her up and down, then stepped back in a hurry, praying she hadn't put paint all over Ally. There were lines of fatigue around Ally's lapis-colored eyes and frown lines around her mouth that Chloe had never seen before. She wore a pair of well-worn khaki trousers and a tan colored shirt with the sleeves rolled to the elbows."Look at you! All you need is a camera on your chest and you'd totally look the part of intrepid adventurer who never missed a place her camera might lead her! When did you get in?"

Ally grinned and glanced at Lila. "I got delayed again so Lila just picked me up from the airport this morning. I just got up from having a nap. Jet lag and all that. There's a lot of hours' difference between here and Zanzibar. She was showing me around the place. At the moment it looks even less like the sketch Lila showed me three years ago."

"That's right. It was just a very bright gleam in Lila's eye when you were here last." Chloe hefted her chin at Lila. "She keeps us informed of all your adventures." At least the ones that were fit to print. Ally was one of those unusual people who seemed to have slept with every man she met and used her sensuality to get what she wanted. At the same time she'd used her connections and her talent as a photographer to raise money for schools, orphanages and environmental in sub-Saharan Africa.

"So what brings you back to Peachland?"

Ally's smile of greeting faded slightly. "Let's just say that I needed to get back to normal for a change. A little peace and quiet would be nice."

"She's come to the right place, hasn't she, Lila. Good thing Kylee moved up to Mom and Dad's house."

Lila nodded. "It leaves the guestroom ready and waiting. I was just explaining that to Allyson."

Ally rolled her eyes. "She practically held me hostage in the car and wouldn't think of it when I asked her to take me to a hotel."

"You'll be comfortable here and there is no place better to relax than Peachland," Lila said.

Chloe nodded, but could feel Lila's relentless regard. Chloe crossed her arms and faced her friend. "You didn't come out here only to show Ally the shop, did you?"

Lila gave a half-shrug.

"Damn, Kylee. The little minx ratted me out, didn't she?"

Lila went over to the wall and seemed far too interested in Chloe's paint job. As usual, she looked the part of a successful business woman even in her casual attire of black capris cut short just above the ankle, white boat shoes and a red, cap-sleeved top. "She told me that she's worried about you, if that's what you mean."

Lila abandoned the wall, and caught her hands. She met Chloe's gaze head on. "Something's happened. I might not be psychic, but I can read my friends."

Chloe pulled away and made herself busy pulling out the cans of stain for the wainscoting. "I don't need to be read, Lila. I'm fine."

"And that sort of attitude is so unlike the Chloe I know, that my assessment stands."

Chloe didn't bother to turn back to her. Instead she turned to Ally. "You must have had all sorts of adventures. I'm going to have to have you over for dinner so that I can hear all about them."

"Do not change the subject, Chloe." The tone of Lila's voice was enough to picture her with her hands on her hips and her lips pressed together, her flow of auburn curls around her face.

"I meant what I said. I don't want or need to talk about it."

"So something did happen."

Damn. She'd never lied to Lila before either. Was she going to now?

Finally she turned around and met her friend's concern. Sighed. "Yeah."

"And you don't want to talk about it."

Chloe nodded. "I'm not sure I know how to at the moment. I'm still processing."

Lila looked thoughtful and patted the back of Chloe's hand. "You know that's usually when you need to talk about it the most. It helps to sort things out."

It was true. Chloe nodded. There'd been a lot of times over the years she'd known Lila that one or the other would have a problem or an idea and talking it through had brought them the answer. They'd been shoulders for each other many, many times, just as Reggie had been.

"Is any of this connected to Corporal Stone?"

What could she say, the instant burn up her face was going to tell all anyway. She sighed. "Some of it does. I kept trying to make it a business lunch, but he clearly wasn't."

"There are worse things than having a handsome man pursuing you."

Chloe swallowed and met her friend's hazel scrutiny. This was one area of her life and her history that Lila didn't need to know. "I suppose there are, but that isn't the issue. Yesterday, at the restaurant, I had some kind of an attack. I'd had one before when I tried to read this." She motioned at the bracelet. "At the restaurant it was worse and Jas was so concerned that he took me home. That was when he called you. After—after, well—stuff happened, okay? It didn't end well. That's all there is to say."

Lila seemed to study her and then put her arms around her. "I'm so sorry. I shouldn't have asked you to try to read the bracelet. I was only thinking it might be some way to gain some insight." She shook her head. "I'm in a quandary. On the one hand I find it hard to believe that the bracelet is responsible for what's been happening, but on the other I want my friends safe. I think the time has come to just get it off you so it can't cause trouble for you or anyone else. It's a beautiful piece, but it might be better to have Reggie melt it down."

"No flipping way!" Chloe ripped away, cradling her wrist against her chest. She backed up until her back hit the cash register counter. Lila loomed through darkness like a dark-haired monster.

"Chloe! Chloe? It was just a suggestion, but you're scaring me now. You've gone deathly pale and your eyes have gone huge. What the heck's happened?"

The darkness passed and now it was a concerned Lila in front of her, but her heart still pounded like she'd run a race. Shadows seemed to flutter just out of her line of vision.

"Oh God," Chloe rubbed her face. "I don't know what's wrong with me—except everything at the moment. I keep having these visions and they're bringing up all kinds of bad stuff and the worst part is..." she hung her head and glanced at Ally. Ally, at least wouldn't judge her, "I slept with him, Lila. Somehow in the midst of all this crap, I was with him even though I know I shouldn't have been."

A twitch found the corners of Lila's lips.

"What? You think it's funny? I went through hell yesterday." Indignation could do wonders to deal with her mortification.

"I'm sure you did, but it explains a lot about what I'm seeing. In all the years I've known you, Chloe, I've never seen you fall for a guy. I've certainly never heard of you falling into bed with one. At least not like this. So I ask you, was it worth it?"

"Worth it? No." How could anything be worth how messed up she felt and yet—maybe it was. He had been so good and kind to her and a terrific lover... A betraying warmth surged up through her neck to her cheeks. Oh God.

"I'd say by her expression, it was." Ally quipped.

Lila's smile had spread to her eyes. "So why's that got you so upset?"

It was like all the warm feelings disappeared and she was that stupid know-it-all girl she'd been at seventeen. She'd re-experienced herself cowering on her shower floor. She'd felt like less than nothing all those years ago. If she hadn't been extremely lucky to have been offered refuge in the New Age church, just where would she be today? Memories of a palm across the face that sent her stumbling against a wall. Of a punch that sent her curling into a ball.

"Dead, most likely," she whispered.

"What? Chloe, what's dead most likely?" Lila's warm, strong hands were on her own and dragging her out from the counter. "Shoot. You're cold as ice."

Ally came up on her other side and, each with an arm around Chloe's shoulders, they led her toward the door and front porch.

"No. This is a business, not a place to get counseling. We need to get the painting done so we can reopen." Chloe ripped away, but Lila was there, hands on hips to face her.

"I think I know how to run a business as well as the next person and I would be happy to leave you to it, but you happen to be my friend, too. And it is very bad for business when you leave a friend in distress. It shows to the customers. That is bad, Chloe. So we are going to deal with this or I am going to send you home until you will."

What the hell! "You can't do that! I'm part owner."

Lila lifted her chin and her greater height made her look like some angry queen with her silver necklace of sterling silver chain glinting around her neck. Ally stood at her shoulder as if offering to back her up.

"Watch me," Lila said. "And if need be I'll get Reggie in here and we can vote you out the door two to one."

It felt like a war of tectonic plates, and she was the plate being shoved under by a greater force. Chloe sagged. "All right. We'll do it your way, but can we please wait until after Kylee gets back. I'm—I'm not sure what good I'll be afterwards."

Just let her have some space to figure out what to say or how to say it. Could Lila really forgive her for how she'd lived her life back in California? She hadn't even trusted her parents or Brett to do that. She wasn't sure she could get past it if she and Lila's situations were reversed. I mean how could anyone ever understand how you could make such bad choices?

Ally sank into the comfy shop chair while Chloe set aside the paints and decided to sort some of the remaining crystals that might work for her healing. She found one of the shop's velvet trays and set the stones in it on the counter. They gleamed softly violet, yellow, green, white, black and blue, each according to their kind. Picking up each stone, she opened herself to assess its potency and potential. The thing was, with her aura so out of whack she wasn't sure with most of them. Each time she failed, she doggedly put the stone down and tried another. Meanwhile, Lila took the broom out and swept the front porch, but her attention was never far from Chloe, as if she suspected her friend would bolt out the back door.

In truth, the thought did cross her mind. Of course Ally was there to watch her.

"You know, she's making a mountain our of a molehill, don't you?" Chloe tried to fill the silence in the shop.

Ally shrugged. "I don't know. It kinda sounded serious. Waking dreams and Kylee's abduction. Who would have thought it could happen in little old Peachland. Not to mention the theft from the shop."

So no support there. Perfect. Just perfect.

Finally a beaming Kylee strode up the sidewalk and turned in at the walkway to *This and That*. The beatific expression on her face clearly indicated she'd had lunch with Brett. The two of them made each other so happy it was almost hard to watch. Chloe's wild baby brother had been caught, hook, line and sinker. Good for Kylee. She deserved to have someone love her the way she was capable of loving.

That was the trouble with her own situation. She might be thirty-four now, with all the reflection and experience that came with rebuilding a life, but no matter the meditations and so on she had done, there was one belief that she hadn't been able to get rid of: how could she ever trust love was real after what she'd been and done.

Kylee positively danced up the front stairs where Lila met her. There was something said and both women looked through the window at Chloe. Oh God. Even Kylee knew something was going on.

Previously, everyone had always commented on Chloe's perennial calm. They'd come to her for help with their problems. But now? Now it was her that was the basket case.

She sighed.

Kylee breezed in with Lila at her heels, like a breath of fresh air against Chloe's churning aura, the little blond was that happy. For a moment, Chloe allowed herself envy. It bubbled inside her, but she pressed it deep down into her belly. Unfortunately that left even her Svadhisthana chakra wobbling. If it wasn't one thing it was another. Her whole system was failing at the moment. Her hands rested uselessly on the tray of glittering stones.

Lila came over and lay her hands over Chloe's. "Let's go do something to help you, instead of pretending you can function."

"But Ally…"

"Ally can help Kylee paint as well as you can," Ally shoved up from the chair. "I happen to be a very good painter."

Lacing her fingers in Chloe's hand, Lila led Chloe out of the shop and down the hall—not to the kitchen, but down the hallway to the peaceful room where Chloe'd done her healing.

"Why are we here?" Chloe asked.

"When you first approached me about starting a crystal healing practice, you mentioned that this room was particularly conducive to healing because of its alignments to energy currents. I don't know anything about that, but it seemed like a good idea to have an upsetting conversation in a place that my dear friend considers calming." Lila nodded at the armchair she usually occupied for reading. "Sit and make yourself comfortable. I'll be back in a few minutes."

Chloe sat and closed her eyes. It was a good room, just as Lila had said. The room seemed to sit right over top of some or other rock formation so there was a glowing sense of purity about it. Or maybe it was the ley line that ran down the valley coming into play. Either way, she breathed in gently, feeling the cool breath on the tip of her nose, then exhaled and let the heated air drain away.

In ten minutes Lila returned with a tray holding two cups and a pot of tea fragrant with orange and peach scent.

"Something warm and comforting for tales that chill the soul," she said and folded into a lotus position on the floor at Chloe's feet. She poured and offered Chloe a mug of the steaming liquid. "I know it's hot outside, but by the feel of your hands you could use a good warming up."

Lila sipped her tea and waited while Chloe sampled it. Fragrant and warm with cinnamon and cloves, the tea was something she might drink on a cold winter's night, or chilled during the summer, but at this moment the heat was what she needed. She sipped and fragrant scent of orchards and oranges filled her up. She closed her eyes. As she swallowed, she imagined the tension flowing out of her shoulders and right down her body and into the floor. She rested there a moment but the room seemed to shimmer around her as if another door was opening. She recognized the feeling from her other times visiting the vision space and opened her eyes to Lila. Nodded.

"So there's something about the bracelet. Since I've put it on, when I open myself, it's like I'm transported somewhere. That has never happened before. I might get impressions, but until now I've never felt like a bystander at the scene of a horrific crime." Chloe told her about the visions and what waited outside the courtyard gate. She shuddered. "In all the excitement, with Kylee's abduction, I don't know if you remember me telling you about a man who came into the shop. He was looking for something—the barest of trinkets, he said—but something that had sentimental meaning to his family. When he looked at me it was like I was looking at something dark and evil that wore him like a man wears a suit." Her fingers twined in the jet beads she wore. "I was wearing these beads at the time and I swear if I hadn't been he would have owned me. I would have done anything for him. As it was I still showed him everything in the shop to appease him. It was only luck that Kylee and the bracelet weren't there at the time.

"Lila, it was those same eyes that looked up at me in the vision, as if he knew exactly who I was and what I was doing." Shivering, she hunkered lower in the chair. "I don't want to go back there, but every time I relax with this bracelet on, it's like I end up there." She swallowed and met Lila's concerned regard.

"I'm sorry. I didn't think it would be quite this big a problem." And normally she could probably manage, but the interlude with Jas Stone had torn apart all her carefully built-up emotional safeguards. How was she supposed to deal with all those emotions when she didn't dare meditate?

End the conversation now, or confess the rest. She met Lila's eyes. "So that's what happened at the restaurant and that's why Jas—Corporal Stone—took me home."

Get out now, while the getting was good just the way a diamond cutter had to know when to stop in his cutting.

She pushed herself up from the chair. "Thank you, Lila. I feel much better now."

"Oh no you don't, girlfriend." From lotus to standing in one easy motion that Chloe didn't quite fathom, Lila blocked the doorway. "You might be able to pull the wool over the eyes of someone like Kylee who barely knows you, but don't try that with me. Something happened, didn't it? Between you and Corporal Stone?

"Why do you need to know what's happening in my personal life? This is a workplace."

Lila grinned. "Well my response to the latter is that I think your state of mind will impact your work. I can't have that. My response to the first question is that you're my friend and I can see you're hurting and I don't want my friend to hurt."

She threaded her arms around Chloe's waist and pulled her into a supportive hug. "Chloe, you know that I love you like a sister. When my sister hurts I need to take action. Did the good Corporal—Jas—did he hurt you in some way, because I'll deal with him if he did."

Lila held Chloe away and looked her in the eye. "Spill."

Oh God, Lila was so open, so willing and her aura was like a warm bath enveloping her, with the diamond of Lila's essence glittering in the middle. So strong. The strongest woman Chloe'd ever met and she'd tried so hard to emulate her. "I wish—I wish I was like you, Lila." She sighed and sank back into the chair to look up at Lila.

"Okay. First off, Jas was a perfect gentleman. He took me home and tried to get me settled. He was—concerned and maybe somewhat confused. After all, what I was experiencing isn't exactly what he deals with day-to-day in police work. I was scared—really scared because I couldn't seem to fully pull away from the vision and he was trying to comfort me and…" She sighed and scrubbed her face with her fists. "I guess I threw myself at him. I don't know why, but I did."

A flush of heat flowed up her shoulders and she so did not want to be the blushing type, but just talking about it brought the heat of the memory of what she—they—had done. What she had revealed about herself and how Jas had left her. How he was likely never coming back again.

"So he took advantage of you, did he?" Lila's voice was tight.

Chloe swallowed back the tears that threatened and shook her head. "No. It wasn't like that. He was tender. It was—wonderful." Oh God, her voice hitched.

Lila was on her knees in front of her again and had pulled her into another hug. "You like him, don't you?"

Nodding into her shoulder, Chloe fought with the tears. Just don't make me tell the rest. Let it stop there.

But Lila, darn her, was too wise for that. She pulled back and grabbed a tissue box, to offer them to Chloe. It was like the stupid tears took that as permission to start falling down her cheeks. She grabbed one and dabbed at her cheeks. Another, and blew her nose.

"You more than like this guy, don't you?"

A swallow and another nod. Then she shook her head. "How can that be, Lila? I barely know him and we're as different as can be. He frowns on everything I believe in. I don't get people who are so blind to the endless possibilities in the world. How do we even stand a chance?"

"Is that what happened? Did that come up?"

"No." Chloe looked away to the philodendron trailing its way over the curtain rod in seeming proof that its will couldn't be contained. Like the truth? She swallowed.

"You're not making this easy, girlfriend. So you made love and it was great. You didn't fight—also a good thing. So you have your differences. People overcome differences in every relationship. You give it a fighting chance and the two of you probably can, as well. If you want that. Or are you telling me the feelings are all one sided. Did he just take advantage of your emotional state?"

Again, the dangerous avenging sister light came into her eyes and Chloe hurriedly shook her head. "No. I think he cared. He cared enough to just hold me when I suddenly—when I—" Darn it, her throat closed up as if a crystal shard was trying to get out and it stabbed her from the inside. She hugged herself and rocked in the chair, tried to breathe to steady herself. What was it the Tibetans said? All life is pain, therefore you must let the pain pass through you and go.

It wasn't quite working for her at the moment, just like the shards of her past had stuck in her, too. The stone in her chest only seemed to get bigger as Lila pulled her into a hug again. Jas had done that, so she'd told him the truth of her history— or part of it—and now he was gone. Would she lose Lila, too, if she told?

The trouble was, she'd already let the cat out of the bag telling Jas. Her sordid secret was going to be making the rounds soon enough and there was no way it wouldn't get back to Lila. Truth was like that. So her friend might as well hear it from her mouth, instead of someone else's.

She struggled free of Lila's comfort, because she really didn't deserve it. Wiping her eyes, she took a deep breath. "Okay. I went off the deep end with Jas. I—I reacted to something that happened and tried to leave him and he wouldn't let me. Like you, he wanted to know what was the matter. So I told him." Try to keep this all clinical and businesslike because Lila valued that. "You see, I have a past and not a pretty one. You and I met when we were twenty-three, right? I remember because you'd just had your birthday, so I bought you lunch. At the time I'd just moved back home and was looking for an apartment."

"That's right. And I offered to let you move in here with me, because Grandma couldn't manage this place after Granddad died and there's lots of space, what with the rooms upstairs."

Chloe nodded, remembering how scared she'd been to have as perfect a friend as Lila. She'd been so afraid that her past shone through her skin and aura, and that Lila would just *see*. Or that maybe she did see and was just taking pity on her. Over the years she'd overcome that feeling and the friendship that had started that summer had solidified into something greater. Hopefully something strong enough to withstand this.

"Let me tell you my story. When we met I told you I'd just come home after living in a New Age commune in San Francisco."

Lila nodded. The light from the window seemed to catch in her aura like mother of pearl. Please let her understand.

"That was only part of the truth. I was there for three years. For three years before that I was—doing other things. You see, I left home at seventeen. Actually it was more like I ran away, but I was smart enough to wait 'til I finished school. I travelled around for about a year and ended up in San Francisco where I ran out of money." Her stomach clenched and her mouth tasted of bile. She so didn't want to do this, but she had to now. She bit back the pain and told Lila the same sordid details she'd told Jas. "Then I ended up with the people from the commune. They put me back together. You know the rest."

She met Lila's gaze for the first time since she got to the heart of her story, and looked for the judgment and condemnation.

There wasn't any. Instead Lila just squeezed her hands—somewhere in telling her story she'd clasped hands with her friend, had found the strength to tell it.

"Thank you. That was very brave. To leave your home, to try it on your own and to get yourself free when you'd taken a wrong turn. It shows just how smart and brave and strong you are, Chloe."

She shook her head aching at Lila's nonjudgmental kindness. "Someone smart would not have ended up almost selling themselves on the street. They would have come home."

"Apparently that wasn't a choice you could make at the time. You were young, Chloe. Give yourself a break. We all make mistakes. The thing is to rise above them and learn from them. Look at Kylee. She always gave her heart away and went chasing after men. When she finally quit, the right one came looking, didn't he?" She shook her head. "I think maybe you've been hating yourself for a long time about this. Maybe it's time you forgave yourself."

Chloe looked at her and couldn't help but shake her head. "I know what I did and that I'm going to pay for it for the rest of my life."

Lila pulled back. "With that sort of closed attitude you will. Isn't it you who talks about balance in life? And don't you also say that the only way to get what you need in life is to put what you need and want out there into the universe? Isn't part of balance being able to learn from the past, but not let it rule you?" She pushed herself up from the floor and looked down at Chloe. "Think about it. Now there's a lot of work to do out front. I'm going to give Kylee and Ally a hand and maybe we can get all the wood staining done today. I just want you to know that I love you, Chloe. We all do. We wouldn't feel that way if you were the horrible person you seem to think you are, and if Jas—Corporal Stone—is the quality guy you seem to think he is, then he'll see past it, too. Or he wasn't worth it in the first place. You got that?"

Chloe swiped at her tears and inhaled, trying for strength when she felt like an emotional wreck. "So you're giving me the tough love thing, are you?" She found a weak grin.

"Damn straight. Now up and at 'em. Fix your makeup in the bathroom and let's get out there. We've got lives to live."

Lila left, her lithe figure swaying down the hall as Chloe picked herself up off the chair. Trust Lila to accept the past and then just move forward. That was the business person in her—ever practical and no-nonsense. Time to practice it herself.

If she could.

She went into the bathroom to check herself in the mirror. The damage wasn't as bad as she'd thought, probably because she wore so little makeup to begin with. She dabbed her eyes with damp towels to get some of the redness out, undid her ponytail and swiftly braided her hair. There. She looked almost like the woman who had come to work all the other days *This and That* had been open.

Strong, Chloe. It was all in the past and she could put the past behind her. She looked down at the bracelet and shivered

Maybe.

CHAPTER 14

JAS STRODE THE OFF-WHITE HALLWAY THAT RAN a loop around the hushed open well of space in the center of the Royal Canadian Mounted Police detachment. It was lit by a pyramid-shaped skylight and by daylight from the large glass rotunda reception area on the first floor, which was supposed to be healthier for employees as well as reducing electricity bills. Chloe would probably have a heyday about the pyramid and all the supposedly mystical properties of that shape. Hell, some of the members had even mentioned it.

Jas shook his head as he returned from the OIC's office. The infuriating Chloe Main had obviously had too much impact on him if he was even noticing things like the pyramid. Its shape reminded him of the end of the large crystal she had in her apartment. Maybe the shape thing was related to the energy she sensed and *Holy Mother of God* what was he thinking?

Get a grip, Mister.

The door to the General Investigation Squad office that he shared with Forester was just ahead. Maybe he'd just pass it by and leave. Forester had been entirely too happy at having detected that Chloe was to blame for Jas's AWOL yesterday. How the man had known, he hadn't given Forester the satisfaction of asking. Instead he'd struck out for the OICs office for *that* scintillating conversation.

As if any officer likes to snitch on their brother officer.

And now to make things better he was going to have to face Forester and probably play twenty questions. He really should have just stayed in bed this morning or taken a sick day and gone to check on Chloe.

There it was again. Chloe. He couldn't seem to get the woman out of his brain. Even the nice neutral nothing scent of the building seemed to carry a hint of incense, but he suspected it was just her scent that had gotten stuck up his nose. Damn pheromones.

He stuck his head in the office, but Forester was still there. He just couldn't seem to catch a break. Sighing, he stepped inside and slumped in his chair. "Well that was fun."

Forester just quirked a brow and ran his fingers through his mess of hair.

"I lied. I told him you were just fine except for the minor thing of alien possession."

"Thanks a bunch, Pal."

"Seriously. I told him you passed muster. You're just as sane as I am." Which wasn't saying a lot at the moment. He stabbed a computer key and the screen sprang to life.

"Thanks, I guess. I owe you."

"Yeah. You do and don't expect me to let you forget it." Jas opened the Zeiss jewelry theft file figuring it was the safest and scanned down the file. "What's this?"

Forester leaned back in his chair and put his size eleven feet up on his desk. "What happens when your partner's out playing footsy with witnesses. A neighbor called it in—the Zeiss jewelry was tossed on their patio sometime early this morning. Thankfully the elderly woman was honest and called us instead of taking the stuff to a pawn shop."

Jas stretched and put his hands on his head. "This isn't making any sense. Why the hell would someone go to all the trouble of casing the apartments to know who's away when, but then risk being seen scaling those balconies to break in. And not even keep what's taken. I can't think of one self respecting burglar who would do that. Can you?"

"Nope. Not one. And everything's there, too. Not one single thing taken. The Zeiss and his girlfriend came in and verified it." Forester shook his head and sipped a mug of coffee he'd found while Jas was talking to the OIC.

"There anymore where that came from? I could use a cup." He nodded at the mug.

"Nope. You wouldn't like this at all. Tastes like horse piss." Forester hauled his legs off his desk and stood. "How about we go get a better cup of coffee and put our thoughts in order?"

Sighing, Jas stood. "Sounds like a plan." Even if Forester was going to grill him about something other than police work. "I wonder what apartment's going to be hit next."

Forester wasn't the sort for one of the 'fancy' coffees as he called them. Good old-fashioned gut rot was what he always hankered for, while Jas preferred his triple Americano. They'd found a hole-in-the-wall spot next to an Indian restaurant in downtown West Kelowna, away from all the usual Gen X types who clogged up the better known establishments.

Betty's Diner was a small place with only five tables. It served coffee and Italian food all prepared by Betty, or Elizabetta di Maria as her birth certificate said. She'd come over from the old country as a teenager and had married, raised five children and lost her husband all in West Kelowna. She'd started the small restaurant as a way to keep busy. Her homemade Italian food and excellent coffee had a small, but loyal following.

"The usual," Jas called as they pushed into the tiny place. Each table was wrought iron with the cliché Mateus bottle with melted candle on the top and some of the most uncomfortable chairs Jas had ever sat in. The chairs still weren't enough to stop him from coming back.

He and Forester took the table in the back corner underneath a bevy of old photos of West Kelowna when it had been called Westbank and her father had owned an orchard. There were shots of Betty, too, as a young black-haired beauty posing as Miss Westbank.

The proprietress fussed with an espresso machine that took up most of her counter space and soon brought them their drinks. She was a tiny woman, all sinew and sun-dried skin, but with a luxuriant mane of now-gray hair coiled around her head.

"How are you two boys doing?" The faint accent of her childhood still clung to her speech.

"Doing just fine, Betty. Now that I've got this to look forward to. What's the special today?"

She looked back at her kitchen area. "Lasagna if the Gods grace these hands. Everything is ready, I just need to put it all together. It takes attention, just like love, my mama always used to say." Her eyes were black beads in sharp bird-like features.

Jas grinned up at her. "For your lasagna, maybe I'll be back today."

"Good boy." She patted his cheek. "You find the right girl yet?"

"He might have, Betty. But he's being kinda closed-mouth about it. I'm here to pry it outta him."

She turned her black bird-eyes on Jas again. "You bring your girl in here and I cook you both a good meal that you won't forget."

"Yes, ma'am. I'll get right on that." He saluted and she left him, laughing, and returned to her kitchen. Soon wonderful aromas of tomato sauce and grilled meat wafted out to them.

"Someone's playing us for fools, is what I think," Jas said as soon as Betty was out of earshot. "I mean why go to all that trouble and not keep the goods?"

Forester nodded and sipped his coffee, then sighed and set it down. "I've been giving that some thought. It seems to me there's two possibilities. The first is there really is someone playing silly bugger out there. Like maybe it's kids breaking in just to prove they can—that sort of thing. The other idea I came up with is maybe they're looking for something in particular, but don't know where it is."

Jas frowned even though they were reasonable possibilities. "Or else these thefts have only been practice for something else."

Forester frowned but nodded. "Could be. What about asking the watch commander for approval for a stakeout?"

The Americano was rich and dark as Jas sipped and contemplated his answer. "If they see us they won't come. Kind of hard to be invisible in that open garden, and anywhere else *we* won't be able to see."

"What about we ask the apartment manager to let us use one of the empty apartments?"

Jas nodded. "A possibility. Or we could set up camp—literally—in the campground next door. If we could get a space next to the fence we could see everything for sure."

"All right. We've got a plan." Forester sipped his coffee and sighed. "If this is coffee, just what is it they're serving us at the detachment?"

Jas raised his mug in salute. "You got me. It was a good idea coming here. Any thoughts on the Jenson abduction case beyond waiting for someone from *SchwarzeNacht* to get back to us?"

Forester shook his head. From the kitchen came a huge sizzling sound and a cloud of tomato-scented steam as Betty added something to a hot pot. It smelled good, whatever it was.

"You know," Jas said. "There is someone who might be able to give us some information, even if *SchwarzeNacht* won't. Someone who knows better than anyone who was in that limo."

"The driver." Forester sat up. "Of course. Who else held the door for his client every day. He'd have to call him or her something. That gives us another direction to pursue."

"And we can try to talk to Tom Beaton," Jas said, though the idea of talking to someone crazy was about as appealing as, well, talking to a crazy man. He drained his coffee. "Flip you for it."

Forester gave him a calculating look. "No way man. You think I don't see what you're doing, trying to get outta here before we get to the good stuff."

The chair suddenly felt more uncomfortable than usual. Jas shifted. "Good stuff?"

"The woman. The witness. The one with the braid. The Main woman, right? That's the one you couldn't seem to keep your eyes off of."

Busted. "Man, you are so wrong. There's nothing going on."

"And you're a rotten liar. Makes me wonder how you ever do so well on the stand."

Jas rolled his eyes. "Gee. Maybe it's because I tell the truth like I'm s'pposed to?"

"And at the moment you're not."

"If I am, maybe it's because it's none of your business."

"You went looking for her in the house when we were doing interviews. The night we met them you couldn't keep your eyes off of her. It was why we paired off in search teams like we did. Or at least that's what I thought—to give you a chance to get to know her a little."

Deny it? Forester didn't look like he was going to let it go.

"Chloe. Her name's Chloe and I really don't think there's a hope in hell of it going anywhere. She's into all that New Age crap and I'm—not. Not exactly the basis of a relationship."

Forester gave a small hoot. "Relationship is it? Now those are words I never thought I'd hear pass the lips of the great Jasper Stone."

"And you are full of shit, Danny Forester." Jas shoved himself away from the table. "You coming, or do I leave you to walk back to the detachment."

"It's only four blocks," Forester gloated up at him

"Fine. Have it your way. I'll make some calls to reach the limo driver and set up the campsite." Jas turned and marched for the door.

Forester's laughter floated after him. "They say sensitivity is a bad sign, partner."

"Whatever." He slammed outside and realized his fists were clenched.

Dammit, it wasn't true. Forester was full of crap. Okay, Forester *had been* full of crap when he was talking about aliens in his head, but other than that he was a straight-up officer. If he was picking up vibes off of Jas, then maybe there was more to these things he'd been feeling.

"Fuck. Fuck me." How the hell was he supposed to be happy with a woman like Chloe? They were too different. When they were around each other there was constant friction.

Yup. And the sparks it created flew in a pretty interesting ways.

The silk of her skin, the luxury of her hair. Those breasts that were too often hidden in her damn drapery-loose tops. Those incredible legs and how they'd felt around him.

His body flushed with the erotic memory. Dammit, dammit, dammit. Just the thought of her and her incense scent aroused him and he so did not need this. But she'd been so vulnerable when he left her. He shouldn't have done it. As a matter of fact he was an idiot for leaving her and not checking with her this morning.

"You still here?" Forester pushed out of the shop, pushing a cloud of delectable scent in front of him. "What, you have a change of heart?" He looked at Jas's face and shook his head. "Nope. I see you're someplace else. She's really got to you, hasn't she?"

"I don't know what to do." He scrubbed his fingers through his hair and looked out at the traffic idling on the highway waiting for the traffic lights to change. West Kelowna had about the worst situation for a highway, with the town bisected twice by major lanes of traffic. There was talk of doing the same to Peachland, with northbound traffic running right along the town's waterfront. Peachland, however, was fighting back against the provincial highway department. "On the one hand she's about the last thing I need with her far-out beliefs and her personal problems. On the other, I can't quit thinking about her."

Forester shrugged. "So get laid and get it over with."

Jas hug his head. "Didn't work, I'm afraid."

Forester gave a low whistle and clapped Jas's shoulder to ease him to the car. "Bad news all around, partner. The ladies of Kelowna are going to throw a wake in your honor. Or maybe not bad news," he grinned. "There'll be more for me."

§

The afternoon was busy, with the four of them slinging a dark wood stain on the wainscoting. Mid-afternoon when Chloe's hands were stained red brown and Ally finally begged off to take a nap to deal with her jet lag, Lila had to leave to take a phone call and she never came back. That left Chloe and Kylee painting the last wall of wood. Kylee was humming some old Beatles song while Chloe let her mind wander—thankfully without any visions arising. By four o'clock they had the last wall finished and stood together in the middle of the room to admire their work.

"It really looks nice," Kylee said. "The dark wood seems to bring out the lavender in the paint and the gray tone of the paint just makes the wood look luxurious."

Chloe nodded. She was right. It might have been the same general concept as the previous paint, but this simply seemed to be a better match—richer and more extravagant looking for all its simplicity. That left the floor to do tomorrow and then they could set up shop again.

"You're awfully quiet today." Kylee said as she shifted one of the glass cases toward the front door. They'd agreed that tomorrow they'd move the cases onto the porch and then stain the floor. If they were quick enough they could move the cases back at the end of the day and start restocking the day after that.

"Just thinking." Chloe lifted her chin at the walls. "That was a good day's work and mostly thanks to you." She glanced at Kylee and smiled. "We've been very lucky that you wanted to settle in Peachland." Then Chloe elbowed the smaller woman. "Brett's a changed man. You tamed him."

Kylee grinned and shrugged. "It happened somehow. Well, it was mutual, actually. I was lucky initially to have a friend like Lila, but blessed when her friends also became mine."

It was a typical Kylee thing to say. The woman was a charm and finally coming into her own now that she'd gotten the bugbear of low self-confidence off her back. She left the paint cans she was closing, came to Chloe and caught her hand. "You know that if you ever need a friend to talk to, I'm here for you, Chloe. I know you've got Lila and I don't know where I'd be without her, but I know what it means to doubt yourself and I don't know if Lila does. I don't like losing the confident woman I first met when I came into the store. I miss her. I miss you."

She shrugged and cocked her head, but then released Chloe's hand and went back to place all the brushes in a tray in preparation for cleaning and use tomorrow.

She moved with utter confidence, not like before, but it was more than that. There was a balance about her and her aura had taken on a soft white light that spoke of contentment and happiness and solid connections to the world.

"How did you know that Brett was the right one? What made him different from the others?" the question spilled out of Chloe's mouth before she could stop it.

Kylee looked up, surprise on her face. Then she frowned.

"I'm not sure," Kylee said. "There was just something—deeper, I guess. Something like a hook right through my heart and it only felt better when he was around. I thought I'd fallen in love so many times before but I realize now it was only a sad imitation. I *wanted* so badly to be in love that I convinced myself it was the real thing again and again. Silly me."

"So you knew you were in love because it hurt?"

That brought a chiming laugh from Kylee. "Oh, goodness, no. It was the way he looked at me, the way I felt when he was around, as if the world was somehow bigger and better. It was other things, too, like the way I could get turned on just by looking at his hands. But that's all I'm saying about your brother." She grinned and went back to the brushes.

Chloe started folding the drop cloths they'd spread.

"Why do you ask?" Kylee asked casually, just not casually enough.

Because I'm struggling here and I feel like I can't breathe?

"Just interested, I guess. I've never been in love." She shoved loose strands of hair behind her ears and began pushing another of the glass jewelry cabinets closer to the door. The room went quiet with only the sounds of their motions and the summer afternoon outside. The scent of cut grass through the window said that some gardener was hard at work.

"You haven't had any problems with the bracelet have you? No threatening notes or anything?" Kylee referred to the note that she had found in her locked house when she first moved in.

Chloe looked up and pasted a smile on her face. "No. No notes."

She tried to keep her voice light but the memory of those eyes staring up at her in her vision made her legs suddenly weak. She staggered and caught herself, but too late.

"Something did happen!" Kylee was around the counter again to tug Chloe over to the chair that Ally had used. "What was it?" She grabbed Chloe's wrist and brought the bracelet up between them. "Come on, Chloe. I had to wear the darn thing, too, you know."

"Yeah. Sure. I know you did. But I haven't had to deal with anything like you did."

Kylee bent down to peer directly into her eyes as if she could read the truth there. "So what's going on, then? What aren't you telling me?"

She'd already told Lila. She might as well tell Kylee. "It's giving me visions I don't want to have.

Lila asked me to read the bracelet, so I tried. I found myself in a courtyard. There was dust all around, high mud-stucco walls, and fear. So much fear because someone was coming." She shook her head to keep the vision from returning. "I don't know what happened except that the visions keep coming even though I don't want them. There were soldiers and something worse outside that courtyard." She shuddered at the memory and nodded at Kylee. "That's it."

"That's it?! Come on, Chloe. That's momentous! And totally consistent with the bracelet being found by Colonel Bristol in North Africa. They have buildings built of bricks and stucco there, *and* they have courtyards!"

"You're guessing, Kylee. We've got nothing to confirm that theory."

"Well we know he was there fighting Rommel in the Second World War. It makes sense. And that's where his luck changed, too. Just like my luck changed when I put the bracelet on. He got promoted and I got Brett, not to mention a home and friends!"

Chloe sighed. It was all a nice dream, but it was too far-fetched even for her. "Come *on*. It hasn't done a single good thing for me—it's just caused strange visions and made me do stupid things."

"I don't see you having it cut off."

"Well don't tempt me too much." She picked up the drop-cloths and scanned the room. "Are we finished?"

"Pretty much." Kylee grabbed the tray with brushes. "Done."

"Good. I think I'll call Ally and see if she wants to come home with me until Lila gets back. I was thinking of a dip in the pool. You interested?"

A moment of thought and Kylee shook her head. "I'll take a pass. I've got work to do today if I'm going to take delivery of that garden soil I ordered. You remember I'll be in late tomorrow, right?"

Chloe did. She left Kylee to set the brushes to soaking and went upstairs to knock on Ally's door.

"Hold on a moment." The sound of rustling came through the door, and then it pulled open. Ally stood there, wiping sleep out of her eyes, with her great mane of blond hair demurely tangled. Behind her, the bedroom was filled with sunshine. "Yeah?"

"We're done downstairs and Lila isn't back. I wondered if you wanted to come for a swim at my place?"

Ally blinked and then nodded. "Better than hanging out here alone. Let me get my swim suit." She went back into her room while Chloe returned downstairs to collect her purse. Ally arrived with a small daypack a lot like the one Kylee always carried.

Chloe locked up the front door and left Kylee to secure the rear.

They clattered down the porch stairs and out into the sunshine and brisk breeze of Beach Avenue. She headed north in a long, ground-eating stride, Ally beside her.

"Sorry you had to see all that today," she said to Ally. The woman moved with a long, athletic stride like the lions she'd first photographed that got her noticed. Even after all these years and even through the disturbances in her aura, Chloe still sensed the same impression she had when she first met Ally: bold. She had always lived her life larger than everyone else. "I suppose Lila told you all the sordid details of what's been going on here?"

Ally shrugged. "Some. She told me that a bracelet came to the shop through an estate sale and that weird stuff has been happening like people putting it on and not being able to get it off—first Kylee and now you." She glanced down at the silver flashing on Chloe's wrist. "So why'd you put it on when that estate agent might have been run over because of it and Kylee was held hostage?."

"Good question." Chloe held the bracelet up for closer inspection. "I just wish I had a really good answer. The day Kylee brought it back to the shop we were all just so happy that she was safe. The stupid bracelet was sitting there looking all innocent so I picked it up to see how the closure worked. You see, no one had been able to figure that out while Kylee wore the bracelet." She sighed. "It seemed really simple. The key slides through the lock on the other end. To open it you just slide the key shank first back through the lock opening. Easy-peasy. So I put the stupid thing on. Look who was stupid."

"Can I try it?"

Chloe stopped and held out her arm. "Fill your boots. Maybe you'll have the magic touch."

But no such luck.

"It's like the key suddenly grows too big or the lock too small," Ally said after trying twice.

"Welcome to my Alice in Wonderland existence." She kept going and Chloe glanced sideways at Ally. "I figure I'm pretty safe in Peachland. My condo's secure and there're people around pretty much all the time in the shop." A shiver ran up her neck.

Ally eyed her knowingly. "I remember when I went into a poacher's camp to do a photo story on their lives; why they do what they do. This group was already believed to have killed two state conservation officers. I was shivering in my boots, but I didn't dare let them see how scared I was. So I showed them the same bold bravado that they like to show the world. Frankly, I think I scared the heck out of them, too, so they respected me and actually took me deeper into their lives than I'd ever expected." She smiled. "So I totally get what you're doing not having the bracelet removed."

Chloe sighed and held the bracelet up to catch the sun. The patina of age was clearer in the bright light. There were shadows softening the tiny gargoyle face of one door and the ornate iron hinges of the one she preferred. They left the tall cottonwood trees that edged the lake shore behind and now the shore curved around westward toward Trepanier Creek and the Willowview.

"I don't know if that's what I'm doing at all, but there is something about this bracelet. I've had visions that I've never had before since I started to wear it, and they are terrifying. I feel more unsettled and confused than I have since, well, since I wasn't much more than a kid."

Ally grinned. "I always say there's a story in there somewhere when I feel like that. It's the uncomfortable stuff that makes us grow stronger. I revel in the stuff."

Chloe led her across the small bridge over the creek to where the Willowview created a wall of apartments in an otherwise pastoral lakeside setting.

"Whoa." Ally stopped dead in her tracks. "That wasn't here when I left. Where'd all the trees go?"

"Where do you think? Cut down to make way for progress."

Ally shook her head. "I would have thought you'd refuse to live here just on general principle."

Chloe shook her head. "My principles went out the window when I was able to get the condo for a song because everyone else felt the same way as you. But yeah, I miss the old campground." But what did it mean? Maybe she'd been fooling herself all these years. Maybe the principles she'd thought she'd reclaimed after San Francisco had never really come back. Maybe she was...

Ally caught her arm. "So are we going to stand here, or are we going for that swim? The sun's headed behind the hills and I'd like to catch a few rays if possible."

Crossing the street, Chloe led Ally through the Willowview Terrace gardens. Everything just looked so normal. Ally was right about the sun falling fast toward the western mountains, which meant the pool would be in shadow soon. It also meant that people were starting to clear out from the pool. More room for her to do her laps undisturbed.

Inside her building they rode the elevator up and hurried down the hall, through the first set of fire doors. Mitch Flanders, a retired dentist, and his wife, Margaret were at their doorway, fumbling their keys into the locks.

"You're back," Chloe called. "How was the trip? Has it really been a month already? I guess it has, because here you are." God, she was blithering and she never blithered.

"Hawaii was wonderful," Margaret said. She was a slim, petite woman who always dressed like she lived in the Hamptons. "We've never gone this time of year before, but it was lovely and so uncrowded. You should consider it, Chloe. We'll give you the name of our rental company."

"Thanks. Not that I'll get away any year soon, but I'll keep it in mind. I watered your plants day before yesterday, so they should still be fine." She eased Ally past, because Margaret could be something of a talker. Chloe had learned that lesson the first time she invited the woman over for coffee, but they were her right-hand neighbors, with the Singhs on the other side. "Sorry. I want to hear about your trip, but I seriously need to get a swim in."

Margaret shook her head. "You youngsters and your exercise."

Chloe almost ran into her apartment. The need to move—not talk—was almost compulsive. She showed Ally the bathroom to change in, then doffed her clothes and left them on the bed, to pull on her favorite swimming maillot. She grabbed a towel for Ally and herself, threw on a cover-up and waited for Ally. She reappeared wearing about the tiniest bronze-colored bikini Chloe had ever seen. It showed off Ally's long, tanned limbs and her lean well-muscled body, not to mention a few other attributes. Well the other condo owners would get an eyeful today.

Chloe led Ally back to the pool. Shadows had already eaten the sunlight at one end of the pool. Ally frowned, but found a chaise at the opposite end of the pool and settled there like a bronze goddess. A woman wrangled three complaining children toward the building. Someone's house guests probably.

Chloe dumped her belongings on a chaise next to Ally's, pulled a cap over her head, goggles on, and dove.

Cool fluid enveloped her and she struck out for the pool's end. Exactly fourteen strokes and she ducked her head and did a kick turn and kept on going. In the water she didn't have a past except how many laps she had done last time. She didn't have men leaving her after she'd foolishly made love to them.

Made love. Hah. That was a fantasy, or something found by the lucky few like Kylee and Brett.

Jas Stone was the farthest thing from the right kind of man for her to 'make love' to.

Was that five laps or seven? Damn it, what was she doing thinking about the guy. Swimming was when she could set her mind on neutral and just feel her body.

She came up to the end of the pool before she knew it, did a kick turn again and kept going, but something wasn't right. It was like there was a shadow over that end of the pool. She reached the other end and turned, churned back the way she'd come, took a chance and looked.

Ally lay on her chaise catching the rays, but her large round sunglasses were tilted back to allow for a long appreciative look at the man standing before Chloe. Long legs in jeans, a black t-shirt left well-muscled arms exposed as he crossed them over his equally well-muscled chest. She knew because the memory of his naked torso was burned onto the insides of her eyelids. Seeing him made her realize that was part of what had confounded her all day. Her feet touched down and she stood in the pool, raising her eyes from his belt buckle *–get a grip, woman–*up to his face. A flutter she'd never felt before fill her chest and all the doubts about how she felt about this man fell away.

Either that, or she was seriously in lust.

§

The fading sunlight silvered her body and the pool behind her as Chloe stood up in the water, her eyes on him. Across the lake, the tops of the mountains were still bright with sunshine, but the shadows of the hills now stole the worst of the heat of the day from the town. Chloe's mane of hair was somehow hidden inside a neon-blue bathing cap, but otherwise there wasn't much of Chloe Main that *was* hidden in the dark blue bathing suit that clung so completely to her lush curves. Not much hidden in her eyes either: fear, confusion, desire.

And denial.

Well, he'd see about that. During the afternoon, while he'd contacted the limo company and arranged the campsite, he'd decided that the safest bet would at least be to get to know her.

The breeze off the lake had picked up, placing small uneasy waves on the pool a lot like the sensation in his chest. He really wanted to try this, but on the other hand, was it worth it? His heart and body said yes. His head wasn't so sure.

He crouched down to sit on his heels. "Hey. I saw someone swimming and thought it might be you." *Liar. From the campsite you saw her arrive home with the high-breasted blond who currently looked like she wore nothing at all in the chaise behind him. You were trying to get up the nerve to go calling when she came down to the pool.*

"So it's me. What are you doing here? Returning to the scene of the crime?" Her jaw was clenched and her arms automatically covered her breasts as if to hide the way her nipples had tightened when she first stood up.

"Working a case." He shrugged off the jab. He should have phoned her this morning. Hell, he never should have left.

"Let me guess. Like you were working the case the other day?" Her voice was cool and as hard as those stones she so admired. "Maybe you thought you'd come for another visit to my place. Isn't that what happens to people like me?"

"No! Chloe, no. What happened between us, happened—but for good reasons. We're attracted to each other. At least I am to you." He sighed. Might as well get used to looking like a fool. "I've thought about you a lot since last night."

"Well isn't that nice for you." She climbed out of the pool like frigging Aphrodite and grabbed a towel. "Ally, I've just lost my appetite for swimming. The sun's not great, but there'll be more privacy on my deck." She swiftly toweled off, while her blond friend stretched and stood and holy God, the woman was stacked. He swallowed and looked back at Chloe as she headed for the pool enclosure gate.

"Where are you going? You just barely started your laps."

She cast a look in his direction that clearly indicated it was because of him she was leaving. "And just how would you know how many laps I swim?"

"I saw you the other day. During the first break-in. You swam like a mermaid."

At that her lips curved slightly. "Oh." She turned to leave.

"Chloe, don't go. Please." He caught the blond eyeing him speculatively. "I'll leave you in peace. I just thought, you know, maybe there was some way we could see each other again." Fuck. He sounded like a fucking school kid asking out his first girl.

Her expression went serious and she looked away. "I don't think that's a good idea. You'd never be able to get past who and what I am."

And with that she walked away, her friend sauntering after her, but tossing a teasing smile over her shoulder. Chloe's body swaying in a manner that spoke volumes about her incredible femininity. Damn. He wanted her. He wanted to learn more about what made her believe in healing stones. He wanted to watch her as she performed her healing. He wanted to sit and tell her about his day and have her place those gentle hands of hers on his shoulders. Most of all he wanted to hold her once more in his arms.

You're an idiot, Stone. The lady doesn't want you around. Get over it.

Shaking his head at the vagaries of a life that would only let him be certain of what he wanted when he was most certain he couldn't have it, he headed back for the campground.

Forester had borrowed another RCMP member's motorhome while Jas had talked the owner of the campground into renting them a space that sat next to the fence adjoining Willowview Terrace. Thankfully the spaces farther back from the lake were less sought after, but it was high season. The owner had squeezed them in so that Jas now sat on one of the narrow twin beds looking out the rear of the motorhome. He had a good view of the entire complex, but his mind kept going to one end of the building.

Chloe'd be in there having a shower. He remembered the way she'd looked with the water pouring down her luscious body, the way she'd made him feel and the smooth firmness of her under his hands. *Don't go there, man. You've got a long night ahead of you.*

She'd probably make herself a cup of coffee with that espresso machine of hers and then relax with her friend and her cat on the patio. She'd probably think about her stones and other unbelievable stuff like that. Not about him—except he was the idiot who bothered her when she was swimming and who had taken advantage of a sick woman and slept with her. That was most likely what she thought of him. No wonder she didn't want him around. For her, he'd only raised the specter of her past. Not exactly the effect he'd like to have.

He kept watch as the light faded. Outside there was all the clamor of a campground with kids playing, mothers trying to corral them for dinner and then the sound of voices gradually becoming quieter. From somewhere closer to the water came the sound of campfire songs he remembered from his childhood. Across the lake the mountains had gone gray and the lake had gone dark.

He microwaved himself a meal of burritos and poured hot sauce over them, popped a cola and sat back on the bed to eat. The beans were brown mush, the meat not much better, but the hot sauce imparted a hint of flavor. There were lights coming on in the apartments. A glow at the end of the building hinted at lights in Chloe's apartment. Maybe she was cooking. She was probably a good cook, too. He raised his burrito to her in a toast.

It was seven o'clock when the knock came at the motorhome door and for a moment he hoped it was Chloe. But he hadn't seen her and she had no way of knowing where he was. He opened the door to Forester who climbed in carrying a grocery bag and two extra-large cups of coffee.

"Thought we might need these." He handed one to Jas and Jas tasted.

One of Betty's Americanos done up mega-sized.

"You are a good man," he said and touched brims with Forester.

"There's been another break-in," Forester said, setting the bags on the counter and starting to remove packages of hot dogs, buns and sandwich fixings into the fridge. A package of coffee he placed next to the drip pot on the counter. "Couple apparently just got back from Hawaii. I've got patrol taking the particulars and Ident coming in. We can visit tomorrow."

Jas sat down at the kitchen table, an uneasy feeling that wasn't burrito filling his stomach. "Which apartment?"

Forester pulled out his notebook. "Three-twenty-three. The water end of the building."

Right beside Chloe's. He left Forester still rummaging through his bags and returned to the bedroom to peer out at the condos. The light was dimming. Across the dark lake, the mountains had gone gray.

"So what's happening? Anything interesting?" Forester asked from the kitchen.

"Not a damn thing," he said and sat down on the bed with his coffee. "We can see pretty well from here, though."

Forester looked around and spotted the empty burrito package. "Blasted burritos, Batman! We can do better than that." He gingerly tossed the package in the garbage. "We could barbecue and try to fit into the neighborhood."

"We're on stakeout, not vacation."

Forester shrugged and sat on the other twin bed. "Okay, so no barbecue. There's hotdogs we can nuke."

He stared out at the apartment block. "We got a call from the psych ward before I left the detachment. They figure Beaton almost has his head on straight if we want to talk to him." He glanced Jas's way. "I thought maybe you wanted to do the honors. The way I figure it, my episode would make any statement I take a bit suspect."

"Did you set an appointment for tomorrow?"

Forester shook his head. "Tonight. About forty minutes from now. They weren't sure he wouldn't fade out again."

"Shit!" Jas hauled his shoes on and grabbed his jacket. "Keys? To the car?" He'd driven the motorhome out to the campground.

Swearing under his breath he snagged the keys out of the air after Forester tossed them and leapt down out of the motorhome, coffee in hand. The blue sedan started and he hauled ass all the way to Kelowna once he got out of the confines of the campground.

Kelowna General Hospital sat one block off the waterfront in a shady, old-money residential area of the city. The Acute Short Stay Psych Unit was on the fourth floor and accessed through a double set of locked doors. Jas was buzzed inside into the scent of disinfectant overlaid on human excrement. Nice. The low buzz of fluorescent lights and human voices grated on his ears. The locked nursing station sat across from the locked doors so he announced himself. The nurse on duty, a middle-aged woman with short graying brown hair, a gold crucifix, and a no-nonsense attitude glanced up at the clock on the wall.

"You're late. We expected you at eight."

"Sorry. Traffic was worse than I expected."

She nodded as if she didn't really believe him, but then she smiled. "Mr. Beaton is waiting for you. He seems eager to talk."

"So there's been improvement, then. I was one of the arresting officers. There was only nonsense coming out of him then."

"He's not violent anymore, if that's what you mean. He seems more in touch with reality."

Music to his ears. "Okay, then. Where?"

She left the confines of her office and led him down the hall. She wore blue nurse scrubs and white runners.

"How long've you been working psych?"

She looked him up and down. "About since you were in grade school." Grinned.

"That long. How's Beaton stack up for crazy in your opinion?"

She chuckled. "I think of it as a continuum from boring to bat-shit crazy. Beaton? He's you or me on a very bad day."

Interesting and not what he expected. "Guess I haven't seen what you have."

"Guess not." She unlocked a room door for him and motioned to a folding chair beside the door. "Just knock on the door when you're done."

He stepped inside to a simple bare room with a bed and bedside table. Tom Beaton rolled up to sit on the edge of the bed as Jas set up the chair. He sat down and studied Beaton.

He was a slighter man than he'd remembered, with stooped shoulders and a narrow frame. His features were large for his face and he had a habit of blinking as if he couldn't quite focus. Small divots on his upper nose spoke of glasses. His thin blond hair fell over his high forehead. Seeing him like this reminded Jas of seeing a perpetrator after they'd cleaned up for court. This man was nothing like the hissing, struggling wild man he'd apprehended after rescuing Kylee Jensen.

"Mr. Beaton," he began and Tom nodded. "Thank you for agreeing to see me. I understand this must be difficult." He nodded at the locked door of the room.

"I knew you'd come—eventually." Tom Beaton's voice was soft, so Jas had to listen closely. By the look of the man, this wasn't an attempt at control, either.

"I'm hoping you want to make a statement."

The little man nodded.

"Then I'm going to record the interview, okay?" He hauled out his telephone, turned on digital record and set it on the floor between them. "Mr. Beaton, my name is Corporal Jasper Stone and we are sitting in your room at Kelowna General Hospital. Before we go any further I have to warn you." He recited the Canadian Charter warning about right to counsel and that anything he said could be used against him. "Do you understand?"

"I understand," Beaton said.

"Do you wish Counsel to be present for this interview?"

"No," Beaton said.

"Could you please repeat that more loudly for the tape and state your name, please."

Beaton complied. Of course, given the man's suspected mental state, the man might not have capacity to give consent anyway.

Jas took out his notebooks and eyed Beaton. The man already looked beaten and close to tears. "Mr. Beaton, I'd like to call your attention to events that transpired on the night of July first. Can you tell me about that day? Perhaps walk me through what happened."

"The nurses tell me that I took a woman hostage. My wife tells me it was our neighbor Kylee Jensen." He seemed to shiver and shrink into himself.

"I'd like to have you tell me about what you remember yourself. Maybe start with your day before the events of that evening. Tell me about your lunch time."

Beaton looked at him doubtfully, but finally sighed. "We had a lunch at home—Mary and Marika—that's my wife and daughter—and me. It's always easier to eat at home when you've got little kids. It was quiet. A nice day, so we ate out on the patio."

"Tell me about the meal."

Frowning, Beaton described tuna sandwiches and carrot sticks and sun tea that Mary had made on the porch. As he spoke of his wife and daughter he smiled.

Tom Beaton wasn't exactly what Jas had expected. The details of his day were far more specific than suspects usually gave and his love for his family might not be unexpected, but it shone through so clearly that Jas couldn't imagine the man endangering his life with them.

"So tell me about how you came to be in downtown Peachland?" Keep the questions general, let Beaton fill the meaning in. That was the trick with police work: keep them talking and don't talk yourself. At least in these early stages. The interrogation could come later.

"Mary and I—we'd planned to go down for the festivities. After all, that's why we chose to live in Peachland—for the small town feel. Part of that is participating in the small town events. So we loaded up Marika and her stroller just after lunch and drove down. Parking was atrocious, but we finally found something and then we just cruised the street, admiring all the vintage cars and enjoying the parade and the clowns and so on. Marika was really getting into it and Mary was enjoying herself, too. At about six o'clock the place was getting too packed and Mary suggested we leave. But it was getting harder and harder to leave because everyone was pushing in toward the downtown and our car was down beyond the bakery, almost to the Trepanier Creek Bridge. We decided we'd try to ride out the worst press and head for the car when things thinned out a bit, so we went with the flow, hoping to find that having the stroller might give us priority at one of the restaurants. We ran into Kylee then. She seemed happy. She was on some kind of race to beat her boyfriend to the beer garden." He sighed, shuddered, and looked Jas in the eye. "She's a nice lady. I wouldn't do anything to hurt her."

Spoken like so many crazies before him. Not all of them had seemed crazy either, Jas reminded himself.

"So then what happened?" Jas kept his voice quiet and just prayed the recorder was picking up everything. He was taking notes, but had to skip some details to keep up.

"I left Mary and Marika to check on another restaurant. They were near the cenotaph and I ran across the street to check with a restaurant. Of course there was a lineup, so I got to talking to a tall fellow waiting in front of me. He pointed down the street at a woman—it was Kylee—and asked me if I knew her. I said yes, that she was my neighbor."

Beaton fell silent. He shook his head. Then he crossed his arms and he started to rock. "I don't know. I don't know." The guy's shoulders were shaking.

Jas set down his notebook. The man looked ready to leap and run. His expression had changed from the man who had spoken so affectionately of his family, to one of desperation.

"What is it that you don't know, Tom." Jas used his most gentle tone.

The man's rocking increased and he scrubbed his arms as if trying to get warm. His blue eyes had gone huge and dark and he no longer seemed aware of the room or Jas. All of the hairs on Jas' arms stood on end.

"What's happening? What's happening? Everything's dark." Beaton's feet came up onto the bed and he shoved himself back until he was caught in the corner between two walls.

"Tom? Can you hear me? What's happening, Tom?" Okay, things were getting a weird.

Tom's arm jerked in a panicked motion for quiet. "Something's out there," he whispered. "I can hear it. Can't you? It's big by the sound of it. So big it fills me up." His face jerked up. "No! It's here! It's here in my head! So big, it fills the night and it wants me to leave my place in line. Kylee is there. It walks up to her and it moves my lips and I talk to her."

okay, not just weird. *Fucking* weird and a cold wind streamed down Jas's back.

Beaton grabbed his head. "No! Don't listen, Kylee. Don't listen to him—me. Oh God, what's happening? Mary? Mary where are you? What are you doing? I don't care that this is none of my business. I don't care that this will only take a few minutes. Kylee—what are you doing to her?"

He hunched forward with his arms over his head and started moaning. "No. No. No."

Jas scrambled to write down Beaton's words in his notepad to the best of his recollection and then grabbed his digital recorder off the floor. All the flesh on his body seemed to prickle. This was the most fucking creepy interview he'd ever had and he'd had some doozies. Just how did a man go from lucid one moment to a basket case while describing standing in a restaurant line?

He stuck the notebook and phone in his pocket and stood. "I guess that's it for today, Tom."

Tom shuddered and peered out at him from the shelter of the arms he had pulled over his head. "No. No. No. You have to understand. I didn't do it. I didn't. It was him. The darkness. He'll come after it forever."

"Who's coming, Tom?" Jas held his breath. This could be the solution to the crime.

Tom clutched at his head as if it pained him. "Old. So old. I don't know his name. No one does. Long forgotten."

okay. That didn't work. "What's he coming for, Tom? What is it that the darkness wants?"

If anything Tom seemed to collapse further in on himself. "The thing. On her wrist. It's important to him."

The room went chill as if every bit of heat had been sucked out of it. There was only one bracelet associated with the case and right at the moment he was freaked enough at Tom Beaton's performance that he could almost believe his craziness. Beaton and Forester and the suicide note of the man who had run over the estate sales person, Moira Burns, had all spouted almost the same crap. Aliens in their head, making them do things they didn't like. Aliens or not, there was something out there apparently looking for the bracelet.

He pounded on the room's door to be let out. He had to get back to Peachland, no matter how weird this was. Regardless of Chloe's assurances, there was no way she was safe.

CHAPTER 15

Chloe fumed around her apartment while Ally watched a movie. Lila had called to say she was held up in town and could Ally either help herself to food in the fridge or hang around with Chloe for a meal. Together the two of them had feasted on a large tuna salad with butter lettuce, olives, tomatoes and capers. They'd shared a bottle of wine, but that still hadn't calmed Chloe down. As a matter of fact, having Ally around only increased the shudders through her system. She'd seen the way Jas had looked at Ally out at the pool. He'd been like some old cartoon character with the eyes bulging and the tongue hanging out. Of course what did she expect, given that the bronze bikini on bronze-tanned skin made Ally almost look like she had nothing on. She should be mad at Ally but her frustration was focused on Jas.

Stupid. He was just a man acting like what he was.

Tonight the usually calming crystals didn't seem to work and her out-of-kilter aura was no help. She'd tried meditating in her bedroom but her monkey-mind just wouldn't go away and even bringing it back to a quiet place over and over again hadn't worked. In disgust she'd finally let the thing go and now it skittered all over the place like light broken apart through a crystal.

She wandered around her livingroom, touching the amethyst thunder egg, the huge rutilated quartz crystal and dragging her fingers over each of the other small crystals on display. It was like a series of musical notes ran through her, but their usual resonance was off, as if they'd gone off-key.

Not the stones. It was her.

She'd downloaded a movie she'd wanted to see, but it hadn't appealed to her once it was playing. She'd left Ally to it and wandered around the room instead of watching. The soundtrack disturbed her even though it was a pleasant enough romantic comedy. So she'd wandered the apartment from sunny kitchen to her bedroom—scene of the crime—and back out to the livingroom's low couch that had betrayed her into kissing him. Oh yes, and don't forget the patio.

The patio where they'd stood too close together and sipped their wine until they both came to their senses and Jas left. She leaned on the back of the couch and sighed. That was when they both had their senses about them—before they both went mad.

Jas. The whole darn apartment was infected with him. His scent kept coming to her, as if it hung in the air like the gold inclusions in the rutilated quartz crystal.

She looked over at the stone. Its inner light had gone dark due to the western angle of the sun. Stupid stone was supposed to give calmness. It was supposed to stimulate self-healing powers and remove mental blocks, and help people discover the truth so that a person could make changes. Yeah. Right. Like that had happened.

What was the phrase? *Physician heal thyself?*

She was doing such a good job of that. Her hand went to the bracelet on her wrist. "And you haven't helped at all, I might add. You and your visions. Idly she tried to fit the key through the lock clasp. "Of course it doesn't work. You don't plan on coming off at all, do you? Not until you're good and ready."

"Chloe, you're talking to yourself again," Ally said. "You sure you don't want to talk this out? I'm here. I have a shoulder to cry on if you need it."

She made it sound so simple, as if that would help.

Shaking her head no, and saying thanks, she slid open the patio door and stepped outside into the muted evening light. The scent of propane barbecue from the campground and all the patio dwellers in the apartments placed a tang on the heated air. The earlier breeze had turned hot and sultry and she fanned herself as she leaned on the deck railing and looked out at the lake.

Southward, huge stacked clouds were parading darkly toward the city of Penticton. There were more of the thunderclouds stacked up above the mountains, so the sun's rays were splayed golden across the sky. Beautiful, if you didn't understand that the lightning the clouds carried could start forest fires. Half the town had been evacuated a few years back, including her brother, Brett. From the news and the weather reports it was looking like it could be another bad summer.

Darn, it was hot. When she'd arrived home, the one constructive thing she'd done after abandoning the pool was doff her suit and pull on a pair of faded denim shorts and a sleeveless blouse. She'd thought they'd be cool enough, but they hadn't helped in the heat.

Hah. *Get real woman. You're producing the heat yourself.*

Because of Jas. Because just seeing him standing there, in those jeans and t-shirt had made her want to strip them off him and drag him into the pool with her. She'd imagined the feel of his warm flesh in the pool and that was why she'd had to get out of there so fast—in case her mind went the way of her body and betrayed her again.

He was like the pebble in her shoe, the grain of sand in the oyster.

And we all know what the sand grows into...

Get real. God, she was even sounding like him.

She went inside and slammed the door behind her, catching a shake of the head from Ally's direction. Let it rain. The rain would be good for the hillsides. Just don't let the thunder and lightning loose. They were too dangerous.

A lot like the feelings you have for Jas? Clear as day, like a voice in her head. Now where the hell had that come from?

The phone buzzed and she grabbed for it, thankful for any distraction. "Hello."

"Chloe! You're home!" Lila's cheerful voice came through the phone. "I came to collect Ally."

"Come on up." Anything would be better than being with herself at the moment. Even more of Lila's interrogation."We can have drinks."

"Perfect. I've got some news."

Lila signed off and Chloe buzzed her in, then took stock of her wine supply. Still a couple of Brett's good Pino Grigio and Viognier. Should be enough.

Chloe threw two bottles of wine in the freezer, straightened pillows—and corralled the dust bunnies of Clyde's hair in the front hallway. The others were just going to have to be left to their own devices. She quickly chopped some fresh vegetables and put them on a plate with some hummus then ran for her bedroom. "Lila's here," she called. "Would you let her in while I get changed?"

She slid into a pair of spandex shorts and a body skimming, sleeveless purple smock and checked her makeup, then added a smidge of lip gloss. Her hair, there was nothing she could do anything about because it was still in its swim-dampened braid. It would do.

A knock came at the door and she heard voices in the livingroom. She went out to hear Lila's news.

Not Lila.

Jas Stone stood there, obviously deeply enthralled with Ally's conversation.

When Ally held forth it was like she drew the eyes of everyone in the place. It was what had made her so good at fund raising for her various causes. It was also the reason she had been probably the most hated of girls at the West Kelowna Community College— at least among the girls. How could an ordinary college girl compete against someone like Ally. The boys flocked to her. So did men, and she was quite prepared to take them all on.

A chill ran through Chloe as she watched how Jas leaned in to receive Ally's fluttering hands, to the way she just had to touch him and the way she leaned in too close. His expression seemed glazed. It was just Ally's way and meant nothing, she told herself, but it caused a jagged pain in her heart, just the same.

She shook herself. It should mean nothing to her. *Jas* was nothing to her except a problem.

Jas stepped back as Ally touched him one more time. He turned, caught sight of Chloe still in the hallway and a smile curved his mouth.

"There you are! Chloe we need to talk. Some developments have occurred in the case and I..."

Another knock on the door and Chloe held up her hand and went to the door. Lila breezed in, back in her black capris and body-skimming boat-necked striped top. "Chloe, Ally!" She stopped. "Well, look at this. And Corporal Stone. Ally, I see you've met West Kelowna's finest, Corporal Stone of the Royal Canadian Mounted Police." Lila caught Chloe's arm and dragged her into the livingroom, a grin on her face.

Jas was a lone island of macho in a sea of femininity. He looked lost as he glanced from Chloe, to Lila, to Ally and back to Chloe. "I didn't know you were having friends over." He swallowed.

"Neither did I." She managed a smile. Judging by the way Ally stood so close to him, maybe she and Lila should just leave them alone. It would get him out her hair. Her gut twisted at the possibility. "Perhaps we can reschedule for another time?" she managed. "Unless you'd like to join us?" she said, looking pointedly at Ally.

"Another time, schmother time." Ally caught Jas's arm. "Don't let Chloe chase you away. We were just getting into a good conversation. Besides, a good old Dudley Do-Right like you will definitely upgrade the company." She dragged Jas possessively toward the couch, leaving Chloe to turn to Lila. What the heck is going on, she motioned. Lila frowned, but followed after them, leaving Chloe to head to the kitchen for wine. Hell, she'd like something stronger given she didn't know what she was feeling. Angry and upset that Jas was here, or was it that Ally was moving in like a shark on the prowl and Jas seemed quite willing to let her. Either way she was angry and upset and her aura seemed to seethe uncomfortably around her. She felt hot, sweaty, old and unattractive.

At one point Ally raised her hands palm together, chest high and bowed slightly. "That's how they say hello in Thailand." Then she leaned in to give Jas a too-lingering kiss on each cheek. "And that's how they do it in Italia."

Clenching her fists, Chloe turned back to the fridge. "That's not exactly true," she said into the fridge. Because in Thailand a younger person should place their hands higher when bowing to an older person—or to someone in authority. At least that's what the Buddhist monks in San Francisco taught her.

"So tell me, Mr. Policeman. What has our Chloe done wrong that you had to come around and bother her."

Chloe poured four glasses of wine and carried them into the livingroom wishing for hemlock, maybe for Jas and Ally, but more likely for herself. Anything to be put out of the misery of this situation. But Jas's pained expression didn't look much happier than she felt. "I needed to discuss a case with Ms. Main. It seems that we may have underestimated the danger she's in."

"Danger? Really?" Ally turned too-bright, too-inquisitive eyes on Chloe. "Our Chloe? That sounds more like my department." As if danger-seeking was a positive trait.

Emotional fatigue seemed to settle a thousand pound weight on Chloe's shoulders. Just what was it she wanted in this situation? Ally always brought out her worst self doubts and emotions. It was worse this time with everything already off-kilter. The way Ally had her long fingers around Jas's arm when she knew something was going on between Chloe and him, she might just have to kill her—well, hurt her at least. It was like she was the lioness and Jas was the fine-looking gazelle that she had trapped. Not that Jas meant anything to her, of course. She just didn't like to see someone put upon like that.

"Here's the wine," she said, carrying the glasses into the room.

Allyson and Lila accepted theirs, but Jas apologized and waved it away.

"On duty," he grumbled and extricated himself from Ally unlike any man Chloe had seen before. He followed her into the kitchen and cornered her by the counter. "Chloe this is serious," he said, low-voiced. "I spoke to Tom Beaton tonight. The guy's clearly nuts, but he repeats the exact same things that Forester and the suicide note said. And he added something more—that there's someone out there who will do anything to get that bracelet."

It took everything she had to ignore his scent of warm earth and leather and the way her body and her aura responded to his nearness. "Do you want coffee?" she asked, turning to the espresso maker.

"Chloe?"

He caught her arms and the shock almost made her knock the wine bottle off the counter. What was it with this man and his impact on her? Her aura positively burned as he turned her to him.

"Are you listening to me?" he murmured.

"I hear you. And I'm listening with a realistic filter. Isn't that what you'd do?" She looked up at him and was surprised to see real worry in his expression. Shook her head. "Don't worry. I'm fine. Now do you want that coffee or not?"

When he kept looking at her but still didn't answer, in self-preservation she stabbed the espresso machine button on and glanced back at him. Not a cappuccino guy, and definitely not a latte. He would drink something dark, but not quite espresso. She turned back to the machine. An Americano, then. She busied herself making the coffee, but aware all the time of Jas right behind her.

"You don't need to worry. You said he was crazy, right? I choose to believe that what he's saying is the crazy talk." Because there were too many other crazy things in her life right now.

She poured boiling water into the espresso and watched the crema dissipate. "Cream?"

He shook his head and she offered him the cup.

"Sugar?"

"I don't need sugar." But his gaze roamed her face as if he was hungry for her.

"Not fair, Jas. Ally's right there, in the next room."

She pushed past with her wine glass and hoped she showed him how much she didn't care about what he did. In the livingroom Lila had settled in an armchair and Ally reclined on the couch like a goddess.

She beckoned to Jas. "Come keep me company."

He sent a look that sought rescue in Chloe's direction, but she ignored him and sank into another chair. Ally was so much more Jas's type.

If he didn't want to sit with her, he could leave.

He sat, and Ally nestled against him. "It is so nice to sit beside a nice solid Canadian male again." She smiled, clapped his thigh with her palm and squeezed. "Manly and strong. Yum yum," Ally said.

"The poor man is sitting right here." Chloe could have shot herself for coming to Jas's defense. She should be sitting back laughing, except he actually did look miserable. "So what are your plans, Ally? How long will you be staying?"

Get Ally talking about herself and maybe she'd loosen the hooks she set into Jas.

"I really haven't any plans. I just had a hankering for some good old-fashioned home-grown peaches and cherries. There's no place that grows them like here. I was telling everyone back in Zanzibar about them and it got me a homesick. Voila! Here I am." Allyson gave the smile that had made her Miss Peachland back in the day.

"I thought you were here to sort out a few things?" Lila said from where she perched on her chair.

Ally shook out her blond fall of hair and leaned into Jas's side. "Well, I was, but who knows? With yummy guys like this one around, I just might not need to sort things at all. Just try a different kind of exciting for a change."

Chloe stood up and didn't even remember doing it. "Corporal Stone, I believe you wanted to talk to me? Perhaps we could adjourn to the patio and let Lila and Allyson relax together for a moment. Okay by you, Lila?"

A small smile curved Lila's lips as she nodded, and Chloe started for the sliding glass door.

Jas practically leapt up to follow.

She slid the door open and stepped out into cool late evening air. The light had fallen until most of the sky was indigo blue, the occasional star or planet peeking through the spaces between the towering clouds. Southward, rain-heavy clouds filled the sky over the hills, but along the water, the lights on the highway shone like quartz and carnelian. The lights of Peachland reflected in the waves like so many broken beams of light. At the moment she felt just that shattered and confused. Jas inhaled, but his pleasant scent of leather caught in her nose.

She turned to him from her place by the railing. "I hope it's okay. You looked like you could use some rescuing. You'll have to pardon Ally. She can be a bit like an avalanche sometimes, but she's basically good people."

"Really?" he said as he shook his head. He stepped up beside her. Chloe stepped back, conscious of the two potential spectators in the livingroom. He still managed to catch her arm with one hand and her skin tingled as he rubbed his fingertips lightly across her flesh.

"She does a lot of good for a lot of very poor people. She takes pictures and sells them online. The profits go to certain charities. She's received an international humanitarian award for her philanthropy."

Jas shrugged. "All well and good, but I don't flirt with women who aren't my type when the one I want is right in front of me. You."

Chloe had to close her eyes and turn away, out to the coming night over the waters of Peachland's bay. "Why do you keep doing that? Saying that? You don't want me. In fact I'm likely the exact opposite of what you want."

"So you're reading my mind, now? My heart? You're a survivor, Chloe. Strong and brilliant like one of your crystals." His voice cracked as he said it, so it had to be for a laugh.

Hard, she thought. That was what he had to mean. It was what she had done. Surrounded herself with crystals to protect herself. Fingers gripped the railing so hard her knuckles were white, she inhaled deeply. "I can't tell anything at all right now. Those visions and what happened between us..." She snuck a glance at his strong profile, but he was watching her and that just made her throat clench. "Nothing's the way it's supposed to be."

She rubbed the bracelet absently, her fingers coming to play with the door she knew too well. Iron over wood. Something stout that would never open, or perhaps never should—like her heart.

"That bracelet," Jas said and caught her arm, holding her wrist up to the light through the window. "I don't believe I'm saying this, but you have to get this off. If what Tom Beaton says is only half true, then this thing puts you in serious danger. Whatever it was that sent Beaton off his rocker is still out there, and it's coming for the bracelet—and you!"

She finally met his worried consideration. "I appreciate your concern, Jas. I do. But even if I could get it off, and I can't, did you ever think that maybe there's a reason it came to me? I've had days to think about it. Like maybe I'm here to protect it or something. Kylee said that Tom Beaton said he couldn't get the bracelet from her as long as she was alive. Well I'm alive and as long as I stay that way, he—it—whatever it is, can't get the bracelet." It sounded just as lame as when she'd first thought it. Overhead, the dark clouds were eating the stars one by one.

"You're suggesting this bracelet has *intent*?" His body had gone rigid and she could feel his anger. "Come on Chloe. I can maybe buy that some nut might be obsessed with this bracelet, but to suggest that there's some greater purpose—that's—that's nuts!"

His response was just proof to everything she'd been thinking. Especially because the more she thought about it, the more she was certain there was something greater going on. The vision. The fact the bracelet wouldn't come off—she tried it again, but the key still wouldn't fit through the lock. The way her aura was totally messed up. The way she felt so protective of the bracelet.

"If that's all you had to tell me, I think you'd better go. I'm sure there must be something better for a police detective to do."

She retraced her way to the patio door as the first pats of rain fell on her bare arms. She waited for him to join her, then stepped inside.

Ally sat up. "So come here, handsome."

"I'm afraid Corporal Stone has places he has to be, don't you, Corporal Stone?" Her expression felt as petrified as old wood, the only way she could hide the pain the decision cost her.

He studied his hands a moment then sent a thin smile in Chloe's direction. "She's right. I do. Another time, then. Chloe, one more thing; there's been another break-in here at the apartment of one of your neighbors. They only seem to be stealing jewelry, but make sure your doors and windows are locked when you're away, including anything that will help secure your patio doors. They seem to be getting in that way." Spoken with an emotionless police public service delivery. Without another word he left the apartment and headed down the corridor.

It was all she could do not to stop him.

When he'd passed beyond the hallway fire doors, she closed her apartment door and slumped against it. It was better this way. She wouldn't be forced to dredge up the past and deal with it. That whole part of her life—the part that had made her a street-fighter and comfortable carrying a knife—was better left behind and locked inside her.

With resolve, she straightened, scrubbed at her eyes and marched back to the livingroom. Settling on her chair she looked from Lila to Ally. "Now where were we?"

"Lila advised me that I might have gone a bit far in my teasing of the good constable," Ally said. "I'm sorry. I couldn't help myself. He was pretty delectable."

"Corporal. He's a corporal and a detective. He has a tough job. He was here tonight because he's worried." About her. Feeling as hollow as a geode, she turned to Lila. "You said you had some other news."

Lila nodded. "I finally heard from Colonel Bristol's son—the one who was going to write a book about his father eventually."

Fingering the silver cuff on her wrist, she wondered what it meant. There had to be something significant for Lila to stay visiting this late at night. "And?"

"He said the bracelet was something his father always kept in a safe, which was strange because it didn't look like much. The son remembered seeing it when he was a child and getting scolded and told to leave it alone when he picked it up. His father never talked about it much, but the few times he did, he referred to it as his luck."

Chloe sat up. "That was Kylee's theory—that Colonel Bristol's luck changed after he came by the bracelet." She held it up to catch the light from the kitchen.

Ally caught her wrist and tried the closure one more time. "Interesting." She grinned up at Chloe. "I had to try, didn't I? I might have had the magic touch—like Prince Charming or something."

Sighing, Chloe pulled her hand back and repositioned the bracelet so her fingers naturally found the small iron-bound door. "I don't think anyone does. No one took it off Kylee's wrist. It fell off, instead. It's like the flipping thing has to want to come off." She looked back to Lila. "So that was it? All the son knew? Not much to go on."

And suddenly she wanted the bracelet off. Wanted her life back so badly it was like a shard of crystal had embedded itself in her chest. Ever since the damn thing had come to her she'd been faced with challenges; to face her past, to face a man she couldn't have, to face whatever searched for the bracelet.

"There was more," Lila said quietly into the first pat-pat-pat of rain on the window. The building clouds were going to deliver. "The son said his father kept a journal almost until the day he died. He apparently started when he was a very young man because he'd once had dreams of being a writer. He never became the writer, but the journaling continued. Even through the war, apparently."

Lila held up her hand to stop Chloe's questions. "He said that he has a copy in Ottawa."

"Can he send us a copy? Maybe it will have answers." From the patio the pat of rain picked up tempo.

A slow smile formed on Lila's face. "Better than that. He said that after his father died, his mother donated the originals to the Kelowna Historical Society. That's where I was this afternoon—making copies of the lot of them. They're in the car."

§

If there was such a thing as fate, then it certainly wasn't working in his favor. Jas hunched under the first soaking wave of rain as he jogged past the unmarked car and down Beach Avenue toward the campground gate. Normally he'd take the car, but if someone was watching it would clearly connect him with a specific motorhome. That would undermine the whole purpose of the stakeout. As it was, his phone had been vibrating ever since he walked into Chloe's apartment building. When he'd checked the messages were all from Forester and all pretty much the same. *WTF U doing?*

At the moment he didn't know.

The rain started in earnest and plastered his hair against his head and his shirt against his body so that he might as well have leapt in the complex pool. He stepped over the low chain gate the campground used to keep people from indiscriminately slipping in and out during the night and slogged along the dirt roadway to the motorhome. Most of the tents were already lights-out dark, though a few of the larger motorhomes still had lights on. The huge willows and poplar stole whatever light there was and seemed to funnel the raindrops onto his head. On the way he stepped into an unseen pothole and filled his left shoe with water. Perfect.

Just like the visit with Chloe was perfect. That Allyson woman had been like a steamroller. Normally he would have put her in her place, but she was Chloe's friend. He'd tried to be nice, infuriating as it was. What he'd really wanted was for the other women to leave and let him have a nice quiet talk with Chloe. Instead he'd blown it big time. Idiot. Maybe if he'd played up to Allyson he could have at least hung around long enough to finish the conversation with Chloe.

He rapped once on the motorhome side and the vehicle swayed as someone came to the door. Forester opened it. It was dark inside, but the scent of strong coffee escaped.

"Where the fuck've you been, partner?" Forester demanded as Jas climbed inside.

"Where do you think? I went to see Chloe. To warn her." He grabbed a tea towel off the oven door and toweled off his hair. What he really needed was a change of clothes.

"You saw Beaton, then."

He nodded, already in the bedroom grabbing a clean shirt from the small bag he'd brought with him. "Interviewed him. It was the strangest fucking thing I've ever seen. Guy was lucid as you or me one moment. The next he'd gone off the deep end about something big and dark that took him over."

Just thinking about it his skin prickled as he toweled off. He pulled the shirt on, but it didn't help against his inner chill. He sank down on the edge of the narrow twin bed he'd used earlier. "It was weird, man. Really weird. Weird enough I almost want to believe him. Or have to." He scrubbed his fingernails through his hair and looked up at the dark figure of Forester. "Is that what it felt like for you? That you knew something was taking you over, and you were helpless to do anything about it?"

Forester sank down on the other bed. "Something like that. For me it was more like I was gone until the very end, here in Peachland. I just count my lucky stars that for some reason I was able to put myself back together."

"Were you?" Jas studied his partner who was like a shadow across from him. Would Forester fall apart like Tom Beaton had? Was he a time bomb waiting to go off?

The gleam of white teeth showed that Forester grinned. "Sure I was. You told the OIC that exact thing today. Besides, if there's anyone whose sanity needs questioning, it's you. What the hell were you thinking? You come screaming into the curb like the cavalry and then leap out and positively run into the building that we've staked out. You think that might give a clue to the perp that someone's watching?"

"What do you think?" Jas looked away from Forester out to the expanse of the Willowview Terrace building.

"I called Forensics about the third condo break-in. The M.O.'s the same: break in through the patio door while the owners are away, take only the jewelry. Interesting thing here is apparently there was someone watching the place for the owners—the woman who lives next door, named Chloe Main. Patrol wants to know if they should interview her."

Jas let the question hang in the air. At the Willowview a lot of the apartments were dark—it was after ten p.m.—but light still showed around the patio walls of the apartment overlooking the water at the end of the building. Chloe's place. "You know, Beaton went on about how this great dark force was after the bracelet and wouldn't stop until he had it. I had to warn Chloe. I told her to have it cut off. Fat lot of good it did. She spouted off some nonsense about the bracelet being on her arm for a purpose."

He shook his head and repositioned himself to peer out the rear window of the vehicle and grabbed the binoculars sitting there. There was nothing to see. The rain made a thin curtain across the Willowview Terrace gardens that swirled in gusting wind off the lake. Nothing moved in the darkness except a couple of women huddling together as they ran toward a red SUV. Lila Weber and Allyson, so Chloe was alone. He scanned back up to her apartment. The lights were still on, so maybe she wasn't feeling any better about their meeting than he was.

"You should get some shut-eye. I'll watch until one and then get you up. Three hour shifts."

Forester grunted behind him, but the man stretched out on the other bunk. Jas went forward for a cup of the spoon-eating coffee. He tried it and almost put it back. That would keep him up all right.

He settled by the window with the binoculars again. Chloe's lights were still on.

"You know you're going to have to deal with this infatuation," Forester's voice came out of the darkness.

"Tell me about it. It's like one of those cases that won't let you rest." He kept the binoculars to his eyes and kept on watching. Outside the sky lit with lightning soon followed by the crash of thunder. Somehow it mirrored just what he was feeling.

CHAPTER 16

THE NEXT MORNING BROKE BRIGHT AND SHINY AS a new penny even if Jas felt like he'd been through the wringer. He hadn't had a good night's sleep since the Jensen abduction and meeting Chloe Main. Last night had brought it home to him. Usually on stakeout, when it came his turn to sleep, he could sleep the slumber of the dead in no time flat. Last night his head had been too full of Chloe. How she'd looked tired. How her hand kept straying to the bracelet. Her attacks. And her total rejection of him.

Her visions had been like a different kind of possession. Though not as horrible as Tom Beaton had demonstrated, it still wasn't natural.

Sipping another cup of coffee—he'd lost count at how many, he peered out the back of the motorhome as Forester puttered around the small kitchen scrambling some eggs. At least there was that—they could have a warm meal instead of living on doughnuts and gas station coffee.

With daylight they could escape the motorhome and he already had plans for his day: home, shower, a nap and follow-up with the limo company. He'd received the man's name from the highway patrol who had stopped him, but the contact information was the company's. He needed to talk to the man.

After breakfast with Forester, they both stepped out into the soggy campground. Thankfully the ground was such porous sand that there was no more standing water, but tents and firewood weren't so lucky and the scents of wet canvas and smoky fire permeated the area under the trees. They drove into West Kelowna together and parted ways in the parking lot. Forester headed home to his apartment in Kelowna. Jas climbed into his vehicle and just sat there.

So whatchagoin' ta do there, Stone? You got a partner who was spouting crazy stuff except now he mostly keeps it to himself, a perp who seems sane one minute and crazy as a shit-house rat the next, rumors of something supernatural going on, and a woman you like who's involved with mystical mumbo-jumbo.

There was a whole lot of shit going down and the connecting shreds of evidence—if you could call it that—was all the stuff he didn't believe in.

No. That was crazy. He might like Chloe, and he might even believe she was in danger, but from a supernatural force? Come on. If he believed that he'd be as suspect as the rest of them.

He climbed out of his car. He might need a shower and some clean clothes but he needed to get in touch with reality more. The best way to get that was to immerse himself in police work. He strode into the detachment, waved at the front desk clerk and buzzed into the secure area. His office was blissfully quiet as he sat down at his desk.

It was a quick job to dial the limo company and talk to the dispatcher.

"I'm following up on the discussion we had yesterday," he said. "I need the contact information for the driver of the limo that was leased by the *SchwarzeNacht Corporation*."

"Just a moment. I left it for the evening shift to dig out," said the woman who sounded like someone's grandmother. The shuffling of papers came through the phone. "I'm sorry, Corporal Stone, it must have been busy last night. My request is sitting right here, with no action on."

Perfect. Just bloody perfect. "Is there any chance you can dig it out for me? The matter is urgent."

"Well, it's busy here during dayshift, but tell you what. I'll try to get to it and will give you a call if I do. Okay? Now what was your number again?"

He gave it to her, even though he'd given it to her three times when he called the day before. He hung up and stared at his computer screen, trying to get his frustration under control. Why was it that when you really needed something, the whole world seemed to get in the way? He opened his email and read the list of messages and clicked the mail closed again. Nothing he *had* to answer at the moment. Maybe he should leave and go back to his apartment like he'd told Forester, but the way he was feeling there was no way he was going to sleep today.

Oh what the hell. He was accomplishing nothing here. Shoving his chair back until it hit the filing cabinet behind, he stood and headed for the door. In the hall, he got exactly five paces before the office phone started shrilling.

Leave or stay. He swung around to take the call.

"Stone," he said when he picked up.

"Corporal Stone, thank goodness I caught you." The voice of the limo company dispatcher rang through the line. "Right after we hung up there was a lull in the traffic so I looked Gurmeet Atwal's number up for you."

He copied it down, thanked her and hung up. Perhaps things weren't going to be so bad. He stabbed the outgoing call button again and dialed.

The line purred in his ear once, twice, three times. On the fourth ring a masculine voice picked up with a sullen-sounding "hello."

"Is this Gurmeet Atwal?" he asked.

"Who's calling?" The masculine voice sounded cautious.

Jas sighed. It was going to be that kind of day. Nothing was going to be straightforward. Well, all he could do was try. "Corporal Jasper Stone calling from the West Kelowna RCMP. I'm trying to get in touch with Gurmeet Atwal to ask him about a recent limo fare. Are you Gurmeet Atwal?"

There was a pause and then, "I didn't do nothing illegal."

"Mr. Atwal, this is not about any personal actions of yours as far as I know. We are trying to identify a passenger you had in your limousine and we were hoping you could help us."

"Oh. Who?" Perhaps a bit more forthcoming?

Jas rolled his eyes. "That's what we're hoping you can assist us with Mr. Atwal." If the man only lived here in Kelowna they could do this in person and Atwal would likely drop the attitude in the face of official police presence. As it was, Jas was going to have to tread carefully.

"Our investigation shows that you were driving a limousine in or around Peachland BC on July first. Do you recall that occasion, Mr. Atwal?"

There was stony silence over the phone.

"Mr. Atwal?"

"Yeah. I'm here. I was just trying to remember."

And just how hard could it be to remember when the man usually drove in Vancouver and was actually stopped and searched at the side of the highway? "Let me reacquaint you. It's a small town along the lake south of Kelowna. There was a major celebration going on for Canada Day and the town's centennial."

"Oh! That town. Yeah. I was there all right. The fare said he had a package to pick up. He was real antsy when the traffic snarled up. Finally decided it wasn't worth the fuss and yelled at the traffic control folks to let us pull a U-turn and get the heck outta that mess. You know what I mean?"

At least that concurred with what the witnesses at the event had said, so maybe the guy wasn't going to be as much of an obstacle and Jas feared. "Can you tell me who your passenger was?"

"Some foreign guy. He was big. Strong looking. You know— one of those big blond guys like the bad guy clone in *Blade Runner*."

"You don't know his name?"

"If I did, I don't remember it. Hey, it was foreign. And I see a lot of fares in a week."

"So what did you call him?"

"Sir. What'd'ya think?"

Jas bit back a retort at the man's lip. "I think you're taking a little too much pleasure in not remembering."

"That's your problem ain't it?" Atwal lipped back apparently emboldened by the telephone line between them.

"Mr. Atwal, I'd appreciate it if you'd take a minute and think back to the first time you met your passenger. You must have known his name then. I'd like you to think back to a half hour before the pickup and tell me about what happened." Jas held his breath. Would the guy cooperate?

The sigh was audible over the phone. "Fine. I got nothing better to do with my life."

"So I was driving to the airport, international terminal 'cause I had a pickup. It was raining, I remember because there were a lot of assholes on the road. I got to the terminal, parked in the limo zone and made up my sign, then went in to collect my fare. The guy came out and saw the sign and I shook his hand and welcomed him to Vancouver and took his bag. We went out to the car and when we were inside he dropped the bomb that I was driving up to the Okanagan. I mean who drives when they can fly, man?"

Jas sorted through the notes he'd taken and looked at the phone. "Mr. Atwal, you mentioned writing the passenger's name down so that he could find you at the airport. What was the name?"

Dead silence over the phone, then, "Well, ain't that strange. I can see myself writing it down, but when I try to recall what it was, it's like something black blocks it out."

Was the guy scamming him? The voice didn't sound like it. As a matter of fact the guy sounded a little freaked by the fact that he couldn't recall.

"Okay. You said you shook his hand and welcomed him. What did you say?"

More silence and then, "Damn! It's like trying to grab hold of Jell-o, man. It's there, but when I go for it, it's gone. And I usually do remember the names—especially foreign ones."

Jas thought a moment. The guy's attitude had changed partway through the interview. He'd become cooperative. The guy's obvious reaction to being unable to remember made Jas inclined to believe him. He sighed. This case was just getting weirder and weirder.

"Mr. Atwal. I'm going to give you my phone number. If you happen to recall the name, please give me a call. This is an urgent case. We're trying to stop a kidnapper."

"Hey man, I get anything I'll call. This is just so weird, because I can picture my hand writing and I can even remember the feel, but what I wrote just isn't there."

"That's fine," Jas said. "I'd just really appreciate it if you'd keep trying. Now, one more question: can you give me a further description of the man you picked up? Height, color of hair and eyes and so on?"

"Why sure. That's no problem. He was big, like I said. Sort of filled up space. One of those larger than life personalities, I guess, or someone who's used to ordering people around. His hair was blond. Well, no, maybe more brown. In fact it was pretty dark in places."

Jas looked at the phone again. "Mr. Atwal, what are you saying? Was his hair blond or brown or dark?"

"Jeezus, man, I don't know. I have him straight in my head. I know I'd know him if I saw him, but when I go for the details I get Jell-o again. "

Either the guy was scamming him or there was something even hinkier with this case. Given everything that had happened until now, he was betting on hinky. "Mr. Atwal, I think that's all the questions I have. Again, if you can please think about what the man looked like and write down your description, that would be most appreciated. Here's my number." He gave it. "Now there's a chance I may obtain a photo of the man that I'll want to send to you for identification purposes. Will that be okay?"

"Fine man. Always happy to help the RCMP."

"Thank you for your time." Jas hung up and sat looking at the receiver in his hand. What the hell was going on? People who are trying to remember don't generally describe the problems remembering that Gurmeet Atwal did. They get some details straight while others they aren't so sure of. And forgetting a name that you both wrote down and used in conversation, was also less common. The way Atwal described the memory eluding him was much more like a victim of something traumatic where their brain wiped out the traumatic event. Except this wasn't traumatic. It was a name and a face—almost as if only specific things had been wiped out.

Was that even possible?

Hell, there were too many things about this case that weren't possible. And the erasure of memory was too close to what Forester talked about. Danny remembered speaking to a witness at Moira Burns' hit and run scene, and then basically coming-to in Peachland knowing that he was watching Lila Weber, but not being sure why.

A cold air ran down his back and he shivered. He didn't like that he didn't understand what was going on, or the motivation behind what was happening. It went against everything he represented as a police officer. The fact that it all seemed to lead back to the bracelet on Chloe Main's arm just made it worse. He had to talk to her and set things straight because she clearly didn't get just how dangerous this situation might be. Someone or something that could erase memories and make people go crazy was not a good thing. He also needed to set her straight how he felt about her—and that he wanted a chance to fix things between them.

He checked his watch. Coming on noon. No time like the present. If he didn't run home for a shower maybe he could take her for a more successful lunch than last time.

§

Eyes feeling gravelly, Chloe rubbed the bridge of her nose and leaned on one of the glass display cases from *This and That*. It sat on the front porch next to two others, partially blocking access to the stairs. After the rains last night the air felt refreshingly cool, but the sun was raising mist from the damp pavement. The steel-colored still lake promised a hot day to come. Inside the shop, the floor had been swept and they had washed it off. They were just waiting for it to dry in the corners before they started staining. While they were waiting, Chloe had thought she'd use the time to examine more of her crystals, but she was having trouble focusing on the stones in the tray in front of her. Not good, when she had three appointments booked for healing sessions later this week. She needed the right kind of stones with the right kind of resonance if she was going to have the desired effect. She sighed and gave up on the stones and prowled restlessly around the porch, just as she'd prowled around the apartment last night after Lila and Ally left.

Strangely, no boats marred the lake's pristine surface. Just a light dusting of cloud dragged their reflections across the surface. Serene. That was the word for it. Serene as Lila. Serene as she had always prided herself on being. Except today she had a sense of foreboding and these days serenity seemed to escape her.

"Hello!" A female voice called from the back of the house. Kylee.

"Out on the porch," Chloe called through the open front door and pasted a smile on her face.

Kylee breezed in wearing faded trekking shorts and an overlarge t-shirt knotted at the waist that was probably Brett's. In white tennis shoes, her long tanned legs looked oh-so-young and coltish.

"You get the delivery okay?" Chloe asked as Kylee tiptoed across the still-damp floor.

"Yup. It's going to be a heap of work building up the beds, but it'll be worth it. The stuff that will grow in that garden will feed us all, all through next summer. Thanks for letting me come in late." She set her purse in the drawer under the cash register and scanned the room. "Where is everyone?"

"Lila's in town buying groceries and Reggie's off somewhere with Ally."

"She's got a pretty big personality, doesn't she?"

Chloe smiled and nodded and Kylee scanned the room again. "Well I guess that leaves the painting up to us." She looked down at Chloe's tray of stones. There were fifteen in the 'to-be-examined' side and only one in the 'examined' side. Kylee pursed her lips, which looked impish and cute on her. She chewed her lip.

"So. Still not making much progress, huh?"

Chloe shook her head and wished she'd stashed the tray away. She looked out at the lake. There was deep water there and possibly Ogopogo, the lake's fabled monster, just like the potential for this discussion.

"You know you've got us all worried, right?"

Darn it. Kylee was right beside her and how had she done that without Chloe knowing? She *always* sensed people's movements around her, just as she always knew their 'word' when she met them. But it wasn't coming so easily right now. Just this morning she'd almost blown it when a woman had come to the store and Chloe had met her on the walkway asking her to come back next week when they'd be open. She'd almost gotten into an argument with the woman when the woman had asked to speak to the manager—read Lila—and it had only been when the woman produced her card—she was a freelance journalist and doing a piece for a well-known travel magazine on Okanagan destinations—that Chloe calmed the situation. She'd eventually promised the woman an interview tomorrow.

If only she could calm herself.

Kylee placed a warm palm on Chloe's arm. "I know I haven't been around as long as Lila or Reggie, but I've done something neither of them have done. I've worn this. You can talk to me." Her hand slid down and formed a warm link over the bracelet. "There were times I actually thought it came to me for a purpose and that's why it wouldn't come off."

A chill ran up Chloe's back and she nodded. "I know. I get that feeling, too." The question was—for what purpose.

"Doesn't that scare you?"

She looked down and met Kylee's wide blue eyes.

Yes, but... "No. Should it?"

Kylee's hand tightened over Chloe's. "Are you forgetting the day that the man came into the shop looking for it? You were terrified. You said that he was evil." She caught the silver chain with the single large jet pendant that Chloe wore over her t-shirt regardless of the fact she was painting. "You said he totally burned out the protective power in the stones you wore that day. Chloe! Come on! You have to remember *that*! It took you a long time to settle after that."

If she ever had.

For a small woman, Kylee showed considerable strength as she dragged Chloe over to the wicker seating. "You sit down, now." Apparently she could also be ferocious. Chloe sat.

"Chloe Main, when I saw you put that bracelet on I didn't think anything until you couldn't get it off again. I thought the story was over with me. Then I was concerned, but Brett knew I was still upset because of what happened so he took me away for a few days. But now you seem so different—upset, unsettled and now you tell me you're not ever worried..." She stroked the black pendant again and leaned down to catch both of Chloe's hands and look into her eyes. "What's wrong with you, Chloe? Because there has to be something the matter for you not to take care."

Chloe tugged her arms free and held up her hands in a football timeout. "Hold it. Hold on here. I do care. I just don't think that getting all hysterical about the situation is going to serve anyone. Why are you coming at me like this?"

"Because you seem to be drifting around in a daze. You were bad after you put the bracelet on, but now... now, you're a basket case." She motioned at the tray of stones on the counter. "Look at those stones. From what I've seen you usually sort eight to ten a morning, and you've been working on this batch for the past four days and getting nowhere."

Had it really been so bad? Four days since her past came back to bite her. She couldn't meet Kylee's regard. Was it true? She didn't remember being as scared as Kylee described her, but then she barely remembered the man in the store either. Except for the eyes.

A bigger chill ran up her back and she looked down at her hands. "I guess you're right. It's like I remember what you say about being afraid, but I've got this fluffy rose-colored lens between me and what happened. All the terror has been milked away." She sat there trying to puzzle out the meaning. That alone should make her afraid, but she wasn't.

"What if the bracelet somehow affects the wearer? What if the bracelet helps deal with fear because otherwise you might be too afraid to do what you have to do—to meet your purpose. It could make you feel like nothing's the matter."

Chloe looked at her. "Okay... now you are channeling things I might say, and I am officially worried."

An exasperated look was all the comment got her. "For me, it was like the bracelet helped bring Brett and me together. It got me over my fear of trusting somebody again. Tell me something. Have you ever seen a door in real life that was identical to one of the ones on the bracelet?"

"Never." She held up the bracelet, beginning to be tired of this lecture. "Besides, there are no men in my life." And no inner demons that she needed to deal with. *Liar*. Okay, none that she was in any way prepared to deal with.

"Maybe it doesn't have to be a man, just someone you love very deeply."

Chloe rolled her eyes. "So my cat is making my aura go off kilter, is that what you're saying?"

"Ah-hah! So you see it too! You know that something's the matter. Chloe how are you going to protect yourself if that's the case. You said it yourself before. This thing hunting the bracelet is evil. If you'd seen what had stared out of Tom Beaton's eyes, you'd be frightened."

Heaving herself up out of the chair, she looked down at Kylee. "According to you, I have faced that evil, but I'm not afraid now. So I get on with life and don't go all trembly about it." She headed for her stones and packed them up, then abandoned the front porch for the store. The floor had to be dry enough to start painting now, because she seriously needed to be doing more than listening to Kylee's lecture.

"It's that Corporal Stone, isn't it? Something happened between you that frightened you." Kylee said from the open doorway.

Chloe spun around so fast she almost knocked over one of the paint cans she'd opened. "There is *nothing* going on between Corporal Stone and me. Now I'll thank you to keep your amateur psychoanalysis to yourself and let me get on with the work that needs to be done."

But the obstinate woman stepped in front of her again. "Once upon a time a woman I respect said that you have to look inside you to know what you really want and need. Then you have to be true to that and go for it—or something to that effect—or suffer the consequences."

"Don't throw my words back at me." Trying to hold onto her dignity, she shoved the tray of stones under the cash register counter, grabbed a paint tray, paint and roller, and prepared to begin painting the floor.

"You're scared on so many levels just like I was. You might not be throwing your heart to the wind, but you've got a really nice guy who seems to be interested and you're refusing to see it. You're running away, Chloe! I *never* would have figured you for a coward."

Chloe stopped rolling the paint onto the floor and just held on tight to the wooden handle. Rigid with anger, because what right did this strip of a woman have to lecture her like this, she turned around just as the bell over the front door dinged. As if Kylee'd conjured him out of the air, a rumpled-looking Jas stood there.

Not at all what she needed.

CHAPTER 17

Jas almost held up his hands to protect himself from Chloe's angry expression. The store smelled of wood stain and the walls were freshly painted, but the tension between the two women was more like what he'd face at a knife fight. Kylee Jensen looked like she was almost in tears as she stood next to the doorway, while Chloe looked like she might just like to plunge the roller handle she held into Kylee's heart. Her face was alabaster white and hard, hard, hard. Immutable as the stones she so loved.

Typical. Like everything else had gone as planned today.

Kylee took a deep breath and seemed to shake off whatever had her upset. She glanced in Chloe's direction and then back at him. "Corporal Stone. To what do we owe the pleasure? Has there been a break in the case?"

Chloe had retreated behind the cashier counter and was looking at him with those purple-tinged eyes that he simply could not forget.

"Unfortunately, no, but we're pursuing leads. I wanted to talk to Chloe because I seem to recall she spoke to a man who came into the store and was asking questions." He'd planned on asking her for lunch, but in the face of her obvious anger, this at least provided an excuse to talk with her. While mulling over the chauffeur's story he'd remembered Chloe's story from the night of

Kylee's abduction. The lack of information about the limousine's passenger was beginning to bother him.

The two women exchanged glances that indicated something was up.

"Funny," Kylee said, her voice carefully neutral. "We were just talking about exactly that. And it's just about time for Chloe to take her break, so maybe you could have lunch together."

Chloe shot her a look that might have killed another woman, but the little blond only lifted her chin in a 'dare you' motion and smiled sweetly.

If he didn't tread very carefully this could all blow up in his face. "What do you say, Chloe? Let me interview you over lunch?"

She shot a cursed look at Kylee. "You want to interview me, fine. Just fine. But we'll do it here. Lila always has something in the kitchen for lunch."

Marching like someone going to the firing squad, she shoved through the beaded curtain toward the kitchen. The beads clacked softly behind her.

"Walk softly," Kylee said. "For some reason you and the bracelet both set her off. If I didn't know better I'd say that you're somehow connected."

He nodded and looked her up and down. Him and bracelet connected? What was it with these women? Taking a deep breath, he followed Chloe to the kitchen.

As he remembered, it was filled with light, the bright yellow cupboards and white walls seeming to radiate happiness, except for the shadows in Chloe's face as she faced him. She had her arms crossed on her chest. "Okay. What's your question?"

"I, uh, thought you were going to have lunch."

Her lips pressed into a line. "Maybe I've lost my appetite."

He shrugged and went to open the fridge door. A platter of fried chicken lay covered in plastic wrap. "This looks good." He hauled the chicken out. He pulled a bag of spinach from the crisper along with some feta cheese, red onion and a bottle of high-end orange and ginger dressing.

"Just what do you think you're doing?" Chloe said from her spot by the door.

"Making us lunch. I seem to recall you like salad and I'm more of a meat guy. I figured this could work for both of us."

"This is Lila's food. You have no right..."

He spun around and caught her by her shoulders. "Chloe Main, I have every right. I'm in the midst of an investigation—three investigations, actually, and I need to interview a witness—you. If this is the only way I can do it, then I'll do it. I want to find this guy and you may have critical information."

Her gaze edged over his face as if assessing the cracks in his story. Not finding any she finally sighed. "All right. I'll clean the spinach."

She filled the sink and washed the greens while he sliced paper-thin slices of red onion and crumbled a healthy dose of feta. When she was done spinning the water out of the spinach, she claimed a large Italian ceramic bowl out of the cupboard, took an orange out of the bowl of fruit on the counter and chopped it up, then added it to the salad he was building in the bowl. Jas carried the salad and chicken to the old-fashioned breakfast nook in the corner. "Plates?"

She pulled two bright turquoise plates from the cupboard and silverware from a drawer and joined him. Silently she filled her plate with salad, then pushed the bowl and chicken at him. Her eyes had gone amethyst hard. Okay. It was all on him to make this work, but he'd interviewed unwilling witnesses before.

"Thank you for agreeing to speak with me," he said.

Chloe avoided his scrutiny and stabbed her salad with her fork. Stabbed again. And again, but didn't lift anything to her mouth.

All right. Let's see how she did in the face of officialdom. He hauled out his recorder and placed it between them on the table.

"July seventh, 2014 at 12:50 hours. This is the interview of Chloe Main conducted by Corporal Jasper Stone in the kitchen of *This and That* jewelry store. Miss Main, would you please identify yourself for the tape?"

He waited a heartbeat. Finally she looked at the recorder. "This is Chloe Main."

"Miss Main. I am interviewing you regarding events on and around July First, Canada Day. It is my understanding that you were approached in this store by someone claiming to be looking for a family heirloom. Can you tell me about that?"

At this, she raised her eyes to his. "Is that what this is about?"

"I'd like you to tell me the story."

At his explanation, her anger seemed to dissipate. She nodded. "It was about a week before, I think. Kylee had stepped out to lunch with Brett, my brother, and I was minding the store. They were running into West Kelowna to place a printing order, because Kylee and I had just come up with a brainwave for advertising our Canada Day sale." She smiled and got a faraway look in her eyes as she shook her head.

"They were so cute together. We all knew they were going to be a couple even though I think Kylee was fighting it some. But off they went and I was humming around the shop, sorting some of my stones and dealing with the lunchtime customers." She frowned and her throat worked. She looked at him for a moment.

"I remember I noticed a limo double-parked outside and thinking how unpopular the driver was going to be given how busy Beach Avenue can get in the daytime. This man got out of the car and came up the walk and I remember thinking that he looked really out of place because he was in this austere business suit. Then he entered the store like he owned the place."

An involuntary shiver ran through her.

"Tell me more about that." He prompted.

"He looked around the store like it was his and I felt like I was a flyspeck on the wall, beneath notice. Then all his attention fell on me and he asked who I was. I didn't want to tell him. So help me, I felt like if I told him I'd be lost, or an important part of me would be. So I asked him what he wanted and who he was. He told me that the store had come into possession of something that belonged to his family. When I said I didn't think we had anything of significant value in the store, he said it was not something anyone else would notice. He called it a trinket." She clenched her eyes closed and her hand was a fist around her fork.

"He demanded to know where we had it, and he—did something." Her free hand wrapped itself around the black pendant she wore. Then she opened her eyes and they were huge and black and frightened. "He looked at me—into me and I thought I was torn loose from my body. My beads burned against me and I managed to hold on as he demanded that I show him everything. I did, and he seemed to be able to see beyond what was in the shop, as if he searched the house with some other sense. Then he seemed to be disgusted and he turned and left and I was so cold I ran outside onto the porch after he was gone."

Her face was pale and her breath seemed to come in tight little gasps. Her knuckles were pure white around the fork.

"Are you all right?" he asked.

She shook herself at that and the fork clattered to her plate of uneaten food. "I'm fine. Now is there anything else?"

"Yes. Could you please describe this man who came into the store?"

She took a deep breath. "Tall. He spoke with a German accent. Deep, guttural voice, but elegant in the way he enunciated. Crisp. He was fair skinned and his hair was—" she seemed to strain for the answer. "Blond! White blond, almost like it was going white, not gray, but not."

She was actually panting as if she'd had to work hard for what should be a simple answer, and both hands were twined and straining around the pendant. She met his gaze. "That was harder than it should have been."

He nodded. "You're not the first person who's struggled to describe him. One more question for this file. Did this man ever tell you his name? You said you asked him to identify himself." She'd gotten out the description. Maybe she could get the name, too, even though it seemed as if she was dealing with the same unnatural memory loss as Gurmeet Atwal.

Chloe's face turned puzzled and she closed her eyes again. "I did ask him. I know I did. And I'm pretty sure he answered. As a matter of fact I can see him open his mouth to answer, but my head fills with the sound of a million insects clicking, buzzing, whirring when he answers. I can't hear what he says." She opened her eyes again. "I'm sorry. It's like white noise in my head."

It was the oddest description he'd ever heard for being unable to remember. He sighed. "Well, it's more than we've gotten from other witnesses. Thank you. Now can I ask you about another case? This involves your neighbors."

"The Singhs?" Her expression was puzzled again.

"Not the Singhs. The Flanders." He flipped to a previous page of his notebook to reference the names. "Mitchell and Margaret. I believe they live on the other side of you from the Singhs?"

"The corner apartment by the road, yes. Has something happened?" She genuinely seemed mystified.

"I understand that they were away on holidays and just returned yesterday."

"Yes. I just saw them in the hall. They seemed relieved to be home. I—I watered their plants while they were gone."

"Tell me about that," he asked, studying her face.

For a moment she looked totally nonplussed. "They have a number of larger plants and orchids that required care. Margaret left me specific instructions about which plant to water which day. She has quite the system. I followed it to the letter except for one day." She looked away and swallowed. "I was supposed to water three of her orchids after work but it didn't happen." She colored slightly and he could guess which day she referred to. He shifted uncomfortably in his chair.

"Tell me about the apartment, please?"

She shrugged. "It's like the mirror opposite of mine given they face out onto the road. They have a large patio like mine. They've got it decorated much more showroom style than mine, but the plants definitely make it a unique space that speaks of them. I don't know. What do you want to know?"

"Where does Margaret Flanders keep her valuables?"

She stopped dead. "I have no idea. We're neighbors, not good friends. I haven't told her where I keep my safe either." She sat up suddenly. "Allan. Damn. He still hasn't reclaimed his jewelry to take to his safety deposit box."

"What are you talking about?"

Chloe shook her head. "Another neighbor. After the Singhs were broken into he asked if I would hold onto a bunch of his jewelry. I couldn't take it all, but a lot of it is in my safe at home as far as I know. The Flanders were broken into, too, weren't they?"

He nodded, watching her face as she figured it out. She was a quick study.

"I'll bet I was the only one with a key and so I'm a suspect." Her lovely eyes had lost their violet color and were deepest blue.

"You would be, except that the entry was gained via the patio."

"Except I could have tried to make it look like the patio door was the break-in point to be consistent with the Singh's place. That is how the thief broke in, right?"

"It is."

She shook her head. "I didn't know Margaret had any jewelry. I mean she wears costume stuff like things she'd bought here, but nothing I would have thought worth stealing. I feel so sorry for her. She's a pretty sentimental soul. She has plants that are cuttings from one that used to be owned by her grandmother. She said sometimes she talks to them for advice."

She might have had a key, but Chloe Mains was not the perpetrator. She was a million other things, but not that and she'd made it eminently clear that his error the afternoon when he'd taken her out for lunch was a deal breaker. It was time for him to move on. He flipped his notebook closed and stood, his meal still largely uneaten. "Thank you for your time."

Her eyes were the deepest blue he'd ever seen, the lavender a small ring around the edge. Her hands were hidden in her lap, but she had a look of pensive waiting about her. "I'm truly sorry for everything that's happened between us. I won't bother you further." He managed a smile. "You should eat something now that you've murdered that salad."

Without waiting for a response he turned and retreated out of the kitchen, down the hall, to nod at Kylee and head out the front door. Somehow the bright blue sky seemed dimmer and his prospects a little grimmer.

Well, he'd ended relationships before and he'd gotten over it and this—whatever it was—was nothing that anyone could truly call a relationship. It had been a one-sided, unrequited love kinda thing and he was not the kind of man to go mooning around about one woman. There were lots of other fish in the sea. The good-looking blond, Ally, came to mind, but he was *not* going to be stupid enough to get involved with one of Chloe's friends.

He climbed into his vehicle and headed home for his shower, hoping he could move on from Chloe as easily as he could put on fresh clothes.

§

Chloe watched him go, listening to his solid footsteps retreating down the hall, his scent of leather and earth fading from the room. The sunlight through the kitchen window filled the place he had been, strong hands busy taking notes, solid brown eyes ever watching. It hadn't been like a cop watching a perpetrator, it had been like a lover trying to capture a face so he'd always remember it.

Jas wasn't come back—at least not for her. He'd do his job, and that might bring them into contact, but the pursuit was over. She should feel relieved, like she could breathe again, but instead her chest felt empty and her eyes were over-full. She swallowed to clear her clogged throat and considered the spinach tattered on her plate. She wasn't hungry, but Jas had said she should eat. Bossy thing.

No, it was a last caring comment from a man she'd sent packing.

She found her fork, stabbed a few bits of spinach and a cube of feta and put them in her mouth. Even with the orange and ginger dressing, they tasted like nothing. She forced a swallow and shoved the plate away. The chicken she returned to the fridge and the salad she covered and placed next to it, even though the spinach was wilting. The debris on their plates, she threw into the green-waste disposal bag and then put the dishes in the dishwasher. She wandered back to the shop and Kylee glanced up at her from where she was rolling paint onto the floor. She glanced at her watch.

"That was fast. Your lunch break's not over."

Chloe shook her head. "I think I'd rather take a shorter lunch today."

"I saw Jas leave. Everything okay?"

It was like Kylee's words came down a long tunnel. Chloe only shook her head. "He won't be coming back."

"Chloe, no!" Kylee was across the room to her. "How could that happen? Did you fight?"

She shook her head and leaned against the doorway that led to the kitchen. The beads rattled around her shoulders. It felt wrong, just like everything else felt.

"What happened, then? What makes you think he's gone for good? I mean the guy's clearly crazy about you. He'd be a fool to leave."

"Nope. Not a fool. In fact he's a smart man. I made it pretty clear that I didn't want anything to do with him. He finally got the message." She forced a smile. "It's much better this way." She looked down at the bracelet, but in the dimmer light of the store it didn't look so much like jewelry as like a shackle she bore. She drew in a deep breath. Maybe now without the distraction of Jas she could focus on what the bracelet meant.

CHAPTER 18

T‍HE AFTERNOON PASSED IN A FOG FOR C‍HLOE. Reggie returned with Ally at about three o'clock from a spur-of-the-moment horseback riding trip in the mountains on the eastern edge of Kelowna. Both of them moaned about their poor bruised bottoms and retreated to their respective living spaces to shower and change. The floor stain dried so she and Kylee rolled the heavy display cases inside into the proposed new configuration. It looked good. When they were done, she sent Kylee home and that left Chloe to finish cleaning up the debris of their labor. She did and then stood there in the quiet of the shop admiring their handiwork. There were benefits of being the part owner.

At least the empty store was peaceful, even if her mind and emotions churned and her stomach felt like a lump of coal.

At five-thirty, purse in hand, she headed for her apartment, praying that now, finally, she'd be able to find some peace and calm. Jas wouldn't be around to bother her anymore. A good long meditation session amongst her crystals would surely do the trick.

The sun was still bright on the mountains across the lake, but Peachland was caught in the shadows of the western hills. The air was still July-warm, though, and children still splashed in the water, though their parents had pulled on cover-ups and shorts over their bathing suits. Portable gas barbecues had been started on picnic tables, and mothers were pulling food out of coolers.

When she crossed the Trepanier Creek Bridge, the tide of summer people who usually inundated the beach had mostly ebbed back into the campground. She eyed the pool, but just couldn't find the energy to even consider swimming. Nope. It was a good book and then bed for her and maybe dinner, if she could find an appetite.

She didn't find an appetite, but she didn't find a good book either. After trying to reach Allan Green to remind him to reclaim his property, she kept trying book after book. From best sellers and critically acclaimed books she'd taken out of the local library, to well-worn old favorites she had on her bookshelves, none could hold her attention. She finally gave up in disgust and looked for a DVD that interested her. No luck there, either. She turned on the TV and flipped through channels to settle on some documentary about porpoise fisheries that did nothing but add to her depression.

She turned the infernal machine off and planted herself lotus style in front of her crystals and tried to focus on steadying her too-rapid breathing. Darn it, what was wrong with her? She'd wanted Jas to quit hounding her. She didn't want the memories he seemed destined to remind her of. She didn't need that dangerous intimacy. She had enough intimacy with people through her aura reading and healing. She certainly didn't need a man. Sex was *not* everything. She'd ministered to herself over the years.

"A man is *not* necessary!" Her adamant voice seemed to shock the silence. The light had almost fully leaked from the day and her patio was filled with gloom except for the light from the livingroom window.

Oh, who was she kidding? She'd liked Jas Stone. Still liked him for that matter, though being around him was difficult. The trouble was, she could still picture his hard body and feel him inside her.

She shivered. It was hard to understand after all these years of celibacy. She'd like it. It had been different than all those years ago—more mutual, more giving. Perhaps even caring.

This wasn't helping a thing. It was just confusing her more. She closed her eyes and focused on her breathing while opening her senses to the crystals and their effect on her aura. The large, rutilated quartz gave off a deep pleasant hum, while the amethyst geode and the other crystals in the room provided fainter counterpoints that she felt like soft, pleasant vibrations against her skin. She settled herself so her weight sank down through her backbone. Breathe in. Exhale. Another breath, focused on the feel of the air on her nose.

Calm. She was calm and her aura solidified into pale gold around her. There was only the breath. Only this moment, and then the next.

Jas would laugh at her attempts to find calmness. He'd probably say what she felt wasn't real, it was a trick of the mind or something. Damn him.

The steady pale gold shivered and was gone leaving spikes and fissures through the energy around her. Stupid to think of Jas. He was gone, had removed himself from her life. Be happy about it. It was what you wanted all along.

Her breath came in rough hurried gasps. Not from deep within her diaphragm. She'd never get calm breathing like this.

She tried again.

And again.

And again.

Each time, just as she relaxed into calm, her flipping monkey-mind leapt free and somehow landed on Jas. Jas concerned asking if she was all right. Jas holding her as the shower ran down their heads. Jas as his body met hers in a mutual coming together.

She clamped her eyes shut, but it didn't stop the memories. Everywhere she seemed to look, a memory of Jas sprang up.

"Damn it!" She sprang to her feet. "I hardly know the man. I've pushed him away every way I know how and he's finally gone." She turned her face heavenward. "Just what the heck is going on that I can't get him out of my head?"

She paced around the condo again, stepped out on the patio and leaned on the rail. He'd been with her here. He'd tried to find a way to make it work. He'd even made a lot of allowances for her perspectives. Of course he might have laughed about them all the way back to his detachment, but she didn't think so. There was no way she should be attracted to him any more than he should be to her, and yet...

"Oh, damn." She looked up at the smooth expanse of night sky, the rich swirl of the Milky Way like an entrapment in amber. The waters of the lake hushed gently against the gravel shore and the air smelled of sun-warmed water. Clyde followed her out the patio door and threaded around her legs.

She picked him up for company. "Have I been stupid, old man? Should I have encouraged him to come around? It probably would have meant you'd be swept off the bed more times than you'd like."

Clyde just purred and head-bumped her face with kitty-love.

Sighing, she carried the big cat inside and slid the door shut. She snapped the door lock on and headed down the hall for her bedroom, shutting the lights off as she went. She had a long night ahead of her.

The question was whether she could fix things tomorrow.

§

She woke up to total darkness uncertain what it was that had brought her awake. Clyde was a snoring furry furnace snuggled beside her. Her window was open just the slightest bit allowing in the sound of the waves on the lake and the wind in the trees. No other sound, other than the almost indiscernible hum of the digital alarm clock on her bedside table.

But something had awakened her. She slid upright in her bed, pulling the bedcovers around her cotton p.j.s. Her room looked the same—the shadow against the wall was the same old hardwood dresser, same bed she was in and the door, half-closed, that led to her ensuite was just a darker square of darkness. By the closet door lay a litter of shoes and the hamper that she hadn't quite made it to for some clothes.

But the apartment was different. It *smelled* different—like an old beach fire pit. Cold ashes.

She frowned and swung her legs off the bed. Had she left the stove on or something? Hesitating, she went to her bedroom door.

Something rustled in her office and she froze. Clyde was still on the bed, so it wasn't him. The floor creaked outside her room, so this wasn't a mouse and the stench of cinders seemed to fill the air and almost gag her. She'd smelled that scent before with the terrifying man who had come into *This and That.* All the little hairs on her arms stood on end. He—it—was here. It had come for her and the bracelet just like it had come for Kylee. She eased back and slowly pushed the bedroom door closed, then scanned the room for a weapon.

A shoe? A picture frame?

She grabbed her phone off the bedside and ran for the patio door. Pushing past the curtains, she eased the door open and stepped outside into cool night wind and clean air. She heaved in a deep breath and slid the door closed behind her. Fumbling the phone on, she hit 911.

The phone buzzed in her ear. Answer. Answer. Answer. Answer.

From her bedroom came the sound of the door crashing back against the wall.

"Police, Fire and Ambulance."

"Hello. Hello. There's someone in my apartment," she whispered into the phone. She gave the dispatcher the address, trying to keep her voice calm.

"Where are you now?" The voice was so cool and clinical.

"I'm outside on my patio," she whispered. "He's in my bedroom right now!"

"Ma'am is there some place safe you can get to?"

"No. Nowhere." He was moving around her bedroom. "If he shifts the curtains he'll see me."

A crash and a rattle said he'd knocked her beads off her dresser. Her beads. Oh God, no. She didn't have her jet beads. She backed toward the patio railing. Could she climb down? Maybe climb around the separating wall to the Singhs place for help?

"Ma'am stay on the phone. What's your name?"

She nearly dropped the phone as she edged toward the livingroom. If he'd come in through the kitchen patio door, then maybe she could go back in and make it out into the apartment hallway.

"Chloe Main. I'm—I'm friends with Jas Stone. Tell him it's me. He'll know what's happening." She reached the livingroom patio door. Inside, everything was in shadows, the tea cup she'd made just as she'd abandoned it last night on the table by the couch when she'd tried to watch TV

Holding her breath, she tried the door. It slid silently open and she stepped inside. The stench of burning and ashes almost sent her coughing. She held her breath and ran for the kitchen and the hallway beyond. The cool kitchen tiles were under her feet. She was going to do this. She was going to make it free on her own.

A rush of wind blew her hair into her face and then something plowed into her from behind.

CHAPTER 19

Jas's cell phone buzzed just as he was rolling over trying to catch a few hours of sketchy sleep on the too hard, too narrow, motorhome bed. On the other bed, Forester was only a shadow as he used the binoculars to scan the Willowview Terrace balconies. It had been a quiet evening, which was just fine with Jas, except it left him with too much empty space for his brain to spin its wheels thinking about Chloe. It was over. He'd pulled the plug because he wasn't going to waste his time on a relationship that was never going to go anywhere.

It didn't matter that she was the most intriguing woman he'd ever met, like a puzzle that just eluded his solution.

But damn it, he hated not solving puzzles, just like he hated not solving crimes.

Thankfully his cell hummed at him and stopped the mental churning. He grabbed it off the shelf above the twin bed. "Stone."

"This is dispatch. We've got a woman saying there's someone in her apartment. She gave her name as Chloe Main and said to advise you. She said you'd know what is happening. We've got patrol responding, but it's going to be five-ten minutes before they arrive. What's your ETA?"

"Two minutes." He was already off the bed, pulling his shoulder holster and shoes on and running.

"Forester. It's happening. It's after Chloe."

Forester dumped the binoculars and grabbed his gun and the two of them barreled out of the motorhome.

No way was he running around the fence to the road, he climbed the board fence and leapt down into the condo's gardens hunched over and running for the building's front door. The wind was cool on his face, slapping him fully awake as the adrenaline ricocheted through his body. The damn front door was closed this time. He stabbed the Singh apartment and waited. Nothing. He tried his shoulder against the door but it didn't give.

Well, then. He grabbed the brick he'd previously thrown into the bushes, backed up a pace and threw.

The door exploded inwards just as Forester came up to him. "The detachment's not going to pay for that."

"Do I care?"

He was already in the emergency stairwell, leaping up the stairs three at a time, Forester pounding after.

When they came out into the third floor hallway there was silence. Not good. There should be screaming. Every frigging apartment door should be opened at the ruckus. He raced down the hallway, through the fire doors, Forester on his heels. The place smelled strange, like something was burning.

He reached Chloe's door and pounded on it. "West Kelowna RCMP. Open the door."

Nothing, but there was a thump beyond. He glanced at Forester. Danny nodded and raised his weapon. Jas backed up a pace and drove his foot against the door.

Wood splintered and the door drove inward, frame shattered.

Beyond, on the floor lay Chloe, clawing at the face of a man who straddled her chest and had his hands wrapped around her neck.

Jas ripped him off her and threw him against the wall, then drove a fist into his gut. Slim man. Sandy brown hair. The man raised his gaze to Jas.

Jas froze. The room stopped. Chloe's cries silenced. The eyes glowed and something dark and slimy looked out at him from the deepest recesses of the earth. The stink of burning seared his lungs and then the glow, the evil was gone. The brown-haired man seemed to collapse in on himself.

"No. No. No. No. No." The man clawed at his head, until Jas, still trying to understand what he'd seen, swung him around to face the wall. Once he was cuffed, Jas swiftly patted him down, then turned him around. Forester was on the floor with Chloe. Two uniformed members arrived at the door and Jas shoved the prisoner in their direction. He knelt beside Chloe and took her in his arms.

In her struggle, Chloe's long hair had come loose and tumbled in waves around her face and shoulders. Her eyes were huge and violet-dark in the light from the hallway, but her eyes met his and held. Red welts encircled her neck where the perp had strangled her.

He pulled her into his chest and held her so tight he might never let her go. Shudders ran through her and he rubbed her back, stroked her hair. What he'd seen in the perp's eyes—he still couldn't understand what it was. All he knew was that it was a miracle Chloe had survived it.

"I'm here. We're here," he amended as he felt Forester and the uniformed men's eyes on him. She felt so *small* and vulnerable and he desperately wanted her to be safe.

"Chloe, can you tell us what happened? Just a bit?"

Shivering, she nodded into his chest and looked up at him. "I was trying to sleep and not doing a very good job of it." Her voice was strained, barely more than a whisper. She reached up to stroke his face and he knew exactly what she was talking about.

She told how she had woken from a doze and heard something in her office. Forester went to check it out while the uniformed members ushered the man away.

"He hit me from behind and that drove me into the wall. It stunned me so he had his hands around my throat before I could do anything." She rubbed her throat and held out her other wrist. The silver bracelet gleamed against her flesh. "He wanted this, but he couldn't take it unless I was dead." She shook her head. "I don't understand, but I guess I do." She looked toward the now-empty doorway. "I know him. His name's Allan Green. He lives in the building and he's a friend. I was holding some jewelry of his in my safe. He'd asked me to after the Singh break-in."

She looked up at him, her expression desolate. "It was Allan and yet it wasn't. It was whatever it was that came after Kylee, and that visited me in the store. I was so afraid it would just take me over like nearly happened then." She shook her head. "I'm sorry. I know you don't believe any of this."

"Try me," he said as he pulled her in closer. She wore thin cotton pajamas with pink lambs frolicking over them, but they couldn't disguise the lush curves of her body. He wanted to hold her and never let her go, but Forester returned carrying an evidence bag. "Found this in the hallway."

The bag held a mass of small silk bags.

Chloe frowned. "I don't understand. Those are the bags he asked me to keep for him."

Forester nodded. "Ever think it might have been a ruse. An excuse. All of the break-ins might have been to cover the intended target—Chloe."

He could see what Forester was getting at. "She'd just be an unfortunate victim who happened to be home."

"And the jewels were returned those other times because they weren't what it was looking for to begin with." Forester nodded at her wrist. "The bracelet."

She nodded and gave the linked silver a tug. "Still securely on my wrist." She coughed and rubbed her neck again.

"I'm taking you to the hospital." Jas stood up and Forester nodded.

"I'll stick around until Forensics gets here and make sure the place gets secured."

Jas helped Chloe into a coat, and to gather her cell phone and purse. Then he helped her down to the lobby where he left her to reclaim the car and bring it around for her. When he returned to her in the lobby she wiped her eyes, but the red rims said she'd been crying. Above her protests, he picked her up and carried her to the car.

"I can walk myself."

"I'm aware of that. Now quit your complaining. I don't do this for just anybody, you know."

At the car, he helped her in, climbed in beside her, then grabbed hold of the steering wheel because he felt like he was going to be sick.

"Jas? What is it?"

"I could have lost you tonight. He could have killed you."

A slim hand slipped over his. "Thank you for not letting that happen."

"Damn straight." He turned the ignition on and pulled away from the curb fighting back the warring relief that she was okay, and the anger that someone had tried to hurt her.

He took her to Kelowna General Emergency and called Lila for her, so that all too soon there were three other women swooping in to care for her. Chloe didn't need him. She had her friends. He withdrew after telling Chloe he'd want to talk to her tomorrow. Tonight there were reports to be written.

§

He couldn't help himself. The next morning he checked and Chloe had remained in the hospital for observation overnight. She'd had a concussion, but was being released that morning. He made a few phone calls, prevailed upon Lila, and found himself with a bundle of clothing walking down the sterile halls until he reached Chloe's room.

She was sitting up in bed, her long hair a smooth wave around her shoulders, a white hospital gown showing off her tanned skin. When she saw him, she smiled.

"Well, well, well. And here comes the handsome detective. Let me guess. You want to take my statement."

He shook his head. "Actually, no. I'm your ride. And I come bearing gifts." He gave her the plastic shopping bag that held her clothes. "Lila pulled these together for you and I volunteered to bring them up." He looked at the floor. "Actually, I arm wrestled her and thankfully won. She can be pretty tough, your friend."

Chloe grinned, her lavender gaze catching at his. "Well, I guess that's my gain, isn't it?" she said softly.

He pulled the curtain around her bed so she could dress. He didn't need to see the smooth flow of her muscles as she dressed, he knew them by heart already. When she was done, she stepped out from behind the curtain, wearing her usual leggings and form-hiding caftan. Her luxuriant hair was once more confined to a braid but when she signed out of the hospital, she held his arm and walked with him out of the hospital to his waiting car.

She settled into the leather bucket seat of his SUV as he hurried around and climbed in beside her. She was studying the dash and the video screen above the rearview mirror.

"This doesn't look like a police vehicle."

He started the engine and pulled away from the curb. "It shouldn't. It's my personal vehicle."

That seemed to stymie her and she was silent as he steered back over the bridge toward West Kelowna.

"What do you know about Allan Green?" he asked as he drove.

Chloe frowned and looked at him. "He's a retired school teacher and writer. He used to write textbooks, now he's trying his hand at children's books. Why?"

"Did you know that the jewelry he had in your safe was stolen? We checked it last night. It came from all over the Okanagan Valley. We got a warrant for his apartment and found more—including some things that look suspiciously like items off your list from the store."

Chloe peered out at the scenery, at the dashboard, at her hands in her lap—and shivered. "He seemed like a normal guy. Where is he now?"

"Keeping Tom Beaton company in the psych ward. Guy broke down under questioning. He seems to be suffering the same delusions as Tom."

She visibly shivered. When he drove past the detachment and turned off the highway toward the lake Chloe sat forward. "Where are you taking me?"

"Some place we won't be interrupted."

For a moment a shadow of fear crossed her features. "What? You're abducting me?"

He looked at her and what she saw must have reassured her."Maybe."

Then she sighed almost as if she was—not afraid—defeated. "I guess we do need to talk. So where are we going."

"Wait and see." From the direction of the water, he turned up onto benchland still covered with orchard and a few older houses. He turned into the driveway of an older, single-story cedar-sided home and stopped.

"Where are we?"

"My place," he said climbing out of the SUV. "Don't worry. I was up all night with reports and the investigation. I want a shower and I need a clean change of clothes and maybe some lunch."

He closed the driver-side door and came around to hers, opened it and she climbed out. He caught her arms a moment, steadied her to steady himself because he felt like he would always need to steady himself around this woman.

He led her to the front door, unlocked it and ushered her in. "There's food in the fridge. Help yourself. I'm going to take that shower. Back in ten."

He left her standing in the foyer of the house he'd renovated himself, hoping she'd be curious enough to stay, but knowing she could be gone when he came out. The place was close enough to West Kelowna proper she could walk into town or she could use his landline to call a cab, if she wanted. Or she could stay.

If he was a betting man, given all their history, he wouldn't put money on the latter.

§

Just like the cab of his SUV, the house smelled of Jas—all clean, warm earth and leather with maybe a hint leather-cleaner, too. She stood in the entrance to the house, listening to Jas's footfall retreat down the hallway that ran off to the side and trying to decide whether to stay or go. The door to the hot sunny day was right behind her. Inside, there were shadows caught in the high ceilings that went all the way to the dark-stained rafters.

She stood in a relatively small area of terra cotta tiles and dark green walls that, on the inside of the house, were bounded by hip-high railings that looked out on a room below. What looked like it might be the back of a stone fireplace rose two stories beside a set of stairs, up past her level and to the ceiling. Chimney, most likely. The stones were smooth river rock, with flecks of what looked like onyx here and there. That suited Jas a lot, with its responsibility-enhancing properties. A set of stairs led down the inside of the house to the room below where tall windows let in the Okanagan view.

Stay where she was, or go? She could find her way back into town herself, but she and Jas needed to talk. She had things she needed to tell him. After last night he deserved at least that. The truth about why they couldn't be together—why he would be better off without her. Then he could choose.

She headed down the stairs, given there was no sign of a kitchen on the level she was on and, though it might be tempting, she certainly was *not* going down the hall where she could hear shower water running. The stairs brought her down into the great room she'd seen from above. Huge windows looked out over the sloped orchards down toward fields and a narrow road that edged the water. The sun caught in the leaves of the cherry and peach trees that were heavy with fruit at this time of year. A large sundeck with barbeque and single chair stretched out from the front of the house. So Jas Stone didn't entertain outside much, though the house was clearly built for it. Future plans it might have been nice to be part of.

The inside was a work of masculine comfort, dark hardwood floors and a large square Berber carpet of taupe. Sure, there was a big screen TV in one corner with a comfortable-looking leather lounge chair before it, but the rest of the room had a modern, square, brown leather sofa set that faced the huge stone fireplace that also opened onto a modern, stainless steel and marble kitchen that sat under the foyer they'd come in on. So the house was deceptive from outside, looking single story, but actually built into the side of the hill.

Her gaze followed the stone fireplace up the two stories and stopped. Came back to the unexpected decoration hung on the stone and looked away again. It fit so well with the boldly colored artwork on the walls and the large Inuit carving of a raven with spread wings on a pedestal in one corner, and yet it had to be her imagination.

She looked back at the fireplace, for hung artfully above the fireplace against the stone was a gleaming almost-black door made of thick, wooden boards held together with shining brass and iron casings.

It couldn't be and yet it was. No. It was *not*.

She marched into the kitchen and pulled open the fridge. She had to give Jas credit: he was an orderly man. She pulled cheese and sliced ham from one drawer, lettuce from another and tomatoes sat in a bowl on the island counter. She set them out in a row, found bread, but couldn't motivate herself to make a sandwich.

Fingering the bracelet, she returned to the livingroom to stare up at the door. Looked down at her wrist and up at the door. It couldn't be, and yet they were the same. The door her fingers seemed to always travel to. Now its life-sized doppelganger hung in Jas's livingroom. What was it Kylee had asked her? If she'd seen a door that matched her bracelet? She asked it in the context of a conversation about her relationship with Jas.

How the hell could Kylee have known? What did it mean? A shiver ran through her and seemed to set her insides rattling.

The soft pad of bare feet on stairs and she found Jas looking at her as he came down to her level. He looked good in worn faded jeans and a plain brown t-shirt that showed off his powerful shoulders. Swimmer's shoulders, she realized. They had that much in common apparently. His dark hair was slicked back from his face, but fell forward into his eyes when he came up beside her. He touched her arm and something like a chime went off inside her. For a moment she felt weak. What the hell was going on? She scrubbed at the bracelet that seemed too warm on her arm.

"So what do you think? I just finished the renos a couple of months ago and the furniture just arrived last month. I've been getting by with artwork, a TV and chair for the past two months."

She avoided looking at him and instead glanced back to the door. "What is that?"

"Uh, a door? A Zanzibar door, to be exact. I saw them first when I took a trip to east Africa a few years back. Then I tripped over this one when I was investigating a break-in at an antique store. The owner gave me a deal and so it's been living in my office until everything was done in here. I just hung it last week."

And some time a long time ago someone had hammered its likeness into silver. Would Jas's door open onto a secret world if she could get up there to open it? The quiver in her aura almost felt like it—as if she was in the presence of something of immense power.

Jas looked proud and pleased as punch, as if her reaction was just what he'd hoped for and suddenly she realized he was standing too close and she wasn't supposed to be feeling this—this warm feeling of camaraderie and comfort and—drawing. She left him for the window. Thankfully he didn't come after her.

"I see you found the fridge. Did you want a sandwich?"

"I thought I did, but maybe not. I really should get back to Peachland. Lila and the others will be waiting." And she was a chicken. Because the shivering since seeing the door hadn't stopped. She stood close by the window hoping the sunlight would warm her, but the house was too cool. She fumbled with the louvered door at the end of the windows and stepped outside into the heat of the sundeck. Let the sun beat down on her. She stood by the rail inhaling the perfume of ripening cherry and peach.

She felt Jas before she heard him, like a gentle caress on her skin before he stepped through onto the patio dragging a kitchen chair and carrying a plate with sandwiches. He set the plate down on the deck and returned to the house, only to come back with two bottles of beer.

"Come. Sit. It's close enough to noon and before you say anything it's non-alcoholic. I keep some for times I get home for lunch from work." He sat down on the kitchen chair, clearly intending the more comfortable patio chair for her.

Sighing, she sat down and took a drink of the yeasty beer. "So why am I here, Jas?" She was just so tired of everything. It was like the past week had been an emotional earthquake and last night had left her still shaking from it.

"Couple of things, really," he said as he wolfed down a half a sandwich. "One, I wanted to apologize for anything I might have done to hurt or offend you. And to try to take back what I said yesterday. I was angry, but I didn't mean it. For some reason I can't walk away from you. So whatever it was that I did to make you angry, I honestly didn't mean to do it and I'd like to start over."

What was she supposed to do? He was so earnest and concern radiated off of him.

She looked up at him. "There's no need to apologize. What happened between us—it was a mistake. My fault, actually. But the... attack... I suffered in the restaurant seemed to impact my libido. So I asked you to have sex with me, but that's over and done." That's right. Keep it clinical. Even though it hurt like a flint shard shoved under the skin, it was better than the alternative. "As for starting over, I wonder why we should bother. When the case is over, you'll move on."

She paused for a moment and glanced over at him. The sunlight had already dried his hair and his eyes were glittering jet shards in the shadow of his brow. He didn't look happy.

Slowly, he chewed a bite of sandwich and continued to study her. She finally grabbed half a sandwich and bit into it, so that she wasn't sitting there empty handed. She chewed, even though the food tasted like sawdust. "Good," she managed.

Jas sat back and shook his head. "You really are a rotten liar. Maybe it's because it's against your nature. It's like everyone can see through you except you. You're just so determined to keep your secret, but it's out there, Chloe. Everyone can see the way you push away any man who tries to get too close. You keep lying to yourself that you don't need a man and telling yourself that that makes you better than everyone, but really you're scared. You're scared because of those men when you were young—they left you thinking you were no good for anyone. You might not want to admit it, but a part of you believed them. It's a tragedy for a beautiful woman like you. A thing like that cuts you off from great possibilities, like maybe with me. You're cutting yourself off from who you are, Chloe. It was horrible what happened to you and I know you don't want to talk about it or hear it, but it's a part of you, of what led to the wonderful person you are."

"No." She put her half-finished sandwich on the plate. "No." She stood up and almost knocked over the mostly full beer bottle. She placed her hands over her ears. She was not going to listen to this. What she had done—he didn't know the half of it and he wouldn't say these things if he did. But the truth was eating its way through her these days. She stood in the sunshine, her eyes clenched shut, feeling the earthquake eat the stone she'd thought was so solidly protecting her. Damn it, she was falling apart. Maybe she needed to give all this up, this shell of a life she'd created for herself.

"Chloe." Jas's arms came around her and she shrugged him off and walked to the verandah edge.

He caught her again. "Chloe, you are so much more than the terrified woman you must have been in San Francisco. You are beautiful and smart and talented and loved. You are truly loved— by your family, your friends. By me, if you'll let me."

She stiffened. Shook her head. No man could love her for herself. Jas certainly wouldn't if he knew how far down in the mud she'd gotten. Someone like Jas could never overlook that. *So tell him and get it over with.*

"So I lied," she said, her voice thick as treacle. "I lied about how brave and smart I was, because I wasn't. I was a stupid kid trying to pretend I was an adult and my 'boyfriend' back then knew it." She hooked her fingers.

She pulled loose and turned to stare up at Jas. Strangely, he took it, just stood there waiting.

"So he didn't just share me with his friends. By then I was so disgusted with myself I knew my parents would never forgive me. So he turned me out." She nodded, daring him to say anything. "That's right. I worked for a living in the only way I had at my disposal. I worked on my back for him until the first time a John beat me. Then it was like a wake-up call. I ran. Heard enough? Are you disgusted now, because I am." She'd been scared, so scared when she ran into that New Age church. She'd been hiding from her past ever since. Or trying to.

She scratched at her arms. "What I wouldn't do to be able to get rid of this skin. I'll never be able to get rid of the feel of them."

She turned away to look down at the orchards and inhaled the peach scent. Felt the air over her nose on the inhale and exhale, but it didn't help. Nothing would. And the air was too thick and had clotted in her lungs like wet sand.

Oh God, what had she done? A secret once spoken was never secret again. This man, this stranger, could shout it to the moon.

Then warm arms slipped around her from behind and pulled her into his chest. He placed a kiss on her hair and his hands were warm over her frozen ones where she'd crossed her arms. He held on like he wasn't going to let go.

"It's okay, Chloe. It's okay. When you told me the story the other day and were so upset I sorta figured there was more to it. Something darker and really, this was the most logical place it could have gone. Unless you killed someone, but I don't think you've got the killer instinct in you."

His arms tightened just enough for her to know he had her.

"No. I didn't kill. I might have, though. For what they did to me and the other girls."

"But you didn't," he whispered into her hair. "Nope you took up meditation as a way to deal with all that anger."

A strangled laugh caught in her throat. "Yeah. Look how well that's doing for me."

"Pretty well considering how long you've been carrying this around. No one knows? Not even Lila?"

Especially not Lila. She set such high standards for herself and those around her. Chloe shook her head.

Jas's arms rocked her. "Well, then I feel very honored that you trusted me."

At that she turned in his arms to face him. "I told you because I hoped it would keep you away."

His dark eyes smiled down at her. "Didn't exactly work, did it?"

She looked at his arms securely locking her against him and shook her head.

"Is that so bad?" he asked leaning into her.

"No," she felt like a kid cajoled out of a tantrum. She sighed. "Thank you for being there for me. Today. Last night. The other day."

"Now that's what I wanted to hear!" he leaned in and placed a soft kiss on her lips and for the first time in forever a zing went through her and the universe seemed to steady.

He pulled back and she looked up at him. Frowned.

"Don't tell me it was as bad as all that!" He actually looked horrified.

Pretending she had to think about it, she pulled loose from his arms, then stood on tiptoe and truly kissed him back.

His arms came around her and it was if all the power in all the stones sizzled through her down to her core right there and then.

She fell back from him and touched her lips, felt her heart do a solid ba-bump, ba-bump. "Hold on," she said.

CHAPTER 20

Watching Chloe was like one of those time-lapse films of a flower opening. From a woman tightly clenched inside herself, in the space of a moment she suddenly seemed to relax, expand and shine. When she stepped back from the kiss and smiled up at him shyly, he could almost believe light gathered to her in the bright afternoon.

Her lips had tasted of ham sandwich and beer over an exotic perfume that was most definitely Chloe. "There a problem?"

"I—I'm not sure." She caught his hand and he let her lead him into the house where she looked up at the door above the stone fireplace. Then she turned to him and stood on tiptoe to kiss him. Light. Warm. Lips trailing across his in a sensual dance of want and restraint—so like Chloe.

He caught her arms lightly and stepped in close. "There are definite possibilities there, but we might have to work on it." He lifted her chin and her gaze was finally warm, as if life had suddenly infused her. "So what d'you say we work on it together."

When she nodded, he leaned down and kissed her like she deserved to be kissed. Softly at first, steadying her with his hands as he savored her mouth and then slipped toward her ear. He inhaled the sweet scent of her hair, drank in the shadows there. He closed his eyes just feeling the softness of her cheek next to his. Then he slid back to her half-open mouth and set a chain of kisses across her lower lip before taking custody of her mouth again.

She answered him back whole-heartedly, her arms coming around his neck, his hands sliding down her back to pull her more firmly into him. The softness of her breasts, the heat of her and the way she pressed into him all said the need was mutual.

He touched his forehead to hers. "I want you," he said. "And not just today." Her eyes were lavender-blue. "I want to learn all about you and your healing. I want to understand what it is you do."

Something troubled her expression like the ripple of the mythic Ogopogo through Okanagan Lake's deep blue water. "You believe in me now?" As if she couldn't quite believe him.

"Funny thing. After seeing Tom Beaton and Allan Green, I do. There's more than meets the eye in this world."

At his words a smile opened her face so that she seemed to glow in his arms. Her arms came around his neck and she leaned in to kiss him, at first with a bittersweet tenderness that mounted into something more passionate. Then she stopped, eye to eye with him. "I think—I want you right back. For more than today."

A look of shock crossed her face.

"What is it? Chloe?"

She pulled loose from his arms and bent down to the taupe Berber carpet, then up at him. In her hands lay something silver.

"The bracelet. It came off. Just as we were talking the clasp just came undone. How does that happen when we couldn't get it off for trying?" She fingered the silver links.

"Don't ask me."

She stood, the infernal silver doors laying across her palm as she looked up at the Zanzibar door above his fireplace. "Kylee asked me if I'd seen a door that matched one in the bracelet. Yours matches the door I was most attracted to. Iron and wood. Strong, I guess. Like you." She smiled shyly up at him. "I'm sorry I've been so difficult."

"Hey, I've dealt with worse."

She frowned. "Women?"

"Suspects."

A horrified expression came over her face and he couldn't help himself—he hauled her into him and kissed her again. "I like this much better than interrogation."

"Do tell." She cheekily quirked a brow at him.

"That, my dear, is going to have to wait until another time. Now that we've got things straight between us, I unfortunately am going to have to take you home to the care of your friends until I go off shift. Then we can complete this conversation." He snagged her ready mouth with his again and oh God, he could think of a much better way to spend the afternoon. When he stepped back they both seemed to stagger a little. "I think—I think *that* conversation may never be over," he said, caught in the deep lavender swirl of her eyes.

Chloe only nodded her agreement.

§

A long, long time. That was how long the conversation with Jas could continue. It was written in the intense black of his gaze that seemed as if it could swallow her whole. It coursed through her aura with the way his had somehow merged with hers so her chakras steadied and for the first time in a very long time she felt whole.

The sunlight through the tall glass windows placed an amber glow on Jas's skin and his warm scent of leather and earth left her full and complete. Except she wanted him more fully. Wanted to feel that hard body next to her, in her, moving with her. She blinked and looked up at him. "I sure hope you mean what you said, because I think I kinda have my heart set on it. For a very long time."

The kiss he planted on her lips sealed his promise and then he caught her hand and slid an arm around the small of her back before walking her up the stairs. In the foyer he kissed her again and she felt the tug of his bedroom down the hall.

She held up the bracelet between them. "I think we need to get this back to Lila for safekeeping."

"You're probably right. That thing's caused enough problems. I don't want it anywhere near you anymore."

With regret she followed him out to his SUV and he drove them out of West Kelowna, down long Drought Hill, then turned onto Beach Avenue and the tranquil streets of Peachland. Today the sunlight seemed brighter and yet more golden. Okanagan Lake was the deepest lapis blue and *This and That* beckoned with its gleaming white paint and red-trimmed shutters. Jas pulled in to the curb in front of the heritage house-come-store and came around the vehicle to open her door. She stepped out into the warm scent of suntan lotion, barbequed hot dogs and the sound of laughing children.

When she looked up, she found Jas studying her. "You okay?"

"The best I've been in a very long time," she said, nodding. "It's like I can... feel everything and everything is right with the world. Or my world, at least." She leaned up to kiss him lightly on the mouth. "Thank you."

A hoot of laughter came from *This and That's* front porch.

"Lady, you ain't seen nothing yet," he murmured to her. She caught his hand and led him toward the house.

"Hold that thought. You are about to run the gauntlet of my friends and—oh no—my brother."

Lila was at the top of the stairs, Kylee and Reggie flanking her, and Ally right behind them with Brett. As usual Lila was the epitome of the business woman in a navy, knee-length summer dress and navy and white sling-back spectator heels. Kylee was charming in a pink t-shirt and shorts and Reggie wore her ubiquitous black camo trouser and singlet. All three of them were down the stairs and surrounding her, channeling Jas away to one side.

"Are you all right?" Lila asked, looking deep into her eyes.

"Just fine. My throat's a bit tender, but that's all."

"I hardly slept last night worrying about you."

"Brett'll tell you I kept him up all night," Kylee chimed in.

"Yeah, but that was probably to his advantage," Chloe said, grinning up at her baby brother where he stood waiting. Kylee blushed prettily as Brett clumped down the stairs to give her a hug.

"You scared the hell out of all of us, Sis." He felt strong and warm and solid and he looked so happy as he stepped back and pulled Kylee into his side.

"Scared the heck out of me, too." She reached out for Jas and he caught her hand. She could feel the glances of the others lock on their connection and caught Lila and Kylee's satisfied nods.

"So where is it?" Kylee asked. "The bracelet. It's not on your wrist anymore but you had it on at the hospital last night."

Chloe dug the offending piece of jewelry out of her pocket and dangled it in the sunlight. "It came off at Jas's place and before your minds run wild with that piece of information, no we were not doing the wild thing. We just—had a few things to sort out. So we did, and the bracelet fell off. How neat is that?" She gave a 'don't you dare' glare to her friends.

Soft sniggering said her glare didn't quite work.

"This time let's not have anyone experiment with the bracelet closure again," Reggie said. "I think we're better off with this thing in the new safe until we know what's going on." She took the bracelet from Chloe and Lila swung an arm around Chloe's waist to lead her up the stairs.

"Jas? You coming?" Chloe called back to him.

"I really should be getting back to work now that you're with your friends."

"No way." She shook her head. "You at least have to have a cup of coffee with us."

So he clumped up the stairs and found himself a seat on the loveseat beside her so she was hyperaware of his nearness and the Jas-ness of his presence. The bracelet Reggie lay on the coffee table beside a carafe of coffee and a tray of cups. The happy buzz of conversation filled the porch.

"I can't thank you enough for saving my sister." Brett shook Jas's hand. "I've got a bottle of my best wine with your name on it."

Jas seemed a uncomfortable with all the attention. "So what *are* we going to do with it," Chloe asked motioning at the bracelet. "I know you said we should put it in the safe, but that's not going to stop someone from wanting it—and trying to get it. Doesn't putting it in the safe just place us all in danger?"

The conversation stopped and everyone looked at her. Chloe looked at each of them in turn. "I've worn the bracelet now and I agree with Kylee. I'm not sure what it is, but there is some purpose there and some reason it came to us. The bracelet isn't evil, but whatever is after it, is. That tells me that we have to keep it safe."

"Colonel Bristol kept the thing locked up for years," Lila stated slowly. "That seems to suggest that locking it up is feasible—and safe."

Kylee shook her head. "But something changed when Bristol died. Suddenly the evil was there and killed Moira Burns. That suggests that Bristol's death started something by bringing the bracelet to light again. Leastwise that thing, whatever it is, knows exactly where the bracelet is now. It's not going to stop just because Chloe and I were lucky. It wants the bracelet back and it's going to come after it again. It can likely get into the new safe as easily as it broke into the old one. I know you bought a more modern safe, but that doesn't mean there isn't someone out there with the skill to do the job. I think the only place it can't get the bracelet easily is when it's on a living wrist."

Chloe sighed. It made sense and echoed what she'd been thinking. "So I guess that means I keep it on for a while longer. No need to put someone else in danger." She reached for the bracelet but slim tanned fingers beat her to it. Ally swept the bracelet around her wrist and slipped the little key through the lock before the rest of them could react.

"There," she said with a satisfied pat of the bracelet on her wrist. Today she'd shed her khakis and wore a pale chambray silk blouse and crisp white shorts that showed off her long legs. "I think you'll agree I'm the best one to do this. I eat danger for lunch and I can easily take the silly thing somewhere the big bad can't find it." She sat up grinning while Chloe turned Ally's wrist over and tried the clasp. It didn't work.

"Looks like you're stuck," she said.

Lila looked about to launch into a lecture, but Ally held up her hand to stop her.

"So," Ally said. "Changing the subject, just what does one do around here to meet men?"

EPILOGUE

In the silence of his Berlin penthouse apartment the thing that was Johan Fehr sat in darkness on his immaculate white leather couch and contemplated the nighttime view over the city. Too many centuries he'd rested here, waiting for the bracelet to come to light again. Too many years barely holding on, when he should be filled with power and replete in the knowledge that the whole earth bowed before him. He might wear a body that was tall and strong. He might be the chair of *SchwarzeNacht Corporation*, but it. Was. Not. Enough.

All that stood between him and that power was what was trapped in the bracelet at the instant of an ancient curse. That should not be a problem. He could claim the power back as soon as he got the bracelet in his hands. But still he had failed to recover it. Twice.

He knocked back the glass of scotch-whiskey he was drinking and went to pour another at the sidebar in the room. Outside, the lights of the city twinkled and head and taillights on the autobahn were like oxygen circulating into and out of the lungs of the city.

"Damnation! It should already be in my hands!" He drank deeply of the new drink, then set the glass down. No need to get this body drunk. That would solve nothing.

Somehow he had been defeated, and the multiple use of power to leap into other bodies was taking its toll. He felt stretched thin.

It was going to take weeks to regain his strength through the slow process of feeding on this body's life source. And the longer he delayed, the more chance there was of the curse being broken in other ways. The infernal bracelet had already succeeded in bringing two sets of lovers together. No more could be allowed, for each time it depleted the curse's power.

Well, perhaps there was another way that the bracelet's powers could be stopped until he could reclaim it. Fishing his cell phone out of his pocket he keyed in a number. The line at the other end rang once.

"Yes," said a voice, neither masculine or feminine, the voice of the castrata who ran a very special house on the outskirts of the city.

"You know who this is?"

"Of course, Sir. Your phone identifies you."

"I need your very best man." He let that hang. Usually his orders went in a totally different direction. "He must be attractive in all the ways that men are perceived by women. He must be prepared to travel and to stay for an extended time. I will advise him of his target once he has arrived at his destination. I will double the usual daily fee for someone who also has no compunctions about getting rid of problems in very final ways."

There was silence a moment, then, "Very good, Sir. Can you provide the destination? We should be able to have our man in place within the day."

The thing in Johan Fehr looked out over the city and remembered other cities, Cairo, Athens, Rome before the fall. "It is no more than a village, really. A motley group of houses along a lakeshore in British Columbia. Peachland, it is called."

Watch for *Unlocking Her Grace*, coming May 2015 or turn the page for a sneak preview.

About the Author

Karen L. Abrahamson (McKee) is a well-traveled writer who has explored cultures and countries around the world. One of her favorite places to return to is the Central Okanagan of British Columbia, Canada. She is the author of literary, romantic and fantasy fiction. She lives on the west coast of Canada with two Bengal cats that aren't quite as well traveled as she is.

When she isn't writing she can be found with a camera and backpack in fabulous locations around the world.

If you would like to get an automatic e-mail when Karen's next book is released, sign up at her website, _www. karenlabrahamson.com_. Your email address will never be shared and you can unsubscribe at any time.

A Special Request from the Author: Word-of-mouth is crucial for any author to succeed. If you enjoyed this book, please consider leaving a review at your favorite e-tailer, or on Goodreads; even if it's only a line or two, it would make all the difference and would be very much appreciated.

To find more of her writing, visit

www.twistedrootpublishing.com.

Romance by Karen L. Abrahamson
and available through *www.twistedrootpublishing.com*

Ashes and Light
Shades of Moonlight
Judas Kiss
Second Spring
A Different Nightmusic
Shadow Play
Coming Down Christmas
Surviving Safe Harbour

The Unlocking Series:
Unlocking Her Heart
Unlocking Her History
Unlocking Her Grace
Unlocking Her Dreams
Unlocking Her Chances
Unlocking Her Doubts

KAREN L. ABRAHAMSON
UNLOCKING
HER GRACE
Unlocking Saga, Book Three

PROLOGUE

At ten pm he deplaned at the Kelowna International Airport to the fawning goodbyes of the flight attendants. The cool night air swirled around the broad shoulders of the body he wore cleansing him of the tired stink of sweating humans that he had tolerated on the long overseas and transcontinental flights. The body crossed the tarmac, carrying a windbreaker folded over one muscled arm, a single brown leather carryon bag over a shoulder, while he nestled for the moment in the body's brain—its most important passenger.

The airport lay in the heart of a long narrow valley with night-darkened, kindling-dry hillsides of pine to either side. Here and there a lone point of light exposed a lonely dwelling house, the type of place where one could do what they wanted with the inhabitants and no one would hear them scream.

He uncoiled and stretched in the body's brain, sniffed the darkness and welcomed it in, inhaling the faintest scent of silver. What passed for blood in his bloodless existence quickened in his breast.

Silver. Old silver. The body's head turned and he lifted its face to draw in a breath.

Southward. That was where it lay, beyond the backwater city of Kelowna with its too-bright lights that polluted the blessed dark sky. Once Creation had been filled with only darkness, but then day formed. Bright light and heat, and though his kind could exist in such places, they did not like it. They preferred to inhabit the dark cracks of the earth and coil round the minds of others, nursing magic as they gathered power.

But this time the body had to be guided more closely if it was to accomplish the mission he had set for it. It would drain his power dangerously, but it was worth it.

Long athletic legs strode across the concrete and pushed inside the terminal to recycled cool air. Female eyes turned in admiration toward him and he knew that he had chosen well. This body—this body was ripe for the task, with tanned flesh in a form that women found attractive. The body wore jeans and expensive-looking Italian loafers, and a denim shirt he had chosen to match the eyes. It sauntered across the arrival hall in a loose-hipped, confident way. Outside again, the air was heavy with the scents of sage and pine and cool water. Water of the deep cold lake that would play a part in his plans.

At the parking lot before him, the body fished the key fob that had been delivered to its Berlin apartment out of a jean pocket and pushed the button. Out in the parking lot a beep-beep-beep came from the only Humvee he could see.

Inside, the vehicle smelled of new leather as the body adjusted the seat, turned the engine on, and cruised out of the lot. In no time at all he was cruising highway 97 southward through the strip of neon lights that was Kelowna and westward across the lake. It was as unimpressive as he remembered. None of the grandeur of mountains like of Switzerland. None of the roar of waves from the ocean, and definitely none of the night life of Berlin.

This was... small. A small city that undoubtedly housed small people, which would make it somewhat more difficult for this splendid body to blend in. But that was what this body had been chosen for—its skill at blending in until it was simply too late for its targets to save themselves.

If Kelowna was small, the lights of his destination farther south spoke of not much more than a village strung like a beggar-woman's rhinestone necklace along the lakeshore. A few more lights scattered up the hillside behind them. None of the glamour of the City of Lights and none of the salt sea scent of the Riviera.

Just how had his precious possession ended up here in a village named after a fruit? Peachland. The land of peaches. Never his favorite fruit—too easily bruised and made inedible. He preferred enjoyments that did not show their injuries quite so openly.

When the body reached the lone stop light on the highway, it turned the Humvee toward the street that followed the lake shore. A block south it slowed and then pulled over. The dash lights turned the body's hands green as he studied the familiar scene before him. The hedge and small garden separated the large white house from the street. The house's red trim was tarnished black by the night that seemed to claw at the well-lit front porch that ran the breadth of the front of the house. A set of false torches lit the porch with a soft golden light illuminating a group of people seated there.

What he sought was there. His essence thrummed like a sticky spider thread vibrating at the quiver of a fly to alert its owner. He had been right to risk himself by once more coming half way around the world.

The women were there.

There were five, as he remembered. The body pushed a button on the door and the driver's side window scrolled down allowing in the night-tinged scent of lake water and power-imbued silver. For a moment vertigo took him and the body stirred of its own volition. He should not lose control so easily. He reasserted dominance and leaned forward to see whom he faced this time.

One, auburn haired, presided over the group from her seat in a high, peacock-backed, wicker chair, but she, as yet, had been untouched by the curse. Another, also untouched, reminded him of an ancient queen of Egypt he had served, with night black hair cut in ruthless bangs that matched the severe masculinity of her camouflage trousers and sleeveless t-shirt.

The hands tightened on the steering wheel at the sight of the third woman, the tiny blond who had escaped him. Beside her on a loveseat perched another who had frustrated his attempt to recover what was rightfully his. Her hair hung to her waist, and she carried the taint of the curse undone—no longer the haunting scent of the silver she had borne.

The breeze swirled along the lakeshore, stirring the leaves of the trees and the waves on the water. It lifted the long blond hair of the last tawny-skinned female. The currents of the night brought her scent through the window and he inhaled and closed the eyes. Old silver and magic—that was what he sought. Its thread of scent overlaid an aroma of warm cloves, baby oil and sweat that sent a titillating arousal through the body.

The spider vibration increased as the woman raised her hand to shift her hair and the torchlight caught on the silver encircling her wrist. He imagined himself staking that fine tendril of scent, hanging above her, his venom sac distended. He released his hold on the body. It started the car and cruised slowly past.

Her.

His target. The vibration in the spider silk ceased.

The spider—he—was here.

CHAPTER 1

It was one of those blue saturated days: blue sky, blue lake, blue docks floating on the water, as if she'd amped up the blue on the RGB scale of her camera. She stood by the Private Party sign by the front gate and watched the crowd of people—women mostly—fluttering around inthe heritage house's front yard. The two-story white-with-red-trim house gleamed contrast to the blue in the Okanagan sun, its broad, covered front porch offering a welcoming shade. Usually the porch was home to a well-used grouping of wicker furniture, but today—the grand reopening of *This and That: Jewelry and Unsung Treasures*—the furniture had been pushed to one end of the porch to allow room for display tables and circulation of the well-dressed people.

The store stood on Beach Avenue in the small south-central British Columbia town of Peachland, but not in the center of the town. No, *This and That* sat a half-mile along the lakefront on Beach Avenue where the town was slowly being transformed from a place of small, 1950s, single-story bungalows owned by Peachland's old families, to sleek glass-fronted, modern homes and condos owned by new money from the Alberta oil field or offshore riches made in the Orient. Ally knew it was eventually going to happen—from what she'd seen in the world, you couldn't stop progress—but it was still like a gut-punch and hard to see. She'd come home from Zanzibar desperately seeking the safety and sameness of the sleepy small town with its almost empty beaches and despairingly little to do to the mind of a teenage girl. Instead she found a destination spot for day-trippers from Kelowna, and the town she remembered was disappearing under the weight of new housing developments eating the orchards above the town and the gentrification of the old town's heart. But not here.

This and That held onto that comfortable past like an oasis in the desert. The house had been Lila Weber's grandparents'. After they had died, Lila had restored it and, with the partnership of two friends, had been determined to make the jewelry shop work to ensure the house could stay in the family and hold onto the town's old grace. They'd succeeded, too, from what Ally could see. The old copper hanging planters bloomed with red and white geraniums and purple heliotrope, and the store's white paint and red shutters shone in the sunshine. A little soft focus, or less contrast in the photographic post-processing and the place would look like it was filled with magic, and magic was what people wanted when it came to selling the beautiful pieces of jewelry found at *This and That*. It specialized in artisanal jewelry brought from all over the world, as well as specialty custom pieces made by their in-house designer, none other than Regulus, better known as Reggie Lewis to her friends.

After the store's recent unfortunate break-in and damage, Lila and company had decided to turn lemons into lemonade and had seized on the opportunity to update the store and make their grand reopening a publicity event.

Mingling female customers formed shoals like tropical fish, their bright summer dresses setting off their tanned legs and arms as they moved between the porch and the refreshment tables on the front lawn. Two young women, one blonde, one brunette hovered over a display of earrings on one of the lawn tables. With their heads close together, one pointed something out to the other and there was such open longing on their faces that Ally raised her camera.

Click-brrr. The Nikon D4 hummed in her hand as she shot a few frames, then checked the image. It was good. Thank goodness

Lila had agreed to ask all attendees to sign a photo release before attending so that photos could be used in promotional materials. It really was an excellent event. Lila and the others had outdone themselves and the setting certainly helped.

The breeze off 80-mile-long Okanagan Lake dispelled the afternoon heat, the blue waves slapping the gravel beach that was just across the street from *This and That*. Blue sky formed a bowl overhead, held up by the grey-green mountains. Uneven benches of land that terraced the hillsides, spread lodgepole pine forests, orchards and wineries down either side of the lake. Out on the water were the ubiquitous power boats pulling water skiers and their wakes sluggishly behind them. A few sailboats flew before the brisk wind and, closer in to shore, a yellow and a blue kayak cut across the water like dragonflies.

A gust struck her in the face and she turned to shield her camera lens in time to see the wind catch the corners of the tablecloths on two of the refreshment tables. The cloths flapped up and the wind caught hold and began to drag the cloth back over the table. Platters of small quiches and finger food began to slide towards the other side of the table. Ally leapt and grabbed for one cloth, yanked it down. Grabbed another and pulled it back in place as Chloe Main, Lila's partner, rushed to help her. Together they used rubber bands Chloe happened to have in her pockets to loop around the table legs and catch the corners of the tablecloths. When they were done they stopped and took stock.

"You were fast," Ally said.

"Not as fast as you." Chloe looked resplendent in a body-skimming caftan of white with a seed pearl and jet torque necklace and matching earrings, an outfit that was a far cry from the practical khaki trousers and silk shirt Ally wore. But then, when you're a working photographer you don't get decked out. Even Chloe's jewelry would be in the way and Ally'd be scared to move around, get down on the ground in such clothing. Even the silver bracelet Ally had on her wrist felt awkward and in the way.

"You getting any good shots?" Chloe asked. The two of them stood by the table and Chloe sampled what looked like smoked salmon and capers on a tiny curled crisp. She nodded in appreciation.

"A few. People admiring the jewelry. A few of the entire scene. It was a good idea having everyone sign a photo release and having those who didn't want to wear that blue dot on their shoulder. It's given me a lot of freedom to shoot. The shots of the scene will make lovely advertising shots for the place. The people shots are giving me ideas. It might be nice to have a few scattered around the shop or in a portfolio if you think you might want to do other events."

Chloe nodded thoughtfully. "You know we can't thank you enough for helping out with the photography. I mean this is really taking advantage of you—sort of a busman's holiday given you're on vacation and all."

Ally shook her head and felt a twinge of unease that she quickly pushed away. "Not a vacation. More like a sorting period." She sighed. "I haven't really wanted to talk about it, but I just needed some space to regain my focus. For some reason Peachland seemed like the perfect place to do it." And forget all the stuff that had gone bad with her life, not to mention maybe distract herself with some nice down home men. After years of sampling the exotic masculine wares around the world it would be nice to reset her meters on some good old North American beefcake.

Chloe shaded her eyes to study the party. "God, it's hot. How can you stand it in long pants like that? Everyone else is wearing as little as possible."

Ally looked down at her khaki trousers. "Is it? To tell you the truth, after Zanzibar and the humidity of the Indian Ocean, I hadn't noticed. The lack of humidity changes the light, too, now that I think about it. Over there, it's like there's a haze over everything and everything shimmers a little as if it's a mirage." Zanzibar floated through her memory again, like a giant dhow with a tree-colored three-cornered sail. Zanzibar and her ultimate failure. She didn't want to think about it because then she might have to deal with it.

Chloe raised her brows. "You okay?"

To steady herself, Ally raised her camera and took a few frames, though she wasn't really aiming at anything. Looking through the lens had always been a safe place, all that convex optical glass between her and real life. It was why she'd been so attracted to photography as a kid—you didn't have to be involved with family problems or worry about friends. "I'm fine. I'm just getting my sea legs under me again is all. It's taken me longer than I expected to get over the jet lag."

"Didn't figure on landing in the midst of a mystery, did you? You regretting putting it on yet?"

For a moment Ally didn't get what Chloe was talking about. She had to let Zanzibar fade away. Then Chloe nodded down at the bracelet on Ally's wrist. The darn thing had somehow snagged on the camera strap. She gentled the strap from around the silver links.

Ally shrugged. "Mystery? That just makes it more interesting." Regret? She had too many other regrets to worry about a silly bracelet. She held up her arm so the sunlight caught in the row of small, ornately-made doors that comprised the bracelet that had consumed the lives of the women at *This and That* since it showed up in a box of estate jewelry about two months ago.

Each of the doors on the bracelet was unique. While all were made of silver, each looked like a door from a different part of the world—as if, like a photographer—the maker was conducting a study of the graceful forms doors could take. One looked like it was made of wood planks and had an arched top that was surrounded by tiny grape clusters. Another appeared to be the kind of door you found in North Africa, iron strapped with large iron bolts. Another door had leaf-shaped hinges and a fourth had what appeared to be almost elfish hinges. The fifth looked like a traditional Dutch door with upper and lower halves and the sixth had what looked like raised square lintels with a small Fatima hand door knocker. The last, and the one that had caught her eye, had a small gargoyle face for a knocker.

The problem was the bracelet brought trouble. Not only did the darn thing have a nasty habit of refusing to unclasp once it was on, it had come to the store after the apparent murder of the estate sale agent who had sold it to them and the suicide of the man who had run her over with his truck.

Since its appearance at the store, the bracelet's first wearer, Kylee, had nearly been abducted and the second wearer, Chloe, had nearly been killed. All that and the break-in at the store, too.It was enough to make all of them want to lock the bracelet up or destroy it, anything but wear it. But there was something else about the bracelet. Somebody or something was looking for it. In all the years she'd been travelling around the world as a photographer, and with her charity, she'd heard a lot of strange stories. Some had proven true, like how certain Indian Shamans could seem to levitate, certain Amazonian plants seemed to foster psychic powers, or how curses actually seemed to work in some African villages. But this was Canada and the story she kept hearing said that something kept possessing people to try to get at the bracelet wearer. That was, well, just a tad unbelievable. Almost as unbelievable as the Okanagan Lake monster that she had believed in as a kid.

After all, she had been wearing the bracelet for a week now and nothing had happened. At all.

"Still not quite sure what to make of it, are you?" Chloe asked. As the second wearer of the bracelet she'd had a hard time of it.

Ally nodded and touched her own neck. Chloe's still showed faint bruising from where she'd almost been strangled."I keep waiting for the other shoe to drop—or to meet the man of my dreams like you and Kylee."

"You haven't had any bad feelings? Visions?"

"Nah. That's your thing, not mine."

Ally ran her hand around the bracelet. The silver was downright cool and never seemed to get warm. Though she could see its charm, she didn't quite understand why she'd volunteered to put the thing on. No, not volunteered—more like leapt at the chance—snaggingthe bracelet off the table and putting it on before anyone could protest. Everyone else had been afraid, but hey, she was a risk taker. "I figure I'll wear it until it falls off on its own and then I'll get on with my life."

Fat chance of that. She certainly wasn't satisfied with this one anymore. Yes, she helped people through her philanthropic organization, *"Get the Picture,"* and she liked the smiles she'd been able to put on people's faces through the help her organization provided to dig wells, build schools, and protect the environment,but every time she looked in the mirror there was nothing smiling back at her. She felt barren and bleached out, like a photograph that had been seriously overexposed and no post processing was going to fix it. The color was gone and so was the passion. She really felt the urge to just, well, run. Heck, she'd done it a few times before in her life. It wouldn't hurt her if it became a habit.

But she managed a grin for Chloe. The other woman had finally unbound her usually braided hair and the luxurious length reached below her hips. Outstanding as it was, it wasn't even her best feature—that was her eyes, which sometimes turned almost lavender but at this moment were luminous blue. Ally raised her camera and shot a few frames, with Chloe becoming increasingly embarrassed.

"I'm outta here," she finally announced, her fingers held up in a crucifix mode to fend off Ally's devilry. She quickly disappeared towards the porch amongst the customers.

"Excuse me! I hate to interrupt, but I promise I won't take a lot of your time." Lila Weber's amplified voice cut through the conversation and the crowd of women on the lawn went quiet. All eyes turned to Lila, standing on the porch at the top of the stairs with a microphone.

A college friend of Ally's, Lila was a beautiful woman of lustrous curled chestnut hair and hazel eyes. At five foot eleven, she was built like a model and might have once considered such a career, but instead she'd been 'discovered' by a movie studio and had become an overnight sensation in what became a cult classic film. After that brush with stardom she'd removed herself from the spotlight entirely. No one, especially her fans, understood why. What she didn't realize was that just by being Lila a spotlight would always find her.

Today she was dressed simply in a black shantung silk dress that hugged her curves and yet withstood the heat. A single silver pendant shaped like a heart hung on her breast, but the heart was wound with chains and hung with a lock. Her matching earrings were tiny keys. Regulus designs, both of them. They just had to be.

"I'm interrupting all your lovely conversations to say thank you for coming today and thank you so much for your years of patronage. *This and That* has been in operation for five and a half years now. I can't believe it's been that long. We've grown and I like to think you've grown along with us as we've experimented with jewelry and other wonders brought in from all parts of the world.

"Today would never have been possible, if it wasn't for some very special people who are very important to me so I'd like to introduce them to you. First off, the one and only Reggie Lewis of our very own Regulus Designs. Reggie come up here."

The dark-haired woman funneled through the crowd and stepped up onto the lowest porch step. Today, she'd actually eschewed her usual camo pants and black singlet, for a sleeveless vaguely oriental looking, crimson blouse and white flowing trousers. She waved, her Celtic knot tattoos flexing around her biceps.

"In just a few weeks she'll be off to Milan to finalize the first showing of her beautiful creations on the runway there. She tells me I'm going to have to give up this lovely piece, too." She feigned a pout and stroked the necklace.

There was applause all around, and Ally stepped outside the gate, snapping photos as she went to frame the scene. Something made her glance sideways and a masculine figure down the sidewalk looked way too familiar, a ghost remembered from an Irish country road. It couldn't be.

"Next up, is Chloe Main who has been the store manager and the face of *This and That*. Chloe's still going to be here, but she'd stepping back a bit from her store duties to focus on her crystal healing business that will also be operating out of this location." Chloe stepped up to join Reggie with a hug as the applause sounded. Ally kept snapping pictures of applauding bejeweled hands, of the three glorious women standing on the porch.

"Chloe's shift of focus has left a huge void to fill, but we've been fortunate to be joined by my high school best friend, Kylee Jensen. Kylee is a marketing genius and the person we have to thank for this wonderful event, today. She will be stepping into Chloe's role and managing the front of the store most days. She's also going to be responsible for growing our venture into private jewelry parties. Thank you, Kylee!" Another round of applause as the petite sunshine-haired Kylee joined Chloe and Reggie at the bottom of the stairs.

"That's the *This and That* team, but on a special note, we are fortunate to have an old friend of mine join us for at least a short while. She is a philanthropist who has worked with the United Nations in places like Ethiopia, Kenya and Tanzania. She is a world recognized photographer who has worked with National Geographic and used the results of her art to raise money for her charity. Today she is photographing our little event. Please welcome Allyson McVay and, if you're so inclined, I've set out a little donation box if anyone would like to help her in her work."

Ally cringed, but obeyed the call to join the others on the front porch. She stepped up to receive hugs from the other women she had gotten to know so well over the past week of her visit. She'd met Chloe and Reggie five years ago on a brief visit. Kylee, though, was new.

She smiled at the crowd, then made excuses that she needed to get back to photographing so she could slide through the crowd and ease out the gate. She shot like mad as Lila made a show of cutting the ribbon over the front door and announced that the shop was officially open for business. She invited people to come in.

The swirling currents of femininity edged toward the front porch and Ally shot off another few frames as the brightly clad women flowed up the stairs.

"Well, well, well. It's quite the day. If it isn't my very own little Ally McVay." The too-familiar rhyme spoken with a too-familiar and too-wished-to-be-forgotten Irish lilt.

She whirled around, praying it *was* a ghost of her imagination.

Not a ghost and not her imagination.

SéamusO'Hearn, Irishman, hunk and the man who had broken her heart, trapped her in his arms and kissed her in front of everyone.

Disaster.

CHAPTER 2

THE DAMN WOMAN GOT HER ELBOWS BETWEEN them and pointy elbows they were. She wielded them like daggers and forced him to let her go. She fell back from him breathing heavy, her tanned face gone dark with anger. But her hair was still burnished honey gold and her eyes were still the deep, deep blue of the sea that he'd drowned in long ago. At the moment, though, they'd gone stormy.

"Happy t' see me, Ally-girl?" He grinned. By the expression on her face she was anything but happy. "I know, I know, it's been a few years, but I got it into my head that maybe it was time to mend some fences." He shrugged like it really didn't matter when in fact the weight of the world rode on this meeting. Well perhaps not the world, but his world, certainly. A relationship he never should have ended. A little matter of personal redemption. He'd come here to see whether it was possible to fix what never should have been broken and he'd always figured humor and affection were the way to get past a woman's anger—at the moment, though, it didn't seem to be working.

"What. The Hell. Are you doing here?" A nice bit of angry white had formed around her lips as she ground out the words. Not exactly his Ally's best look.

"Why I came to see you, o' course. And the town. You talked a lot about this place before ya took off way back when. Figured I needed to see if fer myself." He took a slow turn around to scan the town. Nice enough. Good big bit o' lake, like a Scottish loch, only kinder-gentler looking. Houses strung along the lakeside. A bit of beach. Sun and warmth and none of the humidity that had made the east coast of Africa damned unpleasant. "Looks good."

He swung back to her, but Ally was gone, her height, blond hair and stiff shoulders making her stand out in the crowd of women in the yard as she quick-marched away.

Not exactly the welcome he'd been hopin' for on the long transatlantic flight. He'd been figuring on something a tad more romantic—maybe a run down the lakeshore into each other's arms, followed by a romantic dinner and a meal of other kinds. It had been a wild bit of fun when they'd fallen into bed together before. He'd thought that with all that time for thinking she'd had over the years maybe she'd have come to forgive him.

Apparently not.

"Damnya, woman. Yer not makin' this easy." He worked his shoulders and set to follow her. After all, an Irishman was always good fer a party.

§

It was Lila who stopped her. Ally let the press of women carry her up the stairs and onto the shady porch, but before she could escape inside the house Lila caught her arm and pulled her out of the crowd, to the relative quiet past the now-empty display tables to the wicker couch and chairs.

"Are you all right?" Lila asked, concern on her face. He gaze flickered beyond the overflowing copper flower pots to the sunlit, oh-so-eminently male figure on the sidewalk.

"You saw that, did you?"

"I'd've had to be blind not to. I take it he's someone you're not particularly happy to see."

Ally glanced back at the sidewalk, but he was still there, tall, tousled sandy-brown hair, with that infernal grin on that devilish mouth of his. He had his hands stuck in the pockets of his low-slung faded jeans and his shoulders looked entirely too fine in the chambray shirt with rolled up sleeves. It was the same look he'd affected on their evenings in Ireland, oh-so-long ago. A devil in disguise: she'd learned that lesson the hard way. All these years later, she was not fooled by him anymore—there was no school-girl urgency as there'd been all those years back. Those chocolate-brown eyes of his were just a trap of the worst kind and she wasn't going to fall for them again.

"He's the one—a guy I met just after I left home. I thought I fell in love—until the jerk dumped me out of the blue and went off with a local girl." And scooped out her heart and stomped all over it. "I really don't need him messing with me right now." She glanced back at the gate and dammit, dammit, dammit, he was coming through the gate. That was Séamus—always pushing in where he wasn't welcome and expecting to use his considerable Irish charm to get him by.

Lila patted her shoulder. "Then why don't you head inside and I'll deal with Mr....?"

"O'Hearn. Séamus O'Hearn."

"An Irishman, Ally?" Lila cocked a brow at her and half smiled.

"I know. I know. I should have known better, but he's damned charming. Watch out for it."

She took Lila's invitation and, feeling something of a coward, ducked through the door into the crowded store. It was a good room, with pale lavender-grey paint on the upper walls and the darkly-stained wood wainscoting around the lower four feet of the wall that matched the hardwood floor. A cash desk sat in one corner, ably attended by Kylee Jensen. Above the desk was a shelf that held a seated golden Buddha and a small brazier that trailed a myrrh-scented tendril into the air so the whole room had a sultry, exotic feel. The windows along the front were open to allow in the breeze, but even that couldn't wholly alleviate the heat of so many bodies on such a warm day.

The effect was like she'd been pulled down in a deep, slow moving current. The way the displays were set up in the store encouraged the shoppers to slowly circulate around the room like worshippers at Mecca. That would work well in a less crowded store, but now the brightly clad women formed clots around the displays that left others unable to see the wares. They'd have to circulate around again. But there were other things to see. Brightly colored pashmina scarves were braided into a dark-stained wood dowel ladder that ran up one corner by the window so the sunlight made their colors gleam. The earring cabinets filled one wall and were an obviously popular destination given the number of women hovering there. Glass cases above the wooden wainscoting carried crystals, and silver and stone pendants of various colors. Chloe was there to describe them.

Reggie was holding forth at a special display of her designs, and she had a pad and pencil handy so that she could sketch a design on the spot for one of the customers. There was an excited crowd around her asking all sorts of questions about her forthcoming show in Milan.

Ally sank back against the wall by the door and let the women stream past and around her as a set of heavier feet trod the stairs outside.

"Excuse me." Lila's smooth husky voice. "May I see your invitation? This is a private party today, but the store will be open for regular business tomorrow."

That was Lila, always thinking about tomorrow. She wouldn't just chase the interloper off—which was a darn shame given Lila could be forbidding if she wanted to be.

"Aah, now. Ya see I'm not a customer at all. I'm an old friend of Ally's come for a visit."

His footfall said he went to move past Lila and Ally froze.

She would not have a confrontation with that man. Not here and not now. What the heck was he doing here anyway? How had he found her? Had it taken thirteen years for him to notice he missed her? Or had he just had a bad day and decided he'd come find her to share his misery? Séamus O'Hearn was one of those men who had slipped into and out of her life. Since Ireland she'd found comfort with someone else. A few someone elses if the truth be known. Well, maybe more than a few. She didn't need Séamus O'Hearn weaseling his way back into her life and her heart like a kid placing rabbit ears above a friend's head in a photo. It was not going to happen. She had other things to worry about, like who was responsible for the collapse of her charity's showcase project and whether the charity could survive what had happened.

So she'd called Lila and come home to do some serious thinking. Who knew an old trouble maker would turn up? He was like an imp from his homeland who brought no good with him.

"Mr. O'Hearn, it seems Ally doesn't want to see you now. As this is neither the time nor the place for a scene, I'm going to suggest you come back after the store is closed or, as I mentioned, tomorrow. I will not have you bothering my friend."

Ally waited, breath held, to see what he would do, because although he was basically a good person, sometimes Séamus could do the stupid thing and truly offend people. She would not let him wreck Lila's grand opening. If she had to, she'd drag him away and deal with him. She chanced a glance out the window to find Séamus busy studying his feet

"Well then, would ya give Ally a message fer me? Tell her that after all these years I've come to my senses. Maybe it's time she came to hers. She could at least talk to me."

Ally fisted her hands. High time indeed. It wasn't her that did the leaving. Sure she left Ireland, but that was only after he'd had time to take her heart and clog it into pieces so small they could never be recovered. She heard the clump of his footfall on the stairs and rolled away from the wall herself as Lila stepped inside and made a show of wiping her hands.

"Dealt with."

"Thank you. Now I'd better get busy." She hefted her camera and shot a jillion more frames of the crowd inside the shop. Happy smiles, faces reflected in glass, with the indistinct shapes of the jewelry beyond. Items selected for purchase lying on black velvet trays next to the antique, scroll-sided cash register that was, in-and-of-itself, a piece of art. The mannequins with their ropes of chains and pendants, the pashmina display and the humanity of delighted faces caught in the light and shadow of the room. Then there was the door closing behind the last customer, the deserted tables out front and the business of cleaning it all up.

The five of them collapsed on the wicker couch and chairs after they'd been moved back into their historical position on the porch near the shop's door. Lila looked pleased, Chloe and Reggie a tad frazzled and Kylee positively elated.

"That was the best sales day we've had since I arrived here. We had $7,000 dollars in receipts and we ended up with about fifteen other more expensive pieces on layaway plans," Kylee said. Her big blue eyes were glowing as she shoved some of her chin-length bright blonde hair behind her ears. "That is a good day of business."

"There was a lot of interest in the crystals, too," said Chloe combing her hip-long hair with her hands and then starting to braid it. "I gave away a zillion business cards for the healing sessions, and there were a lot of questions about the properties of the different stones. I think Kylee's right. We should make sure that with each stone sold there's some information about the stone's properties and also something about how to keep the stone cleansed and charged. We might even want to consider having a small stock of books about the stones so that people who are really interested could buy one." Chloe looked around the group and got nods in response.

"So who's the guy, Ally? He's got a cute accent." Reggie asked. As usual she looked like a modern-day Cleopatra with her black hair cut in stark bangs that set off her dark brown eyes and high cheekbones. The soft silk clothing she wore belied the warrior woman she usually was. Unfortunately, she also took great pleasure in asking hard questions when she wasn't making jewelry or taking care of her ten-year-old daughter.

Ally shook her head, her hand finding the bracelet on her wrist. After the heat of the room it was finally warm, too. "An old—acquaintance, Séamus O'Hearn. And yes he's Irish and has one of those lovely lilting accents that make North American girls want to throw their panties at him, but not me." Her hand closed a fist around the bracelet and heat seemed to radiate from it. She released it and sagged back in her chair. "Sorry. It just makes me angry that he nearly made a scene at your party. He shouldn't be here. Not at all. It's been what—twelve or thirteen years since I last saw him."

She glanced up in time to see glances pass between the other women.

"Before you get any stupid ideas, Séamus is nobody to me. We had a fling once, years ago when I first started travelling. I thought we were in love. He had other ideas and dumped me for someone else so I left Ireland. Stupid of me to let a man chase me out of a perfectly lovely country. But it's over. Ended. So completely ended."

"So what's he doing here, now?" Kylee asked, her eager blue eyes clearly already scheming. "All these years later, a man doesn't just follow a woman out of the blue."

"Stalkers do it all the time," Chloe said softly, her lavender gaze troubled.

Kylee turned to stare at Ally and all the others looked at her, too.

"Is he stalking you, Ally?" Lila asked.

Ally sighed. "Not that I know of. At least I didn't think so until he showed up at the gate. Scared the hell out of me, he did." And just why was that?

Reggie stifled a grin.

"What? What are you smiling at?"

Reggie shrugged. "Nothing really. Just that for a moment there, you actually sounded like him."

To continue reading *Unlocking Her Grace*, ask for it at your favorite bookstore or favorite e-tailer.

Romance and Adventure
from Twisted Root Publishing

If you enjoyed this book, you might enjoy
other romance and romantic suspense titles
available from Karen L. Abrahamson in your
local bookstore or wherever e-books are sold.

www.karenlabrahamson.com